Praise f

"Although I don't rea~~~~~~ genre, I was recommer~~~~ ~~~ ~~~~ and absolutely loved it. It was a fast read, mostly because I didn't want to stop, with an exciting plot, twists and turns, interesting and detailed characters."   Amazon Review

"Perfect novel for the Murder Mystery lover! Once again author Joe C. Ellis reigns supreme in his latest novel, a first installment of the Angie Stallone Detective Series! I was enthralled reading the prior Weston Wolf Detective Series, but now Wes' partner, Angie Stallone, has taken over the business. Let the adventure begin right off the bat with a cold case murder and a kayaking trip to the abandoned Monkey Island in the Currituck Sound."   Amazon Review

"From the first page to the last page, I was on the edge of my seat."   Amazon Review

"The Outer Banks being one of my favorite vacation spots, I knew this book might be interesting, and I wasn't disappointed!"   Amazon Review

"I am always up for a book that takes place at my favorite vacation location. Extra fun when you know all the places and businesses mentioned in a mystery that pulls you in and keeps the pages turning."   Amazon Review

"This was a pure joy to read. I've read his other books and have enjoyed them too."   Amazon Review

"Joe Ellis never disappoints!!! The book was amazing and a great page turner! If you like James Patterson, you will love Joe Ellis!"   Amazon Review

A Nags Head Murder
A Stallone Detective Agency Mystery

A novel by
Joe C. Ellis

Outer Banks Stallone Detective Agency Series
Book 1

Upper Ohio Valley Books
Joe C. Ellis
71299 Skyview Drive
Martins Ferry, Ohio 43935
Email: **joecellis@comcast.net**

PUBLISHER'S NOTE

Although this novel, *A Nags Head Murder*, is set in actual locations on the Outer Banks of North Carolina, it is a work of fiction. The characters' names are the products of the author's imagination. Any resemblance of these characters to real people is entirely coincidental. Many of the places mentioned in the novel—Buxton Village Books, Historic Cottage Row, Monkey Island, Ocean Atlantic Rentals in Corolla, Conner's Market in Buxton and other places mentioned in the novel—are real locations. However, their involvement in the plot of the story is purely fictional. It is the author's hope that this novel generates great interest in this wonderful region of the U.S.A., and, as a result, many people will plan a vacation at these locations and experience the beauty of these settings firsthand.

CATALOGING INFORMATION
Ellis, Joe C., 1956-
A Nags Head Murder
A Stallone Detective Agency Mystery
by Joe C. Ellis
ISBN: 979-8-9853327-2-8
1.Outer Banks—Fiction. 2. Nags Head—Fiction
3. Mystery—Fiction 4. Suspense—Fiction
5. Kill Devil Hills—Fiction 6. Kitty Hawk--Fiction
7. Female Detective—Fiction   8. Detective—Fiction

If you enjoy this book and would like to discover how Angie Stallone began her career in the private investigation business, please check out my previous Outer Banks detective series (Weston Wolf Outer Banks Detective Series). In this three-book series, Angie teams up with Detective Weston Wolf to solve a variety of cases full of twists and turns.

Weston Wolf Outer Banks Detective Series

The Roanoke Island Murders: A Weston Wolf OBX Detective Novel

The Singer in the Sound: A Weston Wolf OBX Detective Novel

Kitty Hawk Confidential: A Weston Wolf OBX Detective Novel

Outer Banks Murder Series

The Healing Place (Prequel to Murder at Whalehead)

Book 1 – Murder at Whalehead

Book 2 – Murder at Hatteras

Book 3 – Murder on the Outer Banks

Book 4 – Murder at Ocracoke

Book 5 – The Treasure of Portstmouth Island

A Nags Head Murder
A Stallone Detective Agency Mystery

Chapter 1
A Strange Letter

"This is the letter I called you about." Mee Mee Roberts held up the yellowed paper.

Angie Stallone Thomas leaned and eyed the faded stationery. A rust-colored symbol that resembled an eagle appeared at the top. "Is that a thunderbird?"

Mee Mee nodded, her brown-framed glasses reflecting the store's overhead lighting. Her long-sleeved shirt matched the color of her sandy blonde hair which was gathered into a ponytail.

"Interesting." Angie took the letter, adjusted her red-framed glasses and read it. "I am writing you this letter from my death bed." She paused and glanced at Mee Mee.

The bookstore owner tilted her head and raised her eyebrows.

Angie refocused on the words and continued: "Of all people, I thought you would be the person to contact. At one time, we had a strong spiritual connection. You understand the mysteries of which I speak.

"When my older brother Ahanu died a few weeks ago, his lawyer sent me a box of articles that belonged to my grandfather, mostly books and papers. Grandfather disappeared in the fall of 1966. His name was Ahote Rowtag. At that time, he was working as a hunting and fishing guide at the Monkey Island Hunt Club. The local authorities found his boat on the Currituck Sound and assumed he had fallen in and drowned. His body was never recovered. I believe he was tortured and murdered." Angie shifted her focus to the signature at the bottom of the page, lowered the letter and returned her gaze to Mee Mee. "Who is this Achak Rowtag?"

"An old acquaintance." Mee Mee's eyes fixed on the window facing the road just beyond Angie's shoulder. "He worked at the Frisco Native American Museum in Frisco. Every once in a while, he'd stop in here and pick up books." She refocused on Angie. "He claimed to be shaman, a full-blooded Algonquin descended from the local Pamunkey tribe."

Angie's brow tensed slightly, and she nodded, her blue eyes refocusing on the letter. "Looking through one of my grandfather's diaries, I found a map. It fell out from between the pages. I have included the map with this letter." Angie glanced up.

Mee Mee lifted a faded piece of paper with tattered edges from the counter next to the computer. "X marks the spot."

"Does it really have an X?"

Mee Mee nodded slowly.

Angie read on: "It is a map of Monkey Island. I believe something is buried there that could offer clues to my grandfather's disappearance. Two nights ago, Grandfather appeared to me in a dream and insisted I seek justice. I don't have any other evidence. As you know, the sheriff and I do not get along. He thinks I follow the path of a sly fox. Perhaps you know an investigator who values truth and justice." Angie lowered the letter. "Is that where I come in?"

Mee Mee shrugged. "You are a private investigator."

"True."

"And you do value justice."

Angie raked her fingers through her pixie-cut blonde hair. "I do, but I'm a businessperson, and justice comes with a price tag."

"Read on."

Angie adjusted her glasses and looked at the letter. "I have included five one-hundred-dollar bills in hopes that you will hire someone to find what is buried on Monkey Island and discover any clues that may help to solve my grandfather's murder." Angie glanced up to see Mee Mee waving five Benjamins.

Mee Mee spread the bills like a poker hand on the counter. "Is that enough payola to paddle out to that island and dig a hole?"

"Paddle?"

"We can take a two-person kayak."

"We?"

"I plan on coming with you."

"How long will this take?"

Mee Mee screwed up her face. "Let's see. It's a two-hour trip to Corolla and a two-mile voyage to the island."

"All day."

Mee Mee nodded.

"And another day of research if we find anything."

"That's a possibility. Of course, we can always pass the baton."

Angie took a deep breath, her black Polo shirt hugging her athletic body. "In other words, we can hand over whatever we find to the local authorities."

"Right."

"That would be an option . . . unless we find a chest of gold."

Mee Mee grinned. "That's another possibility."

"He mentions that you two have a spiritual connection. What's that about?"

"That's a long story. Achak was an environmental activist. He had been arrested several times at protests around the country. Occasionally, the Outer Banks Sentinel hired me to do some investigative journalism concerning local environmental issues. Achak and I found ourselves in the midst of a controversial situation on Ocracoke. A developer threatened to exercise his political muscle to commercialize a large portion of the island's protected beaches. Achak's opposition to the developer's plans caused quite a stir. I admired his courage to stand up to greedy plutocrats on ecological principles."

"So you made some kind of connection with him through this . . . ordeal."

"Yes. Being a shaman, Achak was a very spiritual man. I felt like I was on the same wavelength with him."

Angie rubbed her chin. "Interesting. Have you talked to him since you received the letter?"

Mee Mee shook her head. "I tried calling him at home, but no one answered. Then I figured he might be at the hospital in Nags Head since he mentioned being on his death bed."

"Was he there?"

Mee Mee nodded. "It doesn't look good for him-- pneumonia. He's on a ventilator and goes in and out of consciousness."

Angie hooked her thumbs in her jeans pockets and fluttered her fingers. She glanced around the bookstore, a warm and welcoming place. To the right she noticed shelves featuring Outer Banks books. Above them, a long shelf displaying beach bags stretched across the doorway that led to the back of the store. Angie waved toward the Outer Banks books. "Anything on those shelves about Monkey Island?"

"No. There hasn't been much written about the place. An internet search might give us some info. I know it's stuck out in the middle of the Currituck Sound. According to Achak's letter and map, there's an old hunting club there, but I think it's been long abandoned."

"Hmmmph. It's probably haunted. Let me see that map."

Mee Mee delicately pinched the corner of the map, lifted and extended it to Angie. "Be careful. It's fragile."

"So's my career." She laid the map on the counter and studied the drawing. The ink had faded with time, but the shapes and lines remained clear. The island was shaped like the profile of a man wearing a baker's hat. She assumed rectangles near the middle represented buildings. A path wound its way to the left side near an inlet at the base of the hat shape. There an X was marked in red next to a symbol representing a large tree. The words *two paces* were written next to the tree.

"What are you thinking?" Mee Mee asked.

"I'm wondering how difficult it will be to follow this path. I'm guessing the island has been abandoned for decades. There may not even be a path."

"There's only one way to find out."

"Why are you so curious to find out what's buried on that island?"

"I feel like I owe it to Achak."

Angie's eyes narrowed. "Why?"

"Like I said, at one time we had a spiritual connection. At a critical point in my life, he told me I must make a decision."

"What kind of decision?"

"To live or die."

Angie raised her chin. "And you chose to live."

Mee Mee's lips curled into an enigmatic smile. "I'm still here."

Angie appraised her for several seconds, reached and collected the five one-hundred-dollar bills from the counter. She waved them in front of her face, folded them and stuck them in her jeans pocket. "I'll pick you up tomorrow morning at eight o'clock sharp. We'll rent a kayak from one of those beach equipment stores in Corolla. I'm sure that'll cost at least a hundred bucks."

Mee Mee raised her hand. "I'll pay for the kayak."

"Do you have a shovel?"

"Yep."

"Bring it along. Can you think of anything else?"

"Bug spray."

"Right. Bug spray, long sleeves and long pants. The place is probably swarming with mosquitos."

Mee Mee let out a long audible breath. "One other thing."

"What's that?"

"A thick pair of gloves."

"For digging?"

Mee Mee bobbed her head. "Among other things."

Chapter 2
A Secret to Keep

Angie rubbed her belly, noticing the slight bump. *I'm hungry. Maybe we're hungry.* She could smell the aroma of bacon wafting in from the kitchen. *God bless you, Joel. Bacon, scrambled eggs and hash browns. I'll need a big breakfast.* She stepped into a pair of work jeans. They felt stiff but protective. *Who knows what we'll run into on that island?* She picked out a long-sleeved black t-shirt from the top drawer of the old dresser. The bright yellow Stallone Detective Agency logo glowed in contrast to the black cotton fabric. She designed it herself, a simple arc of words over a magnifying glass centered on the Cape Hatteras Light House. She had opted to use her maiden name for the company. Sitting on the unmade bed, she pulled on thick wool socks and jammed her feet into her leather work boots. She wriggled her toes. *Haven't worn these in a while. Thank God my feet aren't that swollen.*

After lacing up and tying the shoes, she ambled into the kitchen and took a big whiff of the wonderful smell of fried breakfast food. Her husband faced the stove wearing a white tank top and baggy gray workout shorts. "Joel, you are my amazing Stud Muffin." She poured herself a cup of coffee and sat down on one of the old chairs padded with yellow vinyl.

"Are you ready for a hearty breakfast?"

"I'm so hungry I could eat the leg off a low flying duck."

Her husband lifted the large plate of steaming eggs, bacon and potatoes and set it on the Formica-topped table. A handsome man, six feet tall with sandy blond close-cropped hair, Joel Thomas was the anchor in her stormy world. At the end of November they would celebrate their one-year anniversary. He worked as a Dare County deputy for several years. When she opened her new agency in Buxton, they sold their house in Nags Head and purchased a humble cottage along Rocky Rollinson Road. With only a few clients over the last several months, she barely managed to pay the overhead, but they somehow scraped by mostly on his salary. Having a home office helped.

He pulled out the chair across from her and sat down with his piled-high plate. "Wish I could go with you."

"You're on duty this afternoon. Besides, you've got to be exhausted. What time did you get in last night?"

"About one."

She shook her head. "So you got about five hours sleep."

"About five and a half."

"Anything interesting happen yesterday?"

He nodded. "Rocky sniffed out some stinkweed. I pulled over an old Chevy pickup for speeding just north of town. Sure enough, Rocky went nuts. Found a pound of Panama Gold under the passenger seat."

Angie swallowed a mouthful of scrambled eggs. "Nice. Any trouble?" She took a swig of coffee.

"No. It was Squeaky Bob Clemons. Second time I've arrested him. He's just a local hay dealer. Judge Jones will probably give him a couple weeks in the Greybar Hotel."

Angie grinned. "Where is Rocky?"

Joel thumbed over his shoulder. "In the living room sleeping in front of the fireplace."

"I'm surprised he's not out here beggin' for bacon."

"Give him a few minutes." He planted his elbows on the table and leaned toward her. "You know paddling out to that island can be dangerous if the sound water is rough."

She shrugged. "We'll rent an ocean kayak. Those things can handle choppy sound waters."

He sat back and rubbed his knuckles along the stubble of his jawline. "Two miles is a long way to paddle an ocean kayak."

"Mee Mee is a pretty fit gal. I don't think we'll have any

problems."

"You better take my truck."

"Right. Hope you don't mind driving the Civic to work."

"Not at all. I'll fill it up for you."

"Thanks." Angie took a deep breath. "There're five C-notes on my dresser. That'll cover some of our bills this month."

"They already paid you?"

Angie bobbed her head. "The client is not well. It's a two-day job. Hopefully, I can give him some answers before he departs this world for the happy hunting grounds."

"He's a Native American?"

Angie nodded. "Achak Rowtag. Ever hear of him?"

Joel shook his head. "What's wrong with him?"

"Pneumonia. He's on a ventilator."

Joel's lips tightened. "Hate to hear that."

A yellow lab trotted into the kitchen, sat next to Angie and raised a paw.

"What do you want?"

The lab brushed the side of her leg with its paw several times.

Angie lifted a piece of bacon from her plate and held it a couple feet above the dog's nose. "Speak."

The dog yelped.

"You speak up when you want something, don't ya, Rocky? Just like someone else I know." She lowered the bacon, and the dog gulped it down. "Now go bother your partner."

The lab circled the table and gazed up at Joel.

He patted the dog's head. "Be patient, boy. I'll cook you up some eggs in a few minutes."

"Do you have any work gloves?"

"Yeah. Why?"

"We're digging a hole."

"Buried treasure?"

"Wouldn't that be nice."

Joel spread his hands. "That'd be great, but I'm already the richest man in town."

"That's news to me."

He winked and pointed at her. "You're my pot of gold."

Angie laughed. "Fool's gold. I don't have much, but I do have you."

Joel did a Schwarzenegger double-bicep pose and nodded toward his right arm. "What more could you ask for?"

Angie scooted out her chair, arose, circled the table and squeezed the impressive muscle. "Wow. If those peaks were any higher, they'd have snow on them."

"Aw, shucks. You're making me blush." He relaxed, stretched his arms and yawned.

"Now where's the gloves?"

"They're in the hall closet. I'll get them for you." He scooted out the chair and stood.

"Give me a kiss good morning first."

"If you insist." He wrapped his arms around her, drew her close and kissed her passionately.

When their lips broke apart, she sighed. "Whoa. That was some good morning kiss."

"Not bad, huh?"

"I didn't even mind the bacon breath."

Joel laughed. "I'll get those gloves."

Angie tapped his cheek. "Thanks, Stud Muffin."

Rocky followed him down the hallway.

Angie rubbed her belly again and smiled. *Should I tell him? I don't even know for sure. I probably should say something.*

Joel returned and extended the gloves. "Here you go."

"Joel . . . "

"What?"

"I need to talk to you about something important."

"Okay." He knotted his brow. "You're serious, aren't you?"

She nodded. "I . . . well, I think that I . . ."

"Go ahead."

She took a deep breath and blew it out with a low whistle. "We'll talk about it later."

"Come on now, Angie."

She raised her hand. "No, no, no. It can wait."

Joel gripped her shoulders. "Are you really going to leave me hanging?"

"We'll talk about it tonight."

"I won't get home tonight until one o'clock in the morning."

"Wake me up when you come to bed." She stood on her tiptoes, gave him a quick kiss on the lips, about-faced and headed out the door.

Chapter 3
Mother Nature

Their humble three-bedroom cottage along Rocky Rollinson Road was less than a mile from Buxton Village Books. They purchased the place for $180,000 six months ago, barely scraping the down payment together, but it was home. Angie had to admit she had never felt this happy in her life. As she slowed for the stop sign, she smiled and took a deep breath. *Ain't that a kick in the head. Credit card bills sky high, an old vehicle with more than 100,000 miles, very few clients, married to a guy that risks his life every day, yet I'm happier than a fisherman's cat. Must be the irony of life old folks always go on about.*

She checked for oncoming traffic, pulled onto Route 12, drove a few hundred yards and parked in front of the bookstore. The shop was a favorite stop for vacationers and locals. Painted a light gray with white trim, the quaint house was one of the oldest on Hatteras Island. It had a front stoop and delicate wood scrolling on the peaks of the porch and roof gables. Mee Mee had established herself as an astute businesswoman in the community and had weathered more than a few hurricanes and nor'easters over the years. Her store was a great place to find books that detailed local history, which came in handy on particular investigations. When she first moved to Buxton, Angie got hooked on local crime novels that Mee Mee always promoted. It was the kind of place where people felt comfortable browsing and hanging out.

Angie beeped the Dodge Ram's horn, and Mee Mee stepped out the door and onto the stoop holding a shovel in one hand and a pair of gloves in the other. Wearing an olive-green fisherman's hat and a gray Addidas sweat outfit, she appeared raring and ready. She hustled down the steps to the side of the truck and tossed the shovel in the back.

When she opened the passenger door, she said, "I feel like Indiana Jones."

"I hope you feel that pumped up paddling a kayak out in the middle of the Currituck Sound."

Mee Mee stepped up into the cab, sat down and buckled her seat belt. "Getting there won't be that bad. Wind's blowing from the south at about twenty miles an hour. Paddling back will be the challenge."

"Great. When we're exhausted from the day's exertion, we'll face a headwind."

Mee Mee laughed. "There should be a law against anyone under the age of forty complaining about a hard day's work."

Angie backed the truck onto Route 12 and headed north. "I guess suffering is good for the soul."

"We'll suffer together."

Angie chuckled. "I'm sure we will."

In early October, the small town of Buxton, North Carolina glowed in the mid-morning sunshine. The tourist crowd had thinned to less than half of the summer's peak. At this time of year vacationers longed for tranquility and beauty. They preferred a lonely walk along the shore compared to zigzagging between a multitude of sunbathers, kids and beach umbrellas. The small towns along the southern barrier islands offered this laid-back setting in abundance, towns like Frisco, Avon, Waves and Rodanthe.

At a few minutes after eight, the temperature had already climbed into the mid-sixties. Bright sunshine lit the front of humble homes, churches and stores—no McMansions along this part of town, just everyday people going about their business. Route 12 weaved through the village past the Studio Art Gallery, Conner's Supermarket, the Osprey Shopping Center, the Thrift Shop and Lighthouse Road which led to the famous Cape Hatteras Lighthouse. Angie loved the rustic feel of the place.

As they drove out of Buxton, the two-lane road divided the scene into contrasting images: the tall dunes and ocean to the right and the salt marshes and Pamlico Sound to the left. A blue sky with wispy clouds hovered over the view like a cosmic bowl uniting the two worlds. These long stretches between towns created a dreamlike atmosphere that lulled most people into laid-back tranquility. Angie enjoyed the quietude, thinking about Joel, Rocky and that morning's breakfast. She felt more than blessed. Mee Mee sat quietly, too, gazing at the top of the dunes as they passed by.

As they entered the town of Avon, Mee Mee said, "This should be some adventure."

"No doubt. I've done some internet research. Monkey Island is definitely an unusual place."

"I did some Google searches, too. What did you find out?"

"First and foremost, there are no monkeys on the island."

"Right. It's become a rookery for big birds."

"Lots of birds, no monkeys. It was named after the Pamunkey Indians who used it as a hunting camp before the Europeans arrived hundreds of years ago."

"Achak is a Pamunkey descendant." Mee Mee faced Angie. "I wonder if he ever explored the island?"

"I would guess he did. He sounds like a man who doesn't trust the media. The reports of his grandfather's drowning didn't add up. At some point in his life, he probably paddled out there and looked around."

"Yeah, if only to honor his grandfather's memory."

"His grandfather worked as a guide for the hunting club in the 1960's, but its history extends much further back. In 1869 Virginia investors bought the island for fifteen bucks. That's what I call a land grab. Eventually, a group of tobacco executives purchased it and formed the Monkey Island Hunt Club. They built a lodge, a caretaker's house and a boathouse on the island. These were some of the richest and most powerful men in America—George Hill, the president of the American Tobacco Company and Charles Penn, the guy who developed Lucky Strike cigarettes."

"Back then, cigarettes were considered fashionable. Everybody smoked."

"And died in their fifties and sixties of emphysema, lung cancer and heart disease."

Mee Mee grimaced. "Those were the days."

"Anyway, the club welcomed some of the most renowned people of the day, people like the well-known artist, Roland Clark. It was a place of wealth and privilege. In those days the popular seasons were reversed on the Outer Banks. Summers were slow, but in the fall, winter and spring the hunting clubs bustled with activity, and there were nearly a hundred clubs up and down these barrier islands. The Monkey Island club was one of the most popular ones. I'm guessing movie stars and sport celebrities flocked there to hunt ducks and fish."

"People like Ernest Hemingway and Clark Gable?"

Angie nodded. "Possibly. Could be the reason the murder investigation was tossed out and hushed up. Scandal is bad for business."

"If so, business didn't benefit from the cover up. From what I read, the hunting club had to close its doors in the mid-seventies."

"Mother Nature has been reclaiming the island for more than forty years."

Mee Mee straightened and clasped her hands in front of her. "And we're intruding."

"Did you bring your phone?"

"Of course. Why?"

"I had to get permission to access the island from the Mackay Island National Wildlife Refuge." Angie tapped her jeans pocket. "They faxed me the approval papers."

"What's my phone got to do with it?"

"I told them we were photographing wading birds for a

newspaper article."

"What!"

"Don't you write articles for the Outer Banks Sentinel?"

"Occasionally."

"There you go."

"Why didn't you tell them what we were really up to?"

"If I told them this was a murder investigation, they would have insisted local law officials be present. Achak specifically requested a private investigator. In his letter he mentioned he didn't get along with the law."

Mee Mee clasped her hands to her head. "So now I have to write an article about Monkey Island wading birds?"

"You don't have to write the actual article. Just take some photographs in case some official shows up. Besides, most likely it will be just you, me and Mother Nature out there."

"Oh, I'll do what we were approved to do."

"Why?"

"It's not nice to fool Mother Nature."

Chapter 4
A Trip Up North

After passing through the small towns of Salvo, Waves and Rodanthe, they drove along the Pea Island National Wildlife Refuge. Angie enjoyed the rugged beauty of the setting, dunes tufted with seagrasses and an occasional glimpse of the Atlantic Ocean to the right and the wide Croatan Sound to the left graced by the flight of ospreys and cranes gliding above the marshes. Sand drifts encroached upon the road in a few places as if to redeem what man had seized. Angie chuckled to herself. *It's a constant battle on these narrow islands to keep the roads clear and traffic moving. The wind, sea, and storms don't care to cooperate.*

As they crossed the Marc Basnight Bridge over the inlet to Nags Head, Angie glanced to the right at the abandoned Oregon Inlet Lifesaving Station. The gray structure sat atop a tall dune, the roof of its lookout tower a charcoal peak against an azure sky. A lonely sentinel at the north end of the island, the building imparted an air of menace. A little over a year ago, her ex-partner nearly lost his life there in a slugfest with a thug who helped to murder a senator's wife. After that brush with death, he decided to get married and take a break from the private investigation business. On her own, Angie wanted to make a new start, move south and open an office in Buxton.

After crossing the bridge and passing the Bodie Island Lighthouse, she made a right onto Old Oregon Inlet Road. A jaunt through the South Nags Head neighborhood would be good for her soul. She missed her ex-partner, Weston Wolf, and their little office on East Hunter Street. They had been best friends for several years, a great one-two punch in the trade. Angie excelled at research and identifying the small details that could break open a case, and Wolf loved doing the footwork and sometimes the dirty work necessary to get the job done. Their combination of brains and instinct created a successful partnership despite a locale lacking a great demand for private eyes.

"Why are we taking a detour?" Mee Mee asked.

Angie slowed the vehicle as they passed East Hunter Street. "Just checking out my old stomping grounds."

"You worked with Weston Wolf, didn't you?"

"Yes. I was his secretary and then his partner for several years."

"How's he doing?"

"Good. He's a family man now. His wife Freyja convinced him to open up a specialty shop in Nags Head."

"What do they sell?"

"Unusual things. They try to stock their shelves with items no one else offers: Outer Banks antiques, odd shaped driftwood, craftwork from local artists, one of a kind stuff. It's a neat shop. They're always looking for interesting items."

"He stopped at the bookstore during a murder investigation on Roanoke Island. Interesting man. He wanted to know all about the archaeological dig down in Hatteras. It had something to do with the case."

"Wes was a good investigator. However, he didn't do things by the book."

Mee Mee chuckled. "Sounds like some of his ways rubbed off on you."

Angie cringed. "I usually don't cross legal lines."

"Today's an exception?"

"No. That's the difference between me and Wes. He wouldn't have bothered with the proper paperwork. He would have just barged onto the island." She patted her jeans pocket. "We've got legal permission."

Mee Mee shook her head. "Your paper makes us legal by the letter of the law."

"Right, and our extracurricular activity may result in justice being served according to the spirit of the law."

"Guess we've got both sides covered."

Angie laughed. "Now you're learning the game."

Old Oregon Inlet Road merged onto Virginia Dare Trail, the two-lane road that ran along the Atlantic Ocean. For about a mile, gray weathered beach houses loomed atop the dunes. To Angie, they looked ancient compared to most of the colorful newer homes that had been built along the oceanfront over the last thirty years.

"I bet these old beach houses have some stories to tell," Angie said.

"For sure. This stretch is known as Nags Head's Historic Cottage Row."

"I've always wondered about these houses."

"They've been called the Unpainted Aristocracy."

"That's an odd name. Why?"

"Many of them were built more than a hundred years ago to withstand the harsh environment of these barrier islands. Unpainted cedar shingles protected the structures from the weather. Cedar is a tough wood."

"Makes sense, but what's the aristocracy all about?"

"Wealthy planters and businessmen from the mainland built them. They were the first real Outer Banks tourists. Their families would arrive in April or May and stay through October."

"Sounds wonderful."

"I'm sure they had a great time. The kids would play all day on the beach or head over to Jockey's Ridge to climb the huge sand dunes. Parents didn't worry about strangers. Everyone knew each other. The houses were passed down from generation to generation. Many of the original families still own the properties."

"I bet some of the old timers have been coming here since the 1930's."

"I've had some interesting conversations with several of them at the bookstore. They don't care for all the development that has gone on since the 1980's. They prefer the old days and ways."

"Life was simpler back then."

They passed through Nags Head, Kill Devil Hills and Kitty Hawk on the main drag, Route 158, and then turned onto Route 12 for the twenty-mile ride to Corolla. The houses, stores and restaurants along the northern shores contrasted with the Historic Cottage Row. The three-story beach homes, painted with bright colors and outfitted with multi-level decks and pools, appealed to the multitudes who wanted to escape the weary world and spend a week or two along the edge of the ocean in paradise. Between the towns of Duck and Corolla, woods, dunes and scrub brush lined the road with occasional areas of new development: construction crews framing houses and cement trucks pouring driveways.

At the north end of Corolla, Angie turned right on Austin Street and then made a quick left into the Corolla Light Village Shops. The dozen or more stores catered to vacationers who rented beach homes and condos affiliated with the Corolla Light Resort. This end of the Outer Banks appealed to young families with kids who wanted an alternative to the over commercialized beaches along the South Carolina coast. She parked the pickup in front of Ocean Atlantic Rentals, a bright yellow building with rows of bikes in front and kayaks stacked along the rail of a narrow side deck that led to the entrance. They mounted the few steps, crossed the deck and entered the store.

A young guy with butch-cut, bleach-blonde hair and Oakley shades leaned on the counter and smiled at them. He wore a yellow t-shirt with the store's logo: an assortment of umbrellas, beach chairs, bicycles, and watersport equipment arranged on the sand just beyond a crashing wave.

"How can I help you ladies?"

Mee Mee cleared her throat. "We are hoping to complete a three-mile voyage on the Currituck Sound. What kind of kayak do you recommend? We want to be safe but comfortable."

"That's easy." He raised his pointer finger. "You want the Old Town Double. It's fourteen feet long, has a large cockpit for extra gear, and sliding high back seats. Believe me, it's comfortable for extended periods on the water."

"Sounds perfect," Mee Mee said. "How much?"

"A hundred and fifty bucks a week or forty bucks a day."

Mee Mee raised her eyebrows. "Very reasonable. Does it come with a fully stocked wet bar?"

The guy laughed. "No, but it does come with two paddles and life jackets."

"Alright. We'll take it for a day. Ring 'er up." Mee Mee slid a credit card out of her sweatpants pocket and handed it to him.

He took the card, filled out the paperwork, completed the transaction on the card reader and handed her a pen and contract. "Due back in twenty-four hours."

Mee Mee signed the bottom line. "We hope to be back later this afternoon."

Angie thumbed over her shoulder. "I've got a Dodge pickup truck out front."

He nodded. That'll work. I'll load up the kayak for you."

Angie and Mee Mee headed out to the truck. The blond guy arrived about two minutes later with the oars and life jackets. After placing them in the truck bed, he strolled around the side of the deck to where the kayaks were stacked. He hefted a big yellow one onto his right shoulder, toted it to the truck and angled it into the bed so that the backend of the kayak slanted from the top of the tailgate.

"That should ride just fine."

"Thank you, young man," Mee Mee said. "We'll see you later this afternoon."

"You ladies be careful." He lifted his sunglasses above his dark eyebrows and met Mee Mee's gaze. "Those sound waters can get choppy on a windy day like today."

Mee Mee grinned. "If we're not back by four, send the cavalry."

"Will do. Where're you headed?"

"Monkey Island," Angie said.

"I paddled out there once and circled the island. That place is spooky."

"Looks like you made it back in one piece," Mee Mee said.

He shrugged. "Barely."

Chapter 5
On Deadly Waters

At the north end of Corolla, Angie turned left into the Maritime Forest Trail parking lot. The trail was located a few hundred yards south of where the road turned onto the beach and entered the four-wheel drive area where the wild horses roamed. The paved lot offered about a dozen parking spaces for visitors who planned to venture onto the three-quarter mile wooden walkway through the forest to the Currituck Sound. Angie didn't expect too many hikers in mid-October. Two vehicles occupied spaces in the lot, a green Subaru Forester and a blue Chevy Impala, their occupants nowhere in sight. Angie pulled into a space on the far right. They exited the truck and met at the tailgate.

Angie lifted the end of the yellow kayak with both arms. "I'd say it weighs about seventy pounds."

"I think we can handle that."

Angie lowered the tailgate. "I've got this end. She slid the kayak out to the end of the tailgate, Mee Mee lifted the other side, and they lowered it to the asphalt. Angie picked up the shovel and slid it under the high-backed seats. Then she tossed in the oars and life jackets.

"Have you been on this trail before?"

"No, but I checked it out on Google Maps."

Mee Mee chuckled. "Where would we be without Google Maps?"

Angie nodded. "According to the image I viewed, there's a creek that meets the wooden walkway not far from here."

"And the creek empties into the sound?"

"Right. It's a good launching point. I'm guessing the island is less than a mile and a half from there."

Mee Mee picked up her end of the kayak. "Let's get going."

Carrying the kayak, they crossed the parking lot to the wooden walkway. Immediately, they entered the shadows of the woods. Wax myrtle shrubs and ferns grew in scattered patches, and live oaks with their sprawling branches loomed like strange sentinels above the brown-leaf-patched forest floor. Occasional pines towered through the foliage.

Suspended a couple feet above the forest floor, the walkway zigzagged through the woods. Angie noticed a squadron of mosquitoes buzzing above a large puddle. *Glad I coated myself with bug spray.* Butterflies flittered here and there lit by the sun's rays filtering through the canopy of leaves. Birds chirped, twittered and fluttered from branch to branch. After a couple of minutes, Angie's arms ached. *I'm not going to be the first one to complain.* Mee Mee didn't even seem to be straining. *Tough lady.* Finally, they advanced to where the creek edged near the walkway.

"We're here. Set it down," Angie groaned.

Mee Mee lowered the kayak and shook out her arms. "That wasn't too bad."

Angie took a deep breath, made fists and then extended her fingers. "Like the song says, we've only just begun." She stepped off the walkway onto the leaf-covered ground. "There's a clear path to the creek." She reached and lifted her end of the kayak and slid the opposite end to the edge of the walkway.

Mee Mee stepped down and lifted her end. "Lead the way."

They walked about thirty yards and lowered the kayak alongside a shallow creek about six feet wide. Mee Mee tossed Angie a red life jacket, and they both strapped and buckled them on.

They lowered the kayak into the creek, and Angie held it steady against the bank which slanted steeply into the dark water a foot below. Gripping the back of the seat, Mee Mee stepped in gingerly and managed to sit without excessive rocking.

Mee Mee reached and grasped a thick root sticking out of the bank. She pulled the kayak against the shore. "Step in. I'll keep it snug."

As Angie stepped in, her end of the boat drifted from the edge. She stumbled forward, smacking her forehead against the top of the seat. The kayak rocked precariously, but Mee Mee kept a solid hold on the root and steadied it.

"Are you okay?"

"No. I thumped my noggin, and now I got to figure out how to turn around and sit down without sinking us."

"The water's only two feet deep."

"So what? Two feet of water gets you just as wet as twenty feet." With a natural athlete's coordination, she turned and planted her rear on the seat. "Alright. Grab an oar. Let's get out of the shadows and into the sunlight."

After picking up the oars, they paddled slowly along the narrow creek. Occasional rays filtered through the treetops slicing bright shafts of light into the gloom of the woods. A great horned owl eyed them from a high branch of a live oak, turning its head as they passed. The sound of crackling sticks erupted beyond a wax myrtle shrub, and Angie stiffened. "What was that?"

"Probably a squirrel or a raccoon. Nothing to worry about."

"So says you."

Mee Mee paused her rowing, laid the oar across the cockpit in front of her and waved toward the canopy of branches and leaves above them. "You have to admit, this is an incredibly beautiful habitat. It's almost magical."

"Yeah, like the enchanted forest in the Wizard of Oz. I keep thinking the flying monkeys will show up sooner or later."

As they progressed, the creek widened, and they passed a railed deck suspended on posts above an inlet where the walkway ended. A mother, father and two young girls, waved at them. Angie nodded, smiled and waved back.

"Good day for a kayak trip," the father called out. He was tall and angular.

"We're going on an adventure," Mee Mee hollered over her shoulder.

"Stay safe," the petite mother said.

"I want to go, too!" one of the girls, a cutie with light blonde hair, yelled.

Angie felt an odd sensation rise from the core of her being. She figured hearing a young girl's voice released some kind of hormonal reaction. *I ought to pick up a pregnancy test on the way home. I left Joel hanging this morning. We both need to know for certain.*

The creek widened out into the Currituck Sound. Without the protection of the forest, the wind whipped against their backs, and the water became choppy. Angie could barely make out the trees that edged the North Carolina mainland. From her research of the aerial map, she figured the sound was about five miles wide at this point. She squinted and spotted a tuft of land barely visible above the churning water. *That's got to be it.*

Mee Mee lowered her oar and pointed to the left. "I see the island. It's not as far as we figured."

Angie glanced in that direction. "That's not it."

"No?"

"That's Mary Island. From what I could tell on the map, it's just a lump of seagrass in the middle of the Currituck Sound."

"I'm glad you know where we're going."

Angie pointed to the right. "Monkey Island is that way."

Mee Mee shifted her gaze to the northwest. "I can see it. That's a long haul."

"Is that a complaint or an observation."

"Half of one and three-quarters of the other, but people over forty are allowed to complain."

"Uh huh."

After about fifteen minutes of paddling, they could clearly see the island, its tall trees rising above the water's surface.

Angie could tell it wasn't a large island, maybe five or six hundred feet wide. It looked like an oasis in the middle of the gray-green sound waters.

Angie laid her paddle across the cockpit. "Let's take a short break."

"Good idea. We've made good progress." Mee Mee placed her oar in front of her and stretched her arms above her head.

As they drifted in the direction of the island, something cut through the water about fifty yards ahead of them.

Angie took in a sharp breath. "What is that?"

Mee Mee, at the front of the kayak, leaned forward. "A dorsal fin."

"A shark?"

"Yep. A big one."

The fin protruded about a foot out of the water.

Angie could feel her heart ramping up. "What's a shark doing in the sound?"

"Looking for lunch. Probably a bull shark."

Now only about thirty yards away, the fin turned in their direction.

"Oh, fishhooks! It's coming our way." Angie grasped her oar.

"Shhhhhhhhh. Don't move."

The shark angled to their left and brushed the side of the kayak, its black eyes like a ghoul's eyes. Angie gulped and watched the fin as it passed. She could almost touch it. The beast glided through the water for about twenty yards, its fin slicing the surface. But then it made a U-turn. "It's coming back," she whispered.

Mee Mee glanced over her shoulder. "Hand me that shovel."

Chapter 6
An Unexpected Discovery

Angie leaned, grabbed the middle of the handle and edged the shovel forward. Mee Mee grasped the neck of the blade, lifted it and thrust it into the air to catch a better grip on the handle. She flipped the shovel around to angle the blade toward the water. With arms tense, she positioned the shovel and held the blade steady about a foot above the surface. The shark passed slowly, as if daring Mee Mee to make a strike. Then the dorsal fin submerged. They sat frozen on the high-backed seats for more than two minutes.

Finally, Angie let out a long breath and sucked in a quick gulp of air. "Is it gone?"

"I think so. A plastic kayak isn't on its menu."

"The kayak was just the packaging. The monster eyed me like I was a good-sized tuna. I don't think he wanted to mess with you though."

Mee Mee lowered the shovel into the cockpit. "I don't know how much damage I could have done. I was aiming for the eye."

"A slap of its tale, and this kayak would have turned over like the last page of a tragic novel."

Mee Mee laughed. "The End."

Angie picked up her oar. "Come on. We're only about fifteen minutes from the island."

After paddling for five minutes, Angie felt nauseated. She placed the oar across the cockpit and lowered her head. The kayak rocked through the choppy waters, and everything spun.

Mee Mee glanced over her shoulder. "How come you're not paddling?"

"I'm sick."

"That shark really shook you up."

"I don't think that's it."

"Seasick?"

"No. I think I'm pregnant."

Mee Mee stopped paddling, twisted in her seat and stared at her. "Really?"

She nodded.

"Congratulations."

"I'm not certain."

"If you throw up, make sure you lean over the side. We don't want to have to clean your puke out of the cockpit."

"Thanks for the helpful hint, Heloise." She took a deep breath and let it out. "Okay. I think it passed." Angie picked up her oar, and they resumed paddling.

As they neared the island, hundreds of white birds rustled and fluttered in the treetops. Several flew from tree to tree, their long necks and wide wingspan bright against the greenery. About twenty to thirty yards from shore, wooden posts thrust their heads a few inches above the surface like a forgotten fence line peeking above floodwaters. Dead fallen trees, their bark bleached light gray, lay here and there across the shore with their spindly branches cautioning passersby to think twice about encroaching what nature has reconquered.

Angie marveled at the cacophony of squawks and screeches as they drew nearer. "I knew they turned this island into a rookery, but I never imagined I'd see this many big birds."

"It's amazing," Mee Mee gasped. "Snowy egrets, great egrets. Look! I see a tri-colored heron. Over there is a glossy ibis. I bet there's more than a thousand birds nesting here."

"And I'm sure they don't want us bothering them."

"Not at all. We've got to be careful not to rile them up."

"Yeah and avoid being splattered with bird poop."

Mee Mee angled the kayak along the row of protruding posts. "These posts served as part of a bulkhead to protect the island from erosion back in the day." She pointed northward. "They circle the island."

"Obviously, they lost the battle. It looks like half the island has slipped back into the sound."

"The nor'easters that come through here show no mercy."

Angie took her oar and pushed away from one of the posts. "Let's head to the other side where we can see the old hunting club. It'll be easier to follow the map from there."

They paddled around the southwest end of the island, the bottom of the baker's profile according to the shape on the map. The trees and underbrush grew thick and gnarly on that side with hundreds of waterfowl resting and flitting in their branches. As they turned northward on the east side of the island, they could see two buildings through the tangled branches and leaves, a larger dull yellow house and smaller outbuilding. The shoreline in front of the structures was obstructed with dead trees and overhanging bushes. Just to the north of the smaller building, the shore widened.

Mee Mee motioned with her oar beyond the bramble of fallen branches. "There's a clear stretch of sand just ahead. No big trees full of birds."

"That'll work. Let's get onto shore and stretch out our legs."

They maneuvered between the posts and directed the kayak to the edge of the shore. Mee Mee steadied the boat by digging the oar into the wet sand.

Angie climbed out. "It feels good to stand up." She knelt and grasped the side of the kayak and slid it halfway onto the shore. Mee Mee stepped out and stretched her whole body. Then she helped Angie pull the kayak several feet away from the water.

"We better turn it over," Mee Mee said. "There's more than an inch of water in it."

"That's not too bad considering the waves."

Mee Mee removed the shovel from the cockpit and tossed it behind them on the ground. Angie helped her flip the kayak over. They tilted it so it rested on the seats at an angle at which the water could drain. They both removed their life jackets and laid them on the hull of the kayak.

Angie reached into her jacket pocket and slipped out a plastic zip bag containing the map. She peeled open the bag, extracted the map and unfolded it. "We are here." She pointed at the shoreline on the map. "The buildings are to the left. The trail to the big tree starts just to the left of the outbuilding."

Mee Mee picked up the shovel. "We should've brought a machete."

"Hopefully, it won't be that bad. Get your phone ready to take some bird pics."

Mee Mee handed her the shovel. "I almost forgot I'm on assignment from the Audubon Society."

"Follow me." Using the shovel's blade to press back the limbs of overgrown shrubs, Angie entered the shadows. A dozen birds fluttered and screeched in the canopy of branches above them. She could make out a path somewhat obstructed by brush that led to the buildings. She glanced at Mee Mee and pointed to the path. "I think the trail is that way."

Mee Mee raised her cell phone and took several photos of the birds above them. "Oooooh. The sun's rays through the branches produce a really cool effect."

"Wonderful. Maybe you'll win an award."

Angie proceeded down the path, spreading branches apart with the blade of the shovel and her free hand. The ground was sandy and patched with clusters of grass. She edged sideways between two bushes, feeling their sharp branches clawing her back. In a small clearing she caught sight of the main building and outbuilding. The boughs of live oaks leaned over and rested on the back half of the one-story building's gabled roof as if to engulf the structure and eventually crush it. The front of the house looked to be about sixty feet wide with a row of posts supporting an overhang for the porch. Several windows, some still intact and some broken, were spaced evenly across the front. The door in the center, rotting and half open, yawned like an old man's mouth with half his teeth missing.

"I'm glad we don't have to go in there," Angie said.

Mee Mee shrugged. "Could be interesting to take a peek inside. You never know what we might find."

Angie shook her head. "No thanks. I'm heading in that direction." She pointed to the corner of the outbuilding. "The path starts over there."

"Maybe next time."

"Yeah, right."

The outbuilding resembled a small cabin, maybe two or three rooms. Oversized shrubs grew all around it, and branches lay scattered on its roof. Limbs propped a dead fallen tree against the apex of the gable. With her phone held just above her head, Mee Mee pivoted several times and took photographs of the birds rustling in the treetops. To Angie, the place smelled like a chicken coop in need of a good cleaning.

She leaned the shovel against a tree and took out the map. "Okay, I'd say it's only about fifty or sixty yards from here. There should be three tall trees. The X is by the third tree."

Mee Mee tucked her phone back in her jacket pocket. "Lead the way."

Although the path was overgrown, Angie could clearly see where it led. At one time it was probably five or six feet wide. Every few yards she had to squeeze between wax myrtles and bay bushes. The brush of their leaves felt creepy against her hands and face. Occasionally, she stopped and glanced at the map to make sure the path followed the markings on the yellowed paper. Mee Mee used the pauses along the trail as opportunities to take a few more photographs. After about fifty yards, they broke through the thick trees into sunlight.

"We're at the northwest end of the island." Angie could see the sound about sixty yards away. Thick brownish-green grasses covered the ground, and tall bushes edged the shoreline. The few trees left standing were dead, bleached light gray in the sunlight. "Look. There's the three large trees."

"Yeah. All three are dead," Mee Mee said.

"At least they're still standing. Once we get to that third tree, we can figure out where to dig."

They high-stepped through the grasses, swatting away mosquitoes. The ground became soggy in places, but Angie managed to not veer too far from the shortest distance to the tree. As she passed the second tree, she stepped over fallen limbs. Branches jabbed at her ankles, causing a reflex jerk of her leg that almost toppled her.

"Did something scare you?"

"This whole island creeps me out."

They tromped through the high grass to the third tree. It looked to be about forty feet tall, an old skeleton of a pine that once stood proudly against the strong winds and harsh weather that assailed the island.

Angie leaned the shovel against the tree and pulled out the map again. "The X is two paces from the base of the tree in the opposite direction of the water.

"That's easy enough to figure out. You can start digging about six feet from the base of the trunk."

"Me?"

"Yeah. I'm responsible for taking bird pics and writing nature articles."

Angie shook her head, tugged Joel's work gloves out of her jacket pockets, put them on and grabbed the shovel. She pivoted so that her back was against the tree and took two big steps. With the tip of the shovel blade she made an X on the sandy ground. "Let's hope it's not six feet down."

The ground wasn't hard, and within a few minutes she cleared out about a foot and a half of sandy dirt, making the hole about two feet wide. She swiped her sleeve across her forehead. "Can you believe it? I'm actually sweating."

"Do you want me to take over?"

"No. I'll dig for a few more minutes."

After clearing out another six inches of sandy dirt, the shovel pinged against something.

Mee Mee leaned and gazed into the hole. "What was that?"

Angie extended the shovel handle in Mee Mee's direction. "Take this. I'll get down on my hands and knees to check it out." She lowered herself, placed one hand on the edge of the hole and reached down with the other hand to scoop out dirt.

"Watch out!" Mee Mee shrieked.

Angie jerked upwards. "What?"

A brown snake with a large triangular head slithered through the grass and latched its jaws onto Angie's glove. Angie gasped and slid her hand out of the oversized mitt.

Mee Mee raised the shovel and thrust the blade. The swift chop sliced off the serpent's head. The decapitated body writhed in the grass, twirling and twitching. Angie, still on her knees, straightened her body as if she had stuck her finger in a socket.

"Did the moccasin get you?"

Angie shook her head with a jittery motion. "I d-don't think so."

"Let me see your hand."

Angie held out her trembling hand.

Mee Mee grasped and examined it. "Nope. I don't see any fang marks. Aren't you glad I told you to bring gloves?"

Angie glared up at her. "Let's get off of this island."

Mee Mee pulled her to her feet. "We can't leave without what we came for." She dropped to the ground and reached down into the hole. "I can feel something."

Angie planted her hands on her knees and tried to calm herself. Her heart rattled in her chest like an old Ford pickup.

"I'm digging around it. It's about the size of a football." She scooped a couple handfuls of dirt out of the hole. Looking up at Angie, she said, "It's almost loose."

"Hopefully, it doesn't bite."

Mee Mee shifted her shoulders back and forth, trying to

dislodge the object. It broke free. "I got it." She brushed away clods of dirt from around it, grasped the top, raised it out of the hole and held it up for Angie to see.

Her mouth dropped open as she stared into the hollow eyes of a skull.

Chapter 7
Crystal Blue Persuasion

"This thing is heavy," Mee Mee said.

"There must be more bones." Angie leaned and examined the hole. "I don't see anything. We've got to call the sheriff's office"

"That won't be necessary."

"What! Why not?"

Mee Mee extended the skull to Angie. "Here. Hold it."

"I don't think I want to."

Mee Mee knotted her brow. "I insist."

Angie took the skull. The surface was marred with dirt and small clumps of mud. A weird sensation washed over her, as if she could sense people watching from behind the bushes or the shadows of the woods. She panned the area but didn't see anyone. "Why is it so heavy?"

"It's not a real skull. It's a carving."

Angie spit on her thumb and rubbed the skull's forehead. The cleansing revealed a light bluish surface. "It's made out of some kind of stone."

Mee Mee nodded. "The sculptor did a great job. Anatomically, it's life size and fairly accurate."

Angie shook her head. "Why would Achak's grandfather bury a carved skull next to this tree?"

"Hard to say. Maybe it's worth a lot of money. Could be some kind of ancient artifact. Whatever the reason, he felt the need to bury it here."

"But how can a sculpted skull give us any clues to his murder?"

"You're the detective. You tell me."

Angie stared at the top of the skull. That feeling of being watched jangled her nerves again. She glanced around but didn't see anybody. "I know someone who may know something about it."

"Who's that?"

"Freyja Wolf, Weston's wife. They sell carved skulls in their shop in Nags Head. I've seen a few on the shelves."

"We can stop by on the way back to Buxton."

Angie nodded. "Here." She extended the skull to Mee Mee. "You carry Mr. Deadhead. He gives me the heebie-jeebies." She bent over and picked up the shovel and gloves. "Let's get out of here."

Mee Mee motioned toward the ground. "Better fill in the hole first."

Angie put on the gloves and stared at the decapitated snake. "Guess I'll give our friend a proper burial." With the blade of the shovel, she swept the moccasin's body and head into the hole. Then she shoveled and scraped the dirt back into the hole and patted the ground level.

Mee Mee used her foot to spread dead leaves across the surface to cover the disturbed area. "There. No one will know the difference."

"The snake certainly won't. Do you want to offer a eulogy before we go?"

"Sure." Mee Mee cradled the skull in front of her by linking her fingers. "I've always heard that every good tale begins with a snake. Too bad this one lost its head in the early pages. May he rest in peace on this small patch of paradise."

"Amen." Angie turned and headed toward the thick stand of trees that surrounded the hunting club and outbuilding. "Let's get out of Eden before the avenging angel shows up."

They trudged through the tall grass and found the path that wound through the bushes and trees. The birds in the branches squawked, fluttered and screeched, their unease intensifying. As Angie eyed the chaotic agitation above her, a chill ran through her, causing her muscles in her back to tense.

"I don't think these birds like us," Mee Mee said.

Angie glanced over her shoulder. "Maybe it's Mr. Deadhead."

"Skulls do have a way of shaking things up."

"Yeah, they remind us of our ultimate destiny."

As they passed the decrepit building, Mee Mee said, "Are you sure you don't want to stop in and check out the hunting club?"

"Positive. Third time's a charm."

"Huh?"

"The shark didn't eat me. The moccasin didn't bite me. I'm not going to give that rotting heap of wood a chance to fall on me."

"It looks pretty solid to me."

"You can come back tomorrow and spend all day here. I'm leaving."

"Okay, okay, I'm right behind you."

Angie hurried along the path and edged sideways through the sprawling plants and bushes. When she reached the clearing by the kayak, she brushed herself off, making sure no insects clung to her clothing. She could feel the strong breeze blowing from the south. The old Bob Seger song, *Against the Wind*, played through her mind, but she changed the words slightly. *Against the wind, I'll be paddling against the wind. I'll be weak and worn and paddling against the wind.*

Mee Mee dropped to her knees on the bank, cradling the skull in the crook of her right arm.

"What are you doing?"

"I'm going to clean this thing off and see what it looks like." She bent over with one hand anchored on the bank and dipped the skull into the water. Leaning on her elbows, she scrubbed the surface of the sculpture with her fingers. "Oh my . . . it's . . . it's beautiful. I think it's made of crystal." After about a minute of washing the surface of the carving, she raised herself onto her knees and held up the skull. The water draining from its surface made it gleam. Periwinkle swirled through its light blue coloring like wispy clouds.

Angie met the skull's gaze, and that weird feeling returned. "I think it's evil."

"Nonsense. It's a work of art. I'm going to call it Crystal Blue Persuasion."

Angie tossed the shovel onto the ground and flipped the kayak over. "You can keep it on your end of the boat."

Mee Mee laughed. "Come on now. We just dug this guy up, and you're making him feel unwanted."

"He's not the first creepy bonehead I've rejected." Angie picked up her life jacket and slipped into it. "Help me get this kayak in the water."

Mee Mee placed the skull in the back of the kayak behind her seat. After putting on her lifejacket, she helped Angie lift the boat. They edged to the shore and lowered the vessel into the water. The waves lapped at its side.

Mee Mee gripped the edge of the back seat with one hand and the side of the kayak with the other. "I'll hold it steady. You climb in."

Angie picked up the shovel and dropped it alongside the seats. She took off her gloves and stuck them into her jacket pockets. Anchoring her hand on the back of the seat, she stepped in, sat down and picked up a paddle. The kayak rocked precariously, but she jammed the paddle into the wet sand and held it steady against the shore.

Mee Mee climbed in, sat down and picked up her paddle. "Raise the anchor and bring it on home."

Angie extracted the oar blade and pushed off the bank. "Home sounds good. It's the mile and a half of choppy waters that bothers me."

As they paddled between the posts, Angie noticed an osprey atop a huge nest mounted on the pedestal of a fallen tree about ten feet above the water. The raptor glared at them as they passed. She stopped paddling and watched it, shifting in her seat and turning her head. The bird sprung from the nest and swooped down at Mee Mee.

Mee Mee ducked and raised her paddle over her head. "What's wrong with that bird! It's not nesting season."

The osprey flew about fifty yards out and then banked into the wind and turned back in their direction.

Angie dug her oar into the water, to the right and then left, as quickly as her arms could manage. "Let's get away from that nest!"

The osprey dove at them again, clipping Angie's shoulder and brushing her hair with its wing.

They paddled furiously. The bird circled above them. The front of the boat slapped and rocked against the oncoming waves.

Angie felt like she was riding a bronco. She dug harder with the right oar to turn them to a less direct angle into the rolling water. Glancing up, she saw the osprey diving at them. "Here it comes again!" She ducked, held onto the oar with one hand and covered her head with her other arm.

"We must be trespassing. Keep paddling!" Mee Mee shouted.

Screeching, the bird flew between them, circled back to the pedestal and landed on the old nest. They paddled again, making better progress with the less direct angle into the waves. However, with every few waves, water lapped over the edge of the kayak.

"Blasted bird!" Angie glanced over her shoulder. "We're definitely not wanted around here." She faced forward. "In twenty minutes, this boat is going to fill with water."

"You're right. We may have to head into shore and dump it out."

"If we can make it to shore."

"I'd say we're about a half mile from that peninsula."

Angie glanced to her left and saw the narrow tract of land extending several hundred feet into the sound. "Let's make a beeline for it." She eyed the bottom of the boat. "We've already taken on over an inch of water." She dipped the right paddle several times to turn shoreward.

"Paddle like the devil is after us!" Mee Mee hollered.

"He probably is. We stole his skull."

After twenty minutes of fighting the waves, they reached the peninsula. Its steep bank and tall grass made it difficult to beach the kayak. Angie clasped clumps of vegetation and pulled the vessel as close as possible to the edge of the shore. Mee Mee climbed out and held the side of the kayak steady as Angie stepped out. They each took an end and dragged the yellow boat into the tall grass.

Angie stood and stretched her back, heaving air. "I'm exhausted and my back hurts. That was farther than a half mile."

"Distances across water can be deceiving." Mee Mee removed the shovel and skull from the kayak and nestled them in the grass. "We can take a fifteen-minute break. I'd say we're less than a mile from the creek."

Angie pointed to the southeast. "Yeah, if we head straight across the open water. If we hug the shoreline, it will be another mile and a half."

"Help me turn this thing over and dump out the water."

The kayak had collected about four inches of water. They heaved and flipped the boat over and then angled it in the grass so it would drain.

Angie plopped onto the ground and lay back in the lush grass. "I pray no snakes crawl over me in the next fifteen minutes." She stared at the sky. Cirrus clouds drifted against an azure blue. The sun shone down at a slanting angle from the north, warming her face.

Mee Mee sat next to her. "I've been thinking about that skull."

"And . . . ?"

"You don't bury a work of art like that unless there's a good reason."

"Fear? Superstition?"

"I don't think so. In the letter, Achak said he believed his grandfather was tortured."

"Right."

"Someone wanted that skull, and he wasn't willing to give it up."

"So, they tortured him in hopes that he would crack?"

"Exactly. But he didn't."

"And they killed him."

Mee Mee nodded. "That's how I see it."

"Crystal Blue Persuasion."

"What?"

"Nothing."

"Tell me why you said that."

Angie sat up. "That's the name you gave the skull."

"Do you think the skull has persuasive powers?"

"It sure seems like it. According to your theory, people are willing to torture and murder to possess it. For fifty-five years it sat in the ground until we were persuaded to dig it up. There's some kind of persuasion there."

Mee Mee crossed her arms. "If it's valuable, then the persuasion is human greed. Believing *the skull* has the power to persuade is irrational."

"There's a fine line between the irrational and the unknown."

Mee Mee chuckled. "The superstitions of today become the science of tomorrow, huh?"

Angie struggled to her feet. "Right. What would you say if I told you a Harvard study just proved that a black cat crossing your path truly brings bad luck?"

Mee Mee stood. "I'd say you're telling me a fabricated inexactitude."

Angie grinned. "Does that mean I'm lying?"

Mee Mee nodded.

"You're right. I made that one up." She trudged through the grass to the kayak and flipped it over. "Let's get this thing back in the sound. We've got a long stretch of water ahead of us, and that's not a frabri . . . .whatever you said. It's a fact."

They managed to get back into the boat without tipping it and paddled into the open water. The wind whipped into their faces, driving the waves into the bow, so they angled to the left a few hundred yards and then to the right to get back on track. The weaving helped them make progress, but the water continued to lap over the starboard side and collect in the bottom. After about twenty minutes, Angie felt exhausted. However, she could see the deck at the end of the Maritime Forest Trail where the creek entered the woods about five or six hundred yards away. She kept dipping the paddles and pulling them through the water. The pain in her back and shoulders intensified as if a pack of trolls were stabbing her with blunt knives.

"I'm going to down a bottle of ibuprofen when I get home. My back is killing me," Angie groaned.

"Back pain is youth leaving the body."

Angie glanced down. "We've got a lot of water in the bottom of this boat again."

"I noticed that. We're only ten or fifteen minutes away from the creek. I think we can make it."

"Either we will, or we won't. There's no other option."

"Repeat after me: I think we can. I think we can. I think we can."

Angie shook her head. "You've been reading too many children's books."

By the time they got to within one hundred yards of where the creek emptied into the sound, the water had filled the boat to within an inch of the top edge. The shovel and skull wallowed around in the bottom.

"We might have to walk it in from here," Mee Mee said. "It's only three or four feet deep."

"Maybe it's not deep, but it's wet and cold."

They progressed about twenty-five yards before the kayak went under. As Angie slipped into the freezing water, she sucked in a sharp breath. "We're going to catch pneumonia." The footing was solid, but the waves lapped above the bottom of her lifejacket.

"Grab your end," Mee Mee ordered. "Don't let the kayak sink to the bottom."

Angie managed to grasp the plastic handle on her end of the boat. The top of the high-backed seats remained above the water. She could see the shovel sloshing around in the cockpit. "Did the skull fall out?"

Mee Mee held up Crystal Blue Persuasion. "I've got it."

Angie pointed to her right where a narrow strip of land extended a good distance from the shoreline. "There's the closest solid ground."

Mee Mee's eyes grew wide. "You're not going to believe this."

"What?"

"A black cat just crossed our path."

Angie whipped around to see a familiar fin cut through the water in their direction less than thirty yards ahead of her.

Chapter 8
A Cold, Hard Stare

The fin slowly submerged and disappeared. Angie turned and glared at Mee Mee. "What do we do now?"

Mee Mee held the end of the kayak with one hand and the skull lifted shoulder high in the other. She took a slow breath. "Stay completely still."

Angie focused on the skull. Its malevolent grin sent a deeper chill through her frigid body. *The thing is a death magnet.* She eyed Mee Mee. The bookstore owner's face muscles remained rigid, but then her eyes widened. Angie turned to see the fin resurface like a Nazi periscope.

"Don't move," Mee Mee said in a hushed voice.

The bull shark slowly sank and swam under the kayak between them. As it passed, Angie saw the top of its tail swishing just below the water's surface. The monster was at least ten feet long. The dorsal fin reappeared about twenty yards beyond them heading out into the Currituck Sound.

"Okay. Let's get to the shore," Mee Mee ordered.

Angie pointed to her right at the thin finger of land that stretched into the sound. "Over there! Go!"

Mee Mee led the way, charging through the choppy water while holding the skull out in front of her and tugging the kayak. As Angie trailed, she kept glancing over her shoulder to check on the shark. When they got to within ten yards of shore, the dorsal fin reappeared. The beast, about five yards away, zeroed in on her.

Angie let go of the back of the kayak and dove toward the bank. She felt the shark's nose nudge her foot, and she kicked back against it. As she surfaced, she reached for the grass on the edge of the waterline. Seizing a clump, she flipped herself over and drew her legs out of the water. The shark rose up, thrashing and chomping at her feet. She kicked harder as she scooted herself backwards onto the shore.

Mee Mee stepped forward with the shovel and whomped the blade onto the beast's forehead. The monster slung a curtain of water over them with its tail. Then, caught on the shallow bank, it shifted back and forth until it managed to free itself and slip below the surface.

Angie leaned back on her elbows and heaved in air. Water drained from her hair and lifejacket. Trembling, she sat up and eyed her work boots.

Mee Mee leaned over her. "Do you still have all your toes?"

Angie reached and dislodged a triangular object from the rubber tread on the tip of her shoe—a shark's tooth about an inch long. She wriggled her toes. "I think they're all still here."

"Nice souvenir." Mee Mee dropped the shovel, extended her hands and pulled Angie to her feet.

Angie took several deep breaths to slow her heart and steady her trembling hands. "Joel is not going to believe this." She slipped the tooth into her jeans pocket and glanced at the kayak. "You yanked that waterlogged boat onto shore all by yourself?"

Mee Mee nodded. "Adrenaline can turn a one-hundred-and-twenty-pound bookworm into Supergirl."

Angie blew out a long breath. "Thanks for whacking that brute with the shovel."

"Had to. He broke the number one shark attack rule."

"What's that?"

"You can't attack a human unless you hear the Jaws music."

Angie shook her head. "I feel like I just stepped out of a nightmare."

Mee Mee trudged through the thick grass to the kayak, dropped the shovel and flipped the vessel over to drain the water. "I'm thankful you're still in one piece . . ." She reached into the deep grass and lifted the skull. ". . . and Mr. Crystal Blue Persuasion is no worse for wear."

Angie gave the skull a cold stare. "Yeah, he looks happier than a butcher's dog. Bet he got a kick out of watching me do the Frantic Shark Shuffle."

Mee Mee chuckled. "Come on, now. He's just an old chunk of crystal. He doesn't know the difference between a bull shark and a hole in the ground."

Angie shook her head. "Oh, he knows. He knows we were the ones who dug that hole and unleashed him."

"So you think we're cursed?"

"Maybe."

"You're full of beans." Mee Mee motioned toward the kayak. "Let's haul this thing to the walkway. We need to get back to your truck and get warmed up. I feel like I just went skinny dipping in a snowstorm."

Angie walked to the kayak and helped Mee Mee turn it over. After placing the oars, lifejackets and shovel into the cockpit, she reached for the handle on the front end.

Mee Mee carefully secured the skull behind the back seat and picked up her end. "Lead the way."

Angie peered at the walkway deck. It looked to be about two hundred yards away. She high stepped through the tall grass and weaved around an occasional bush. Her arm muscles ached from all the rowing, and now the weight of the kayak threatened to pull her elbow joint apart. The narrow strip of land that extended from the main shoreline was only about thirty yards wide. She strained to see through the knee-high grass to the ground. *There's probably a thousand water moccasins between here and the walkway.*

After about a hundred yards, she stopped. "I need to switch arms."

"Me, too," Mee Mee groaned.

They lowered the kayak and shook out their arms.

"How much am I getting paid on this case?" Angie asked.

"Not enough."

"You got that right."

They picked up the kayak and plodded the last hundred yards to the walkway. The deck, mounted on piers, extended from the shore into the mouth of the creek. Raised about five feet off the ground, it presented a challenge to climb up and over the railing and then somehow get the kayak with its highbacked seats up and over.

"I'll climb onto the deck," Mee Mee said. "You can tilt the kayak on its end and lean it against the railing."

Angie glanced from the top of the railing down to the kayak. "That should work if my arms don't give out."

They lowered the kayak into the grass and removed the equipment and skull. Wooden benches lined the perimeter of the deck, offering hikers a place to sit down after traversing the three-quarter mile walkway through the maritime forest. Angie clasped her hands together to give Mee Mee a foothold and boost up over one of the benches. Then she lifted the front end of the kayak and   heaved it up against the back of the nearest bench. Mee Mee handled the front while Angie clasped the handle on the backend and lifted it like a weightlifter doing a press. Mee Mee managed to slide the boat across the top of the bench and set her end down. Then she scurried to the other end, picked it up and lowered it to the deck.

Leaning against the back of the bench, she peered down at Angie. "There. That wasn't too bad. Hand me up the equipment."

"I wish you weren't so peppy." Angie picked up the oars and shovel and extended them to her. Then she tossed up the lifejackets.

After putting the equipment in the cockpit, Mee Mee leaned over the bench again. "Remember, there's always a light at the end of the tunnel."

Angie picked up the skull and stared into its hollow eyes. "Just hope that light isn't Engine Number Nine."

Mee Mee reached and took the skull. "Mr. CBP could be the

puzzle piece we need to solve this cold case."

"Mr. CBP?"

Mee Mee grinned. "Mr. Crystal Blue Persuasion." She placed the skull into the back of the cockpit.

"Help me get up onto the deck."

With a hand up from Mee Mee, Angie managed to mount the deck and climb over the bench. They faced a half mile tramp to where they originally stepped off the walkway and lowered the kayak into the creek and then another quarter mile along the walkway to the parking lot. Using both hands extended behind her to grip the kayak handle, Angie led the way. Every couple hundred yards they lowered the kayak and rested. By the time they got to the truck, Angie's arms felt so elongated she should pass for a chimpanzee.

Mee Mee removed the skull and placed it on the front passenger seat while Angie rubbed out her elbows. Then they lifted the kayak and angled it down into the bed of the truck from the top of the tailgate.

Once they both climbed into the cab, Angie glanced over and saw the skull in Mee Mee's lap. "That thing doesn't bother you at all, does it?"

Mee Mee patted the top of Mr. CBP's head. "Nope. I think he likes me."

Angie started the truck, backed up and pulled out of the parking lot onto Route 12. "Maybe he'll tell you who killed Achak's grandfather."

"In some roundabout way, he just might."

It only took a few minutes to get to Ocean Atlantic Rentals. The young clerk came out and unloaded the kayak for them. He lifted his Oakleys and spied the shovel in the cockpit. "What did you do? Go treasure hunting?" He picked up the shovel and handed it to Angie.

"More like grave digging," Mee Mee said.

The young man straightened. "Huh?"

Angie gave Mee Mee a perturbed glance and then eyed the

salesclerk. "She's just jerking your leash. We brought the shovel along in case we ran into snakes."

"Or a nasty shark," Mee Mee added.

The guy laughed. "Yeah, right."

Angie turned and headed back to the truck. "She's not kidding about the shark," she grumbled.

They climbed into the cab, and Angie backed out, drove through the shopping area and turned south onto Route 12. The drive to Nags Head would take about forty-five minutes. Angie zoned out as they cruised along the two-lane road, her mind and body numb from the unsettling excursion. The warmth of the truck's heater helped to ease her shivering but lulled her to the edge of drowsiness. Sharp turns brought her back to consciousness as she tensed up and refocused. Mee Mee hummed along to the old rock ballads on the satellite seventies station, Elton John's *Goodbye Yellow Brick Road* and Bread's *Everything I Own*.

At the north end of Kitty Hawk, she turned onto the four-lane Route 158. The lively traffic flow and multitude of stoplights snapped her out of the zombie zone and reengaged her concentration. She took a quick peek at Mr. Deadhead. "I hope this escapade was worth the risk."

Mee Mee cradled the skull in her lap. "I've been thinking about that. I'm convinced CBP has some juju."

"Some what?"

"Juju. You know, magic powers."

"Didn't you tell me it was just an old chunk of crystal?"

"I'm not saying *I believe* it has magic powers. There are objects in this world that are venerated by certain groups of people who are convinced the object possesses supernatural capacity."

"I know the thing freaks me out."

"There you go. That demonstrates my point."

"How so?"

"You are supersensitive to the vibes Mr. CBP emits."

"Wait a minute. You just said you don't believe it has magical powers."

"I don't, but its very appearance throttles you. I imagine it has the same effect on others."

"And so, people with similar reactions conclude the skull can project power or control like some kind of ancient idol?"

Mee Mee held the skull up and peered into its eye sockets. "Right. And you never know how far true believers will go to possess something like this."

"Do you think Achak's grandfather was a true believer?"

"No doubt, but he wasn't the only one."

Angie shook her head. "That seems extreme: murdering someone over a superstitious notion about a hunk of crystal."

"Being a detective, I would think you should entertain such a possibility."

"Why's that?"

"The act of murder is extreme."

"Aren't you jumping to conclusions?"

"What do you mean?"

"It's only murder if we find a body. Until then, Grandpa Rowtag is just a missing person who buried a crystal skull."

"What do you think, Mr. CBP?" Mee Mee shook the skull like a Magic 8-Ball. "He says, 'Signs point to yes'."

"But he's a bonehead."

At the north end of Nags Head Angie spotted a Wendy's on the left side of the road. "I'm starved. Let's stop and get something to eat."

"Good idea. I love their apple pecan salad."

"Salad? Going to Wendy's for a salad is like going to Denzel Washington's house to get the cleaning lady's autograph. I'm getting the double bacon cheeseburger, large fries and a Coke."

"What do you think, Mr. CBP?" Mee Mee shook the skull again. "He says the journey of a thousand pounds begins with a double bacon cheeseburger."

"I've had enough of the bonehead's comments. Besides, I'm

eating for two."

Mee Mee laughed. "I hope you are pregnant."

Angie nodded. "Me, too."

After going through the drive-thru and picking up their food, Angie turned right on Dean Street, right again on Wrightsville Boulevard and then left onto Neptune Drive toward the sea. At the stop sign she turned south onto Virginia Dare Trail, the two-lane road that ran along the ocean. As she munched on her fries, she noticed the unpainted beach houses of Historic Cottage Row. They sat atop the dunes, their brownish-gray cedar shingles looking drab in the bright sunshine. Most of them had become larger structures over the years, their owners adding rooms to accommodate growing families. She sensed an austere doggedness in their stubborn stance against the constant battering of wind and waves. Their dark shapes raged against the background of beige sand and blue sky, defying nature's fury. To Angie, they possessed an uncanny aspect like weathered gravestones in old cemeteries.

The Wolfs' specialty shop, the Lost Lagoon, was located in the Surfside Shopping Plaza along Virginia Dare Trail. The plaza had a good size parking lot surrounded by more than a dozen shops. As Angie slowed to make the right turn into the plaza, she spotted a young brunette pushing an elderly lady in a wheelchair across the street. Angie stopped the pickup and allowed them to pass. The brunette's beige turtleneck and tight jeans accentuated her slim but shapely figure. The older woman swiveled her head and stared at Angie. Frost gray streaked her long black hair, and her eyebrows peaked like the wings of a raven. She had sunken eyes, wizened cheeks and a hooked nose. Her black dress reached almost to her ankles, and a white pinned laced collar encompassed her neck. The woman's stare startled her, but Angie maintained eye contact until she looked away. The brunette pushed her toward the first shop on the left, the Wolf's Lost Lagoon.

"I recognize them," Mee Mee said. "They've stopped by the

bookstore a few times. They must live in one of the historic houses across the street."

Angie nodded. "I think I've seen her in a few horror movies."

"That's a mean thing to say."

"I'm in a mean mood." Angie turned into the plaza and parked in the middle of the lot facing the store. Twenty or so motorcycles filled the spaces around them. "Looks like the Hell's Angels are here."

Mee Mee laughed and thumbed over her shoulder. "Noooo. The Harley Davidson shop is right behind us. You're gloomier than an abandoned amusement park."

"You'll have to bear with me. The events of the day have convinced me to expect the worst. Hand me that double bacon cheeseburger."

Mee Mee extracted the paper-wrapped burger out of the bag and gave it to her. "I'm sure this dead cow will improve your mood."

"It couldn't hurt." As she took a big bite of the burger, she watched the brunette push the old woman into the open door of the Lost Lagoon.

As Mee Mee picked at her salad, Crystal Blue Persuasion stared up from her lap. "This is delicious."

"Don't you mind Deadhead watching you eat?"

"I could set him on the dashboard. I think he'd really enjoy seeing you scarf down that burger." Mee Mee set the skull on the dashboard. "There you go."

Angie eyed the skull's empty eyes. "Now I'm getting indigestion."

"Don't blame Mr. CBP. It's that ground chuck churning in your belly."

After finishing their lunch, they exited the pickup and headed to the store. The shops on the left side of the lot were aligned in a long one-story building with a flat roof. Large windows fronted the Wolf's shop with a couple orange

Adirondack chairs and a glider bench in front. A large neon OPEN sign hung in the middle window with a variety of odd-shaped pieces of driftwood along the shelf at the bottom. Necklaces with sea glass pendants hung from silver chains on the branches of the driftwood. Carrying the skull in front of her, Mee Mee opened the door and entered. Angie followed and stepped up beside her near a rack of t-shirts.

As the door closed behind Angie, the old woman turned her wheelchair and faced them. Her eyes caught fire, and she spun the wheels, charging toward them. The young brunette pivoted away from the counter, and her mouth dropped open as she watched her slide to a stop a few feet away.

The crone's face lit up like an arsonist watching a house burn. "Where did you get that skull?"

Angie straightened, chills shooting up her back. "I don't think it's any of your business."

The old woman's eyes froze into a cold, hard stare.

Chapter 9
Buckle Up, Buttercup

"Grandmother!" the brunette rushed to the back of the wheelchair. "What are you doing?"

The old woman took a deep breath. "The . . . the . . . skull looks so familiar. I . . . I wanted to get a closer look."

The girl's emerald eyes widened as she lowered her delicate chin, her face flushing. "You'll have to excuse my grandmother. She collects carved skulls."

"Not a problem," Mee Mee said.

"Don't I know you?" the pretty girl asked.

Mee Mee smiled graciously. "Yes. I'm Mee Mee Roberts. I own the bookstore in Buxton."

"Of course. We've visited that store a few times. I'm Charlotte Crane. This is my grandmother, Olivia Crane."

"Nice to meet you." Mee Mee nodded toward Angie. "This is my friend, Angie Thomas."

The brunette smiled and bobbed her head.

Olivia Crane raised her bony hand and pointed. "Is the skull for sale?"

"No." Angie crossed her arms.

"Not at this time," Mee Mee said.

She raised her raven-wing eyebrows. "Then why are you bringing it here?"

"My friends own this store," Angie said. "They've handled a few crystal skulls. We want them to take a look at this one."

"I've handled a few myself. Can I hold it?" She held out trembling hands.

Mee Mee eyed Angie.

Angie shrugged. *Maybe this old shrew knows something about the murder.* "I guess so."

Mee Mee lowered the skull into Olivia Crane's hands. "We call him Crystal Blue Persuasion."

She nestled the skull in her lap and clasped her fingers across the dome of its head. Her eyes rolled up, and she closed her lids. She took several deep breaths, and her bottom lip trembled. "This is one of the Thirteen! He is number Ten."

Angie glanced at Mee Mee and raised her eyebrows. She refocused on the woman. Olivia Crane lifted the skull to chest level, her arms shaking slightly.

"Grandmother . . ." Charlotte touched her shoulder.

"Shhhhhhhh." The old woman's face muscles tensed. She opened her eyes and gazed into the empty eye sockets.

"Grandmother, you're acting strange. We're in a public place."

She lowered the skull. "I know where you found him."

Angie raised her chin. "Where?"

"Not on this island but on another."

A cold tingling prickled Angie's shoulders and shot down into her legs. "What island?"

"One not far from here." Her lips formed an odd smile. "Your journey was perilous."

"How did you know that?" Mee Mee asked.

"He spoke to me when I gazed into his eyes."

Mee Mee leaned forward, planting her hands on her knees. "Mr. Crystal Blue Persuasion spoke to you?"

She nodded.

Angie cleared her throat. "We did have some difficulties on the way there and back, but I think you're making good guesses."

She swiveled her head. "How did you know where to dig?"

"What?" Angie's mind scrambled for an answer.

"You dug him up. How did you know where to dig?"

"We were treasure hunting and got lucky, I guess," Mee Mee said.

"No." Olivia Crane handed the skull back to Mee Mee. "It was not luck. It was fate."

Footsteps echoed from the back of the store. Angie peered up to see Weston Wolf approaching them. A few streaks of gray highlighted his unruly brown hair. He smiled, and some slight wrinkles sprouted from around his eyes and creases formed on the sides of his cheeks. In his early forties, Wolf still looked trim and fit, wearing gray cargo shorts and a blue button-down denim shirt.

He raised his thick brown eyebrows. "Well look who's here, my good buddy, Angie Thomas."

The familiar voice caused a smile to break up her sober demeanor. "Hi, Wes."

"And Mee Mee Roberts. Good to see you again."

"Hello." Mee Mee swept her arm like a gameshow prize presenter. "I love your new store."

"Thanks. We're making a go of it."

Olivia Crane took hold of the wheels and edged forward a few inches. "Excuse me. We must be leaving."

"It was nice meeting you," Mee Mee said as she stepped aside.

Angie took a few steps backwards and opened the door.

Charlotte grasped the handles on the back of the chair. "It was nice meeting you, too." She pushed her grandmother toward the door.

Olivia Crane raised her hand. "Stop, Charlotte!"

She halted the chair beside Mee Mee.

Olivia Crane reached up and caressed the side of the skull's face. "I'll be seeing you soon."

"Uh . . . okay," Mee Mee said. "Stop by the store any time."

Charlotte cringed and pushed her grandmother out the door and into the parking lot.

Angie slipped back into the store as the door closed. "I don't think she was talking to you."

Mee Mee appraised the skull and nodded. "I think you're

right."

"She's a strange one," Wolf said.

Angie stepped up beside Mee Mee. "Does she come in here often?"

"About once a week. She's always looking for something unusual." Wolf pointed at the skull. "How'd you get your hands on that gem?"

Mee Mee lifted the skull with one hand. "We dug it up, just like Mrs. Crane surmised."

"We're on a murder investigation," Angie said.

"Interesting."

"A cold case," Mee Mee added.

"*Very* interesting. Where did you find it?"

"Monkey Island," Angie said.

"Can I take a closer look?"

"Sure." Mee Mee handed Wolf the skull.

"It's crystal. We've sold a few of these."

"Are they common?" Mee Mee asked.

"Not at all." He raised the skull to eyelevel. "Life-size ones are very rare . . . and expensive."

Angie rubbed her chin. "How did she know we dug it up on an island not far from here? That freaked me out."

Mee Mee shrugged and pointed at the skull. "She said that Mr. Crystal Blue Persuasion told her."

"I don't think so." Wolf brushed the side of the skull with his thumb. "I can see remnants of sand and dirt. Mrs. Crane probably noticed it, too, and figured the thing had been buried."

"That makes sense," Angie said, "but how did she know we found it on another island?"

"Your clothes look wet, and your hair is matted down." Wolf grinned. "I'd guess you were kayaking on rough waters."

"Of course," Mee Mee said. "Mrs. Crane picked up on our appearance right away. She even commented that our journey was perilous."

Angie stared at her damp boots. "Smart lady." She felt a rush of blood to her face. *Wes just gave me a lesson in Observation 101. I feel like an amateur. Why didn't I catch on? I was too spooked by the skull and Olivia Crane's dramatics. Unless . . . unless . . . she knows something.* "Her fascination with the skull makes her a person of interest."

Wolf nodded. "That's a relevant consideration. You said it was a cold case. When did the murder take place?"

"1966," Mee Mee said.

"On Monkey Island?"

Angie bobbed her head. "On or nearby. The victim's fishing boat was discovered floating in the sound. The body was never recovered."

"No body? So, it wasn't officially booked a murder."

"Correct," Angie said. "The grandson of the victim has his suspicions. He hired us."

"Mrs. Crane has been around a long time. I'd say she's in her late seventies. She owns one of the older houses along Historic Cottage Row."

Mee Mee scratched the top of her head. "If I can do the math, then she would have been about thirty when Grandpa Rowtag went missing."

"Sounds about right." He handed the skull to Mee Mee.

With her hands linked, she bobbed it slowly. "Mr. CBP just may open a door for us."

Angie cleared her throat. "I'd like to know more about crystal skulls before we go knocking on that door."

Wolf thumbed over his shoulder. "Freyja knows all about them. We've got several for sale on a shelf in the back."

"Where is your wife?" Angie asked.

"In the office working on the books. I'll go get her." He about-faced and sauntered toward the back of the store.

Angie glanced around the establishment. To the left she saw Mermaid Corner: a number of paintings and sculptures featuring mermaids, some sensuous and some fanciful. On the right side of the store a long glass case featured necklaces, rings and bracelets fitted with polished stones and sea glass. The back left corner displayed colorful clothing: hats and handbags hung on several rows of hooks along the wall; several sleek and faceless mannequins sported jackets and exquisitely designed blouses; a couple racks offered a variety of shirts and outfits.

In the middle a huge lazy Susan with several levels, displayed lighthouses and seashells. A replica of the Cape Hatteras Lighthouse stood on top and almost reached the ceiling. Large whelk shells circled the next level down. Smaller lighthouses and shells filled the remaining levels.

The items and shelves in the back right corner caught her attention. Carved from wood, a life-size Black Beard stood in a long black coat with his captain's hat tilted back on his head. He held two flintlock pistols, and red bows adorned the ends of his braided beard. Behind him, pirate ships and skulls crowded several shelves. Most of the skulls, wearing eyepatches and bandanas, appeared to be manufactured for retail sale. A number of Day-of-the-Dead skulls, brightly painted and decorated, smiled down from the top shelf. The middle shelf featured a row of glass or possibly crystal skulls, most of them three or four inches in height. However, a large black skull in the middle dominated the shelf.

Freyja Wolf entered the store through a rear doorway. Her sheer teal dress and matching tunic-length jacket flowed as she walked toward them. A string of white pearls flashed against her tanned neckline. Her long legs and shoulder-length ash blonde hair added to her world class looks, marred only by the pinkish and white scars that scored the left side of her face. Her husband followed a few steps behind.

"Hi, ladies," Freyja said with a smoky voice that reminded Angie of Cher.

"Love your shop," Mee Mee said.

"Thanks."

"It's definitely unique," Angie added.

"So are we." Freyja smiled, the taut scarring tugging at the corners of her eye and lips.

Wolf reached and grasped her shoulder. "She's unique. I'm just an old chunk of coal."

Freyja elbowed his ribs. "Yeah, I found him in my stocking on Christmas morning."

"What can I say?" Wolf winked. "You've been a naughty girl."

"I'm hoping he'll turn into a diamond one day."

Angie chuckled. "That's not going to happen."

"That's a beautiful skull." Freyja extended her hands. "Can I hold it?"

Mee Mee handed the skull to her. "We call him Mr. CBP."

Freyja took a deep breath and closed her eyes. After a few seconds, she nodded. "This one is special." She rubbed the top with her thumb. "It looks to be carved from Dumortierite quartz."

"Why did you close your eyes?" Angie asked.

Freyja shrugged. "Just trying to make a connection. This is the same material used in hard drives for memory storage. Crystal quartz microchips can hold incredible amounts of data and last forever."

Mee Mee narrowed her eyes. "Are you saying Mr. CBP has memories?"

Freyja nodded. "Many people believe they record what's going on around them. The question is: How do you access the information?"

"Obviously," Angie said, "computer scientists have figured out how to do it. You turn them into memory disks."

"Right." Freyja raised the skull slightly. "But I'm talking about crystal quartz in this state. When I close my eyes, I'm trying to make a connection to the skull's memories."

"So you become a human computer accessing the hard drive." Mee Mee reached and gently touched Mr. CBP's forehead. "Not working for me. Don't feel a thing."

"Most people don't," Freyja said. "It's an inborn ability. A person must have a certain kind of sensitivity."

Angie tilted her head. "Like a horse whisperer or a psychic?"

"Exactly."

Wolf held out his hand. "Let me try holding it. A lot of people say I'm psychotic."

Freyja handed him the skull. "A truer statement was never spoken."

Wolf cradled the skull in both hands and closed his eyes. "I see something round. Within the circle are many other red circles." He took a deep whiff. "It's causing a reaction. My mouth is watering. I see a number — a phone number."

"That's enough." Freyja pried the skull from his hands. "He's envisioning a pepperoni pizza from Nags Head Pizza Company."

Wolf grinned. "With extra cheese and anchovies."

Angie spread her hands. "So people buy these skulls to make some kind of connection with them?"

Freyja shrugged. "They say every skull has its own personality. Each can produce a different kind of energy depending on the type of quartz and how it was carved. Some are used for healing, others to look into the past and others to predict the future."

"Why did you say this one was special."

"Just the vibe I got. Who knows? This one might be classified as old or maybe even ancient."

"Classified?" Angie asked.

"There're three classifications — contemporary, old and ancient. A contemporary skull has been carved in the last hundred years. Most of the ones we sell are contemporary. The old classification goes from one hundred years to nine-hundred and ninety-nine. Any skull more than a thousand years old is considered ancient. Of course, the older the skull, the more valuable."

"What would an ancient skull be worth?" Mee Mee asked.

Freyja knotted her brow. "Some are considered priceless. Most of the ancient skulls were used by priests to perform ceremonial rites — the Maya, the Hindus, the Tibetan Buddhists. Ancient skulls are worth millions to certain people."

Angie narrowed her eyes. "Olivia Crane said the skull was number Ten out of Thirteen? What was that all about?"

"Hmmmm." Freyja eyed the top of the skull. "That's a reference to the Thirteen Skulls of Atlantis."

"The lost city of Atlantis? I thought that was a fairytale," Angie said.

"I'd call it a historical myth." Freyja handed Mee Mee the skull.

Mee Mee patted the top of the dome. "So, Mr. CBP could be worth millions if he's from Atlantis?"

"It all depends."

"On what?" Angie asked.

"On what a collector believes. You'd be surprised at the number of wealthy people in the world who believe the legend to be true."

Wolf raised his hand. "I believe in Bigfoot."

Freyja shook her head and blew out an annoyed breath.

Wolf's thick eyebrows slanted upwards. "Hey, I once found a big pile of leaves in the Nags Head Woods. What more proof do you need?"

"Ignore him," Angie said, "and tell us about the legend."

"According to the legend, thousands of years ago thirteen master craftsmen gathered in Atlantis to carve skulls out of crystal quartz. Because they were an advanced civilization, the craftsmen had the technology required to shape the crystal. Upon completion, the skulls became the repository for the secrets of the universe and the origin of humankind. They were sent to various locations throughout the earth to provide advanced knowledge to different cultures. Over the millennia they have been lost or hidden. However, in the last hundred years many of them have been found."

Mee Mee grinned and lifted Mr. CBP with one hand. "And we found number Ten."

Freyja nodded. "There is an organization called the Atlantean Skull Society whose aim is to gather all thirteen skulls in one place. They believe that when all the skulls work together in unity, their knowledge will be concentrated, and their secrets will be revealed to those who are present. The members believe it's a race against time."

"What's the hurry?" Angie asked.

"The combined knowledge of the Atlantean skulls will offer the world a means by which humankind can prevent the Apocalypse."

Mee Mee's eyes grew wide. "So, we're talking about the end of the world here."

Wolf grinned. "Buckle up, Buttercup."

Chapter 10
A Test

On the way home the drive across the Marc Basnight Bridge and through the Pea Island National Wildlife Refuge helped to ease Angie's nerves. The long stretch of concrete and steel spanning the Oregon Inlet bothered some people, but the wide blue sky above and turbulent waters below made the passage seem transcendent. Of course, the beauty of Pea Island enchanted most people. Two-lane Route 12 divided the dunes and sea from the marshlands and sound, the perfect pathway to enjoy nature's artistry.

"You're awful quiet," Mee Mee said.

"It's been a long day."

"What's our next step?"

"We've got to find out what Olivia Crane knows about your friend there."

Mee Mee patted Mr. CBP's head. "That was a creepy encounter."

Angie glanced at the skull. "This whole day has creeped me out."

"Freyja helped fill in a few blanks."

Angie nodded. "I'm amazed at what she said about crystal quartz and its memory capacities."

"When you think about it, crystals grow like living things."

"True. What seems odd is the possibility that a crystal skull can record what's going on around it."

"Maybe Olivia Crane can tap into Mr. CBP's memories."

"Maybe."

"How about you?"

"Me? What about me?"

Mee Mee lifted the skull. "I don't feel anything when I hold him, but you seem pretty sensitive."

Angie recalled the unsettling feelings she experienced on Monkey Island and at Wolf's store. "I did get a weird sensation when we dug that thing up—the odd feeling we were being watched. I felt it several times today."

"There you go. Mr. Crystal Blue Persuasion projected his memories of the people connected to this cold case into your mind. When we get back to my store, you should have a sit down with him. You know, one of those Vulcan mind melds."

"No thanks. I'm going to drop you off and head straight home. I'm one skull tango away from losing it."

Mee Mee laughed. "You could always take him home with you and mind meld on your own time."

"Nope. He can hang out with you for now."

"Whatever. I want to find a safe place for him though. Freyja said he could be worth millions."

"We could forget this cold case, put him up for sale and split the profits."

"That's a possibility. If he truly is one of the Ancient Thirteen, we'll be rolling in the clover."

Angie chuckled. "Right. We probably should try to prevent the Apocalypse before we sell him though. That way we can enjoy the proceeds."

"Decisions, decisions." Mee Mee raised the skull and gazed into its eye sockets. "Mr. CBP, you sure have complicated our lives. Are you a path to evidence or opulence?"

"Seriously, though, his value may have been a motive for Grandpa Rowtag's murder. Do you feel safe keeping him?"

"Only a handful of people know I have him."

"I can think of six: you, me, the Wolfs and the Cranes."

"I trust Wes and Freyja. Olivia is wheelchair bound, and her granddaughter is just a kid."

"A kid? She's a grown woman in her early twenties."

"To me, that's still a kid."

"Where will you keep the skull?"

"I'll put it under my bed. Nobody'll know he's there except you and me."

"And him."

Mee Mee smiled. "Let's hope Mr. CBP doesn't project his location to some diabolical ancient skull devotee."

Angie grimaced. "Let's hope not. Freyja said the Maya used ancient skulls in their ceremonial rituals. Joel and I watched a documentary about those rituals. The Maya practiced human sacrifice."

"I know all about it. Back in the 90's I spent a winter backpacking through Central America. Walking through those Maya ruins was very mystical and at times ominous."

Angie gave her a doubletake. "Dip me in butter and roll me in cracker crumbs. Who the heck are you?"

"You'd be surprised to hear about some of my adventures."

"I guess so. What did you learn about the Maya ceremonies?"

"The high priest would cut the heart out of the victim while it was still beating. Then he would put a carved skull in the heart cavity."

Angie put her hand to her chest. "You better put that skull in a lead-lined box."

Mee Mee snorted. "I don't think quartz crystal is akin to kryptonite. I'll be fine."

They drove for another thirty minutes without saying much. Passing through the small villages of Rodanthe, Waves, Salvo and Avon brought back a sense of normalcy to Angie. People shopped, filled their gas tanks, walked, jogged and greeted each other along the street and in front of the stores. A return to normalcy sounded good to her, a prescriptive path to ease the anxiety. *I just want to go home, take a hot bath, relax, watch some Gilmore Girls and wait for Joel to get home.*

At the south end of Buxton Angie pulled into one of the few empty parking spaces in front of Mee Mee's bookstore. "Looks busy. Who's minding the shop?"

"Cathy Fields. She's a great gal. Knows books like a barista knows coffee."

"Don't tell her about the skull."

"Don't fret. I may be new at this investigation game, but I don't plan on making any rookie mistakes."

"Good. Maybe you'll make rookie of the year."

Mee Mee tucked the skull under her Adidas jacket. "Mr. CBP is going right into the back of my Jeep." She opened the door, stepped out of the truck and faced Angie. "Should I give Olivia Crane a call?"

"Do you have her number?"

"No, but it might be in the phone book."

Angie shook her head. "Let's just pay her a surprise visit tomorrow morning. We'll take the skull with us."

"Good idea. Mr. CBP might be able to get a foot in the door."

"It'll be one of ours. He doesn't have any feet."

"Right. We'll be his arms and legs. All he has to do is look good. What time tomorrow morning?"

"I'll pick you up sometime after ten."

"I'll be here." Mee Mee closed the door and hurried around the right side of the store to where her Jeep Wrangler was parked in the rear.

Angie backed the pickup onto Route 12 and headed north. *Good looks? The thing is hideous. I'm glad he's not sleeping under my bed.* She tried to shake the image of the skull out of the back of her mind, but it lingered like a fading shadow. *What if he is worth millions? Does he belong to us? Finders keepers. I'm sure the U.S. Fish and Wildlife folks will kick up a fuss if they find out we dug him up on an island they own. But oh, what a difference a few million bucks would make. Joel and I could focus on raising a family and take a break from the daily grind.*

As Angie approached Rocky Rollinson Road, she reached for the turn signal. *Wait a second. I wanted to stop and get a pregnancy test.* She regripped the wheel and continued up Route 12. *Conner's Supermarket should have them.* After driving another few hundred yards, she made a left into the store's parking lot.

Stepping out of the vehicle, she sensed a shift in the mood that had plagued her most of the day from apprehension to anticipation. *What if I am pregnant? It would be wonderful and exasperating. How would we make ends meet on a deputy's salary?* Crystal Blue Persuasion reappeared from the shadows of her mind. *Maybe I should be nicer to that creepy skull. He could turn into a cash cow.*

After picking up a one-step pregnancy test, she headed home and filled the bathtub almost to the top with hot water. She slipped the shark's tooth out of her jeans pocket and laid it on the corner of the vanity. Wriggling her toes on her right foot, she shook her head. "*We can paddle a kayak to the island,*" she said. "*It'll be fun,*" she said. *Yeah. Right. I've had more fun getting my molars pulled.*

She took off her clothes, stepped into the tub and soaked for half an hour, falling asleep momentarily a few times. The bath rejuvenated her. She stood in front of the mirror above the sink and eyed her slim body. Patting her stomach, she said, "Is it goodbye sixpack and hello baby bump? Only one way to find out." She picked up the pregnancy test box from the edge of the vanity and read the instructions on the back. "Urinate in a clean, dry cup. Place the test wand on a flat surface. Using the dropper, pour three drops of urine into the sample well. If you are pregnant, two red lines will appear within three minutes." Angie nodded. "Simple enough."

She went through the steps, set the test wand next to the shark's tooth and waited. The seconds ticked by like the drip of an old faucet. *Will I be eating for two? Is there a pea in the pod?* She took a deep breath, closed her eyes and counted to sixty. She opened her eyes. *Come on now, it's been at least two minutes.* Two red lines appeared. "Tin roof rusted! I'm pregnant!" Her heart thumped against her ribcage. *Whoa! Joel will flip out. He won't get here until after midnight. Should I call him? No. I'll wait. I want to see his reaction in person.*

The rest of the day felt like a foggy dream. She watched several episodes of the *Gilmore Girls* on Netflix. As the familiar faces appeared and stories played out on the screen, her mind drifted to baby plans: painting the spare bedroom, shopping for a crib, planning a shower, picking out names. Occasionally, flashes from the day's excursion infiltrated her happy thoughts: the snake attack, the osprey onslaught, the shark encounter and the grinning skull. Every time the disconcerting images trespassed, the joy of bearing a child flooded over and washed them away. For dinner she ate a heaping plate of leftover spaghetti and downed a large bowl of chocolate ice cream without feeling an ounce of guilt. *Eating for two won't be a problem for me.*

A little after ten, she crawled into bed, exhausted. Within a few minutes, she was out. Her sleep, dark and dreamless, went uninterrupted for a long while until a fog developed, clouding the blackness. Slowly moving objects materialized within the fog. As she closed in on the scene, she made out two forms — Charlotte and Olivia Crane. Charlotte pushed her grandmother's wheelchair but halted in the middle of a two-lane road. Angie hit the brakes and skidded to a stop about ten feet in front of them. In the glare of the headlights, Charlotte turned the wheelchair to face Angie. Olivia Crane stood and staggered toward the Ram pickup.

She planted her hands on the hood of the truck and glared at Angie. "You are a pretender. The blue skull does not belong to you. We are coming for the blue skull." She extended her hands. "Give us the skull!"

The skin of the old woman's face began to shrink over her bone structure. The color of her complexion shifted from gray to blue. Her eyes sank into her head and became empty holes. She grinned, and the flesh around her mouth rotted and fell away. Her long black and gray streaked hair fell out leaving only her skull. With her bony fists she pounded on the hood of the truck. Angie opened her eyes and sat up in bed, her heart pounding.

She heard thumps and footsteps. Somewhere in the house a door opened. She shifted her legs from beneath the covers and sat on the edge of the mattress. The nightlight cast a weak glow over the nightstand to her right. She reached, eased out the drawer and picked up her Colt .38 special. Slowly standing, she tilted her head and listened. More muffled noises came from beyond the door. *Someone is searching for that skull.*

Chapter 11
Midnight Caller

She tiptoed to the door, turned the knob and inched it open. The hallway was empty, but light sliced through a crack in the darkness. *The bathroom.* The noises grew louder. *Someone is searching in the bathroom.* With the gun aimed at the sliver of light, she edged down the hallway. Inhaling slowly, she tried to calm her pounding heart. When she reached the door, she took a deep breath, threw it open and pointed the gun at the intruder. Looming over the corner of the vanity stood her wide-eyed husband.

"Joel!"

He put up his hands. "Don't shoot. I didn't mean to wake you."

She lowered the gun. "I'm so sorry. I thought someone broke into the house."

He lowered his hands. "Why? You knew I was getting home late."

She shook her head. "I had a bad dream. I'm still wound up."

"Geesh! You're jumpier than a cat on caffeine. What kind of dream?"

She closed her eyes, and Olivia Crane's rotting face reappeared. "One I want to forget. Anyway, I'm glad you're home."

"Me, too." He examined the items on the sink counter. "What in the world?"

"Kind of a shocker, huh?"

"The shark's tooth?"

She rolled her eyes. "That was a shocker but not the biggest jolt."

"Is that a pregnancy test?"

She nodded.

"Are you . . . ?"

She nodded again.

He spread his arms. "I'm going to be a dad?"

She placed the gun on the sink counter and stepped up to him. "Yes, you're going to be a father."

He wrapped his arms around her and pulled her tight against him. "Wow! I'll say it backwards. Wow! This is incredible!"

"Really?"

"Of course. Our family is about to grow."

"But how are we going to afford it?"

He released her and stepped back. "We'll find a way. My parents struggled to pay the bills when I was a kid, but we got by somehow."

"So did mine. We were lucky to make it from pay to pay."

"See. It's a family tradition."

They embraced again, and Angie let out a deep sigh. "I'm so glad you're not all shook up about this."

"Oh, I'm all shook up, but it's a good shake up. We'll figure out a way to keep the lights on."

She gazed up at him. "There is a possibility I may cash in big on this new case."

"Really? How big?"

"A few million."

Joel laughed, released his embrace and stepped back. "Very funny. You are kidding, right?"

She shrugged. "Yes . . . Maybe . . . I'm not sure about anything at this point."

"Let's go out in the kitchen and get something to eat. You can tell me all about it."

"Good idea. I could go for another bowl of chocolate ice cream."

Joel stepped back to the corner of the sink top, picked up the shark's tooth and test wand and held them in the palm of his hand. "Now here are a couple things that don't quite go together."

"Sure they do." She bobbed her head and sang, "Baby shark ta doo ta doo ta doo, Baby shark ta doo ta doo ta doo. It's a kid's song. Once you start singing you can't stop." Joel sang along as they shuffled down the hallway and into the kitchen.

"Have a seat," Joel said. "You've had a long day. I'll dish out the ice cream."

Angie plopped down on one of the yellow padded chairs, planted her elbows on the table and propped her head in her hand. "Three scoops, please."

"Three scoops coming up." Joel placed the shark's tooth and wand in front of her. "You've told me about our baby. Now tell me about the shark's tooth. Did you find it on Monkey Island?"

"No." She picked up the tooth. "It found me."

"Huh?"

"Did you know there're bull sharks in the Currituck Sound?"

"Uh huh. They find their way over through one of the inlets to feed."

"I was on today's menu."

Joel leaned on the table and met her gaze. "Are you serious?"

"I'm not kidding. Dish out the ice cream, and I'll tell you all about it."

After Joel scooped out two bowls of ice cream, he slid one in front of Angie and sat down. Between bites, she recounted the day's perils and pitfalls. She wondered if the weird clashes with the snake, osprey and shark had something to do with the skull. Then she felt silly for even entertaining the notion. When she told him about Freyja's insight into crystal skulls and the appraisal of Mr. CBP's possible value, his eyes grew wide, and he let out a low whistle. She capped off her account by describing the odd encounter with Olivia and Charlotte Crane. Recalling the old woman's seemingly psychic knowledge of their exploits, Angie stiffened as chills shot through her. Of course, the ice cream intensified the sensation.

Joel brushed the stubble on his chin with the back of his knuckles. "Olivia Crane is either some kind of crystal skull mystic or possibly an accessory to a murder."

Angie shrugged. "Maybe both."

"Did you bring the skull home with you?"

"No way. I left it with Mee Mee."

"Too bad. I'd like to take a look at it."

"I don't want the thing in this house. Mee Mee doesn't seem to mind at all. For some reason, it spooks me. Mee Mee thinks I have the gift."

"What do you mean?"

"Freyja told us some people can connect to the skull's memories. I get weird sensations when I'm around it."

"What makes it so valuable?"

"Do you remember that documentary we watched on the History Channel about the Maya priests?"

"Yeah. That was gruesome."

"They used skulls during their human sacrifice ceremonies. Any crystal skull more than a thousand years old is considered ancient and worth tons of money. Some people believe master craftsmen from the Lost City of Atlantis carved thirteen of them."

"And yours might be one of the thirteen?"

"Olivia Crane thinks so."

Joel nodded. "So, when you heard me stumbling around in the bathroom, you figured someone broke in to find the skull."

Angie nodded. "You never know what some crazy fanatic might do."

Alan Parsons Project's *Eye in the Sky* instrumental played from the back bedroom.

Joel checked his watch. "Who could be calling you at one

o'clock in the morning?"

Angie scooted out her chair and stood. "I have a feeling things are about to get weirder." She hurried down the hallway, and Joel followed.

She flipped on the light, stepped to the dresser, picked up the phone and checked the caller I.D. "It's Mee Mee Roberts." She tapped the answer icon and put the phone to her ear. "Hello."

"It's me."

"I know. What's up? Did somebody try to break in?"

"No. Mr. CBP is fast asleep under my bed. Did I wake you?"

"No. Are you okay?"

"I'm a little hyped up. Sorry to call so late, but I couldn't sleep."

"What's the matter?"

"I got a phone call at midnight."

"From who?"

"Olivia Crane."

"What did she want?"

"She invited us for lunch tomorrow at her beach house."

"I wonder why she called so late?"

"I don't know. When I picked up the phone, I checked the time. It was exactly midnight."

"Very strange, but a fitting ending to this weird day."

"Look on the bright side. Now we've got an open door."

"Maybe we can find some answers. I'll pick you up about eleven tomorrow and we'll head over to Historic Cottage Row."

"There's something else."

"What?"

"She wants us to bring the skull."

Chapter 12
The Crane House

Joel set the plate of scrambled eggs, pancakes and bacon in front of her. "Are you sure you don't want me to come with you?"

"Positive." Angie took in a big whiff of the steaming breakfast food. "That smells soooo good."

"It's my day off. I could follow you and watch from a distance."

Angie pointed at the kitchen sink. "I'd rather you change that leaky faucet and cut the grass." She dug into her scrambled eggs.

"Aren't you worried about hauling that skull around? This could be a setup."

She picked up a slice of crispy bacon and chomped until the last bite entered her mouth. She patted the side of her loose fitting knit sweater. "I'm carrying my Colt .38. It's small but mighty."

"Good. Self-preservation is no joke."

"If it were, death would be the punchline."

Joel wobbled his head. "That's true but not funny."

"I'll be fine, Joel. Olivia Crane may be obsessed with the skull, but I don't think she plans on committing murder to get her hands on it."

He shrugged. "Somebody did, according to Achak Rowtag."

Angie gobbled another strip of bacon and wiped her mouth with a paper towel. "The question is: Does Olivia Crane know anything about Grandpa Rowtag's missing body. Her family has owned that beach house since the late 1800's. Rowtag disappeared back in 1966."

"How old is she?"

"I'd say late seventies to early-eighties."

Joel eyed the ceiling and squinted. "I'm guessing she was around thirty back then. Certainly, she heard the news stories."

Angie nodded. "Any missing person case along the Outer Banks would have been front page headlines. I'm anxious to find out if her family had any connection to the Monkey Island Hunt Club."

"How are you going to get around to that subject?"

"Good question. If we tell her we're investigating a cold case, she might clam up. We'll have to come up with some believable story. We definitely need to be selective in what we say."

"Makes sense. Don't reveal your hand. Play one card at a time."

"Problem is we don't have all the right cards."

Joel winked. "Then you might have to bluff."

Angie chuckled. "Wes was always a good bluffer. He could bluff his way through a horde of zombies."

"Wes didn't play by the rules."

"That's true. He believed rules were for fools." She checked her watch. "It's almost ten-thirty. I better get going."

After putting on some makeup and brushing her teeth, she kissed her husband goodbye, headed out the door and climbed into her green Honda Civic. The car had some years and lots of miles on it but still ran like a stubborn marathoner. On the short ride over to Mee Mee's bookstore, she tried to come up with a believable story line to feed Olivia Crane, but nothing held water. Digging up a crystal skull on Monkey Island didn't fit in a standard shipping box when it came to explanations. *We've got a forty-five-minute drive to Nags Head. Hopefully, we'll come up with something.*

Angie pulled into a parking space in front of the store and beeped her horn. Toting a bowling bag, Mee Mee stepped onto the shop's front stoop, descended the few steps, climbed into the Civic, set the bag between her feet and shut the car door.

Angie stared at the bag. "Are we going to stop and bowl a few frames at Nags Head Lanes?"

"Mr. CBP would enjoy knocking down a few pins, but we don't have time to *spare*."

"Very funny."

"So, what's our plan?"

Angie backed onto Route 12 and headed north. "I was hoping you figured out some brilliant strategy."

"I've been thinking about it. She made the first move by inviting us over. Now we've got to make the right play."

Angie smiled. "That's one way to put it. It's like a game of euchre. You can win with an average hand if you know what you're doing."

"An average hand? I think we've got a great hand."

"No way. She knows we dug up that skull on Monkey Island, and dumb luck doesn't account for it. She suspects something and wants to find out what we know. She may be wheelchair bound, but, believe me, she'll put on a song and dance."

"I'm not so sure about that. More than anything, she wants to get her hands on our crystal skull. She thinks it's number Ten out of the Atlantean Thirteen. We've got the high trump card. All we have to do is tell her what she wants to hear."

"And what does she want to hear?"

"That we are true believers."

"And how do we convince her of that?"

Mee Mee scratched her chin. "I think it's up to you."

"Me?"

"That's right. You've got some kind of connection to Mr. CBP. Use that sixth sense to pull this off."

"The thing does give me the creepy crawlers."

"And Olivia Crane will sense that synergy."

"I wouldn't call it synergy. It's more like dread."

"Dread'll work. She'll link into what you're feeling and that will establish some credibility."

"And credibility leads to trust."

"And trust leads to revelations."

"Hmmmm." Angie focused on the long stretch of road that divided the dunes and marshlands. *Mee Mee may be onto something. Olivia Crane is one of those fanatical types that sees a demon in a dumpster fire. All I have to do is tell the truth in my own words. The skull speaks to me. When I'm around it, I feel people are watching me, perhaps people from the past trapped in the skull's memories. That sounds good. Now all we need is a good story to go with it.*

They drove through the small towns of Salvo, Waves and Rodanthe in silence. Angie juggled several different scenarios in her mind, but the rubber balls turned into chainsaws. She couldn't keep more than two in the air at one time without cutting off a branch of rationality. As they neared the Marc Basnight Bridge, a sense of panic stirred in the pit of her stomach and rose into her chest.

Angie pounded the steering wheel with her fist. "I'm coming up with half-baked ideas that a five-year old wouldn't believe."

"Don't worry. I've got it covered."

"You do?"

"Yep." Mee Mee tapped her temple. "Here's the story."

For the next ten minutes she detailed an unusual account of how Mr. CBP came into their possession. Angie listened carefully with some doubt but had to admit that Mee Mee's fabrication outshone any of her creative jumbles. By the time they reached the big intersection where Route 158 crossed over to Manteo, Mee Mee had put the final ingredients into her bizarre concoction.

"There you go." Mee Mee sat back in the seat and rubbed her hands together. "That should do the trick."

Angie turned right, following Route 12 toward the ocean. "That's not half bad."

"Not half bad? It's a great story."

"We're less than five minutes away from the Crane's. We'll go with it."

"If you got something better, let me know."

Angie blew out a long breath. "I've got nothing."

"Well then?"

"I said we'll go with it. I'll do my best to convince her I'm a true believer."

"Good. You'll see. It'll work."

"Just remember to keep your cards close to your vest."

"Of course. Only say what needs to be said."

"That's right."

Mee Mee rubbed her hands together. "My first interrogation. This is going to be exciting."

Angie shook her head. "Interrogation? I'd call it a visit, maybe an interview." To her right, the repetition of colorful beachfront homes ended as they entered Historic Cottage Row. One after another unpainted, cedar-sided houses loomed above the dunes.

The Crane house was located across the street and about five or six houses down from the Seaside Plaza. A wooden two-railed fence fronted the property, and a long cement driveway led to the hulking structure. Angie turned onto the driveway and noticed a separate two-car garage sided with the same dark shingles to her left. Ahead, the massive house cast its late-morning shadow toward them. The driveway widened at the base of the house, but no cars occupied the available parking area. As they slowly approached, she gazed up at the three-story building. Five windows were spaced evenly across the top floor of the main section, each with a green awning propped open to let the sea breezes flow. An ell extended from the left side of the structure. Unlike the main section, the bottom floor of the ell was not enclosed but stood on thick piers ten feet above the ground. A wide porch wrapped around the second floor of the entire house, overhung by a hipped porch roof. The landscaping that edged the cement driveway consisted of scrub brush and waving sea oats over several humps of sandy ground—nothing fancy.

Angie parked to the right of the wide wooden stairway that led up to the second floor of the main section. "Remember to keep your cool and stick to the story"

Mee Mee lifted the bowling bag and placed it on her lap. "Don't worry. Me and Mr. CBP are cooler than an outhouse on an iceberg." She popped open the door.

Angie shook her head, got out of the Civic and waited for Mee Mee at the bottom of the steps. Mee Mee circled the front of the car, smiling like an ace bowler ready for the lady's league championship. They mounted the steps, crossed the porch and faced the windowless cedar door.

Seeing no doorbell, Angie pounded on the door with her fist. After about a half minute, she knocked again. The door swung open, and a tall black man faced them. He had close-cropped salt-and-pepper hair and a gray goatee. Lanky with a slight paunch, he wore a button-down white dress shirt and loosely fitting gray slacks. His thick eyebrows hooded his dark eyes. Staring at them, he didn't say a word.

Angie cleared her throat. "We're here to see Mrs. Crane."

He nodded slowly and shifted his focus to the bowling ball bag. "She's on the back porch. Follow me." His voice had a Morgan Freeman quality, mellow but authoritative. He pivoted and strode through the entrance hall toward the back of the house. Dark wood paneling covered the foyer walls, and more than twenty old black and white photographs of family beach scenes hung at various levels, breaking up the pattern of the paneling. Immediately to the left, a stairway ascended to the dark regions of the third floor. The house exuded the smell of age, not off-putting but somewhat fusty.

Light from the next room blazed in from an open back door, radiant against his tall silhouette. Angie took a quick glance to her right and noticed a large dining area and kitchen, and to the left, a spacious great room. Wood paneling continued the vintage character of both rooms, and the old furniture, appliances, cabinets and shelves gave her the impression that the place hadn't been updated for decades. The man turned and faced them, his hand on the knob of a wide screen door. He lowered his eyebrows and said, "Lunch will be ready in a few minutes. Mrs. Crane is enjoying the view." He opened the screen door, stepped onto the deck and motioned to his right. "She's sitting at the far table."

Straight ahead, steps descended from the deck to a gap between two dunes crowned with sea grass. Beyond the dunes, the waves tumbled, rolled and roared. The porch roof shielded the deck from the sun's brilliant rays, and a sea breeze cooled Angie's face. Wooden benches substituted for porch railings around the entire perimeter. Angie turned to see Olivia Crane in her wheelchair sitting at a small round table and staring out to sea. Mee Mee sidled up to her, and the man stepped into the house and closed the screen door.

Mee Mee elbowed her and whispered, "Feels like we just entered a time portal."

In a low tone Angie said, "Yeah, mid 1960s."

They walked across the deck to where Olivia Crane sat, and Mee Mee placed the bowling bag on the table and said, "Thanks for inviting us over for a little get together."

Olivia Crane shifted her focus from the sea to the bag. She took a deep breath. "Is my friend in there?"

Mee Mee nodded. "Do you want me to take him out?"

"Yes. Place him in the middle of the table."

Mee Mee zipped open the bowling bag, carefully lifted the blue skull, which was wrapped in a white towel, removed the towel and placed the skull in the center of the table. Olivia Crane gazed at it, eyes tense.

After about a half minute, Angie said, "Do you mind if we sit down?"

The words broke her trance, and she eyed them. "I'm sorry for being an insensitive host, but I don't think you understand the significance of the moment. Please sit down."

Two empty chairs were spaced evenly around the table. When Angie sat down and stared at the back of the skull, she felt like an outlier at a séance. She twisted in her seat and glanced over her shoulder. "Nice view of the ocean from back here."

The old woman bobbed her head slowly. "I've been enjoying it since I was a child."

"How old is this house?" Mee Mee asked.

"My great grandfather built it back in 1875. A large addition was added in the 1920s to accommodate our growing family."

Angie turned and faced her. "Do many family members live here now?"

She wagged her head. "Just me, my granddaughter and Isaac."

Mee Mee raised her chin. "Is Isaac the man who answered the door?"

Olivia Crane nodded.

Angie said, "Sure is a big house for three people."

"That's true. Ten bedrooms: one occupied and nine empty. Charlotte is my caregiver. She stays in my room in case I need her at night. Isaac manages the property. He prefers to live in the apartment above the garage. Extended family gathers here on holidays, but for most of the year I appreciate the solitude."

Mee Mee scanned the horizon as a flock of seagulls glided above the dunes. "You do have a little piece of paradise back here."

"It's my Eden." She reached, placed her hand on top of the skull and closed her eyes. She bobbed her head, and her lips tightened into a thin line.

After a minute's silence, Angie asked, "Is the skull speaking to you?"

She opened her eyes and removed her hand. "Yes."

"He speaks to me, too."

She met Angie's gaze. "I know."

Angie swallowed. "When I am near him, I can sense the presence of others."

An odd smile broke across Olivia Crane's crinkled face. "There is someone else here. I want you to meet him."

Angie and Mee Mee briefly looked at each other and then returned their focus to the old woman.

"Sure," Mee Mee said. "One of your relatives?"

"No, but he is my closest friend." She reached beside her wheelchair and grasped the handle of a metal box about the size of a toaster. Her face muscles straining, she lifted the box and placed it on her lap. She flipped up a clasp, opened the lid, reached into the box, lifted out a life-size clear crystal skull and set it next to the blue skull facing Angie. "I would like you to meet the Skull of Doom."

Chapter 13
The Skull of Doom

Angie stared into the eye sockets of the Skull of Doom. She felt needles prickle her shoulders and descend her back like a thousand small knives. Through the sockets, she could see into the depths of the crystal. The subtle variations caused by the refraction of light through the natural fissures resembled shadowy figures. She closed her eyes and heard soft murmuring, the sound one hears in a crowded theater before the show. The odd sensation that she was being watched nagged at her again. She opened her eyes.

A wry smile raised the corners of Olivia Crane's lips. "You feel something, don't you?"

Angie nodded. *Time to put this sixth sense to work.* "There are others here. I don't know if they are memories or spirits."

The old woman's eyes narrowed. "Both. They are spirits conjured by the skull's memories."

Angie shook her head and shifted her focus to a window just beyond the old woman's shoulder. "Please turn it away from me. I don't like looking at it."

Olivia Crane lifted the skull and placed it on the table facing Mee Mee. "Have you ever heard of the Skull of Doom?"

Mee Mee shrugged. "Can't say I have, but he's cute. Is he famous?"

"Yes. He is world renowned."

Mee Mee raised her eyebrows. "Wow. Didn't figure on meeting a celebrity today. What's his claim to fame?"

"He has been tested for authenticity in the labs of the most prestigious universities, museums and technological centers. He even went through exhaustive analysis at the Hewlett-

Packard Laboratories in Santa Clara, California. They determined him to be an ancient skull of Maya origin."

Mee Mee let out a low whistle. "So, he's the real deal?"

Olivia Crane bobbed her head. "They just got one thing wrong. He's not of Maya origin. He is one of the Atlantean skulls. He is One of the Thirteen, the Master Skull."

Mee Mee lowered her head and stared into the eye sockets. "He's top dog?"

She gave Mee Mee a perturbed glance. "He is the Master of the Thirteen, and now he has been reunited with number Ten."

"I didn't mean any disrespect," Mee Mee clarified, "but why didn't the labs confirm his Atlantean origin?"

"Science doesn't recognize the city of Atlantis as historical. Without physical proof of its existence, it is categorized as a legend."

"Then how did the Mayas gain possession of it?" Angie asked.

"The Atlanteans were highly evolved beings. Their connection to the spirit realm unlocked the possibilities of humankind's future. Using advanced technologies, their master craftsmen carved the thirteen skulls from quartz crystal. They programmed them with the consciousness, knowledge and wisdom that had been gathered since the beginning of their existence as a people. The skulls possess the divine blueprint for humanity. The Atlanteans understood man's destructive nature and foresaw the Apocalypse. They laid out a plan of preservation. They distributed the skulls throughout the world and envisioned a day when the Thirteen would be reunited. People from different cultures will come together to prevent Armageddon."

Mee Mee leaned forward on the table and gazed into the clear skull's eye sockets. "So, Mr. Doom has been programmed to save the world?"

The old woman nodded. "Their knowledge will be unleashed when all thirteen have been gathered and placed in correct order in a circle with the Skull of Doom in the center. The chosen people will then be given the master plan to save our planet."

"Who are the chosen people?" Angie asked.

"The ones chosen by the skulls are called Guardians."

Mee Mee raised her eyebrows. "Us?"

"Possibly. One by one the skulls are allowing themselves to be found. The time is near. The question is: Were you chosen?"

Mee Mee spread her hands. "I guess so. We're the ones who found Mr. CBP."

Olivia Crane raised a bony finger. "But how did you find him? Tell me exactly what happened and don't lie. I will know if you lie."

Mee Mee glanced at Angie. They both hesitated, waiting for the other to begin their concocted story. Finally, Mee Mee spoke: "About a month ago I stopped at an antique store in Edenton. Occasionally, I'll find old Outer Banks history books in some of these shops. That day three books caught my eye. One was about the multitude of hunting clubs that were popular along the Outer Banks back in the good old days. I purchased the books and finally got a chance to look through them a couple weeks ago. When I was paging through the one about the hunting clubs, I found a hand drawn map tucked at the beginning of a chapter about Monkey Island."

Olivia Crane's eyes grew big. "I knew it! That's where you found him, isn't it?"

Angie nodded. "Mee Mee asked me to come over and take a look at it. Occasionally, we go kayaking together. On the map there was an X under a big tree on the west side of the island. We had no idea what could be buried there."

The old woman gulped and coughed as if water had gone down the wrong pipe. She cleared her throat. "Go on."

Mee Mee leaned against the table. "I wanted to paddle out there right away to see what was buried under that tree, but Angie didn't feel right about it."

She shifted her focus to Angie. "Why not?"

"The island is off limits. It's owned and managed by the Mackay Island National Wildlife Refuge and designated as a protected bird sanctuary. I didn't want to break the law just to satisfy our curiosity."

"But you did anyway."

Angie nodded. "Something bothered me about that map. I couldn't sleep at night. The X under that tree kept appearing in my dreams. It was as if I had no choice but to paddle out to that island and find what was buried there."

Olivia Crane's eyes narrowed. "You were being called."

Mee Mee thumbed at Angie. "She kept telling me about these strange feelings that came over her."

"What kind of feelings?"

Angie glanced at the wizened woman and then refocused on the back of the skull. "They were just odd feelings at first, but when we made it to the island, they began to intensify. The map was easy to follow. We started at the old hunting club and wound our way along the path to the big tree. I began to get this strange sensation that we were being watched."

Olivia Crane bobbed her head slowly. "You were being watched but not by any living person."

"Now I understand. Our friend at the Lost Lagoon told us that crystal skulls record memories like a computer's hard drive. For some reason I could access those memories."

"You have the gift." She reached and placed her hand on top of Angie's hand.

The old woman's icy touch revulsed her, but she did her best to remain motionless. "Does that mean I have been chosen?"

Olivia Crane nodded. "You have been called to be a Guardian. It is a serious and dangerous responsibility."

"Why dangerous?" Mee Mee asked.

"There are unseen forces in the world that oppose the Atlanteans' intentions and welcome the destruction of humanity. Have you encountered any kinds of struggles or threats since obtaining the skull?"

"Yes, several." Angie slid her hand out from under the woman's grasp. "At the tree where we dug up the skull, a snake almost bit me. Then the birds on the island became agitated. An osprey flew down at us several times. The worst thing, though, was a shark attack while we were paddling back to shore. The beast almost took off my leg."

"You see what I mean? We are in a spiritual battle with forces that can even influence primeval creatures which otherwise would go about their natural routines."

Angie straightened and gripped the edge of the table. "I'm not so sure I want the responsibility of a Guardian. Why me?"

"For some reason the map fell into your hands." Olivia Crane eyed Mee Mee. "Do you know the original owner of the book in which the map was inserted?"

"His name was written on the first page along with the person's name who gifted him the book."

"What were the names?"

"Achak and Ahote Rowtag."

"Rowtag?" The old woman took a quick breath and stiffened. "That is a Native American name."

"Yes," Mee Mee said. "Originally, Monkey Island was an Pamunkey hunting camp."

Her eyes shifted, and her lips tightened into a thin line against her teeth. She stared at the Skull of Doom. "Some Native American tribes know about the Atlantean skulls. The one who buried the skull was probably an Algonquin shaman."

Angie leaned against the table. "Perhaps he worked at the Monkey Island Hunt Club. Have you ever visited the island?"

"Yes. For many years my family belonged to the club."

"They may have known Mr. Rowtag," Mee Mee said.

Olivia Crane shifted her eyes and rubbed her knuckles against her pointed chin. "That's possible."

"Are any still alive?" Angie asked.

She straightened and blinked several times. "Most have passed away."

"Sorry," Angie said. "I didn't mean to stir painful memories. I'm sure you miss them."

"Life goes on," she said in a flat tone.

Mee Mee reached and patted the top of the blue skull. "Anyway, that's how we found Mr. CBP. Now the question is: What do we do with him? Should we have him tested like Mr. Doom here?"

"That won't be necessary."

Angie tilted her head. "Why not?"

"Obviously, we can sense his power."

"But what does that prove?" Mee Mee said.

"The first time I saw him, I knew he was an ancient skull." She reached, rested her hand on top of the blue skull and closed her eyes. "I can see his memories. He speaks to me. The proof is in the power."

Mee Mee pointed at the clear skull. "But your Mr. Doom has been tested and verified. Why would anyone trust the authenticity of Mr. CBP without proof?"

"Believe me, the Guardians will know. Besides, we don't have time for months or perhaps years of testing. Cataclysmic destruction is drawing near."

"How do you know that for sure?" Angie asked.

"Certainly, you've seen the state of the world—hatred, division, crime, disaster, terrorism, war, nuclear threats. Humanity is on the verge of total annihilation. We must gather the Atlantean skulls and attempt to forestall the Apocalypse."

Mee Mee's eyebrows tensed. "Have all thirteen skulls been found?"

"No. Yours is only the tenth one."

"Then how can we activate their power with three skulls missing?" Angie asked.

Olivia Crane reached and grasped their hands. "Please, hold each other's hand so we can make an undivided circuit around the two skulls."

Angie and Mee Mee eyed one another and then clasped hands.

"Thank you." The old woman closed her eyes and took a deep breath. After about a half minute she said, "Yes, yes, I hear you. I understand. I will do all that I can to make it happen." She bobbed her head slowly. "Soon. Yes, very soon." She released their hands. "The Skull of Doom has instructed me."

Mee Mee let go of Angie's hand. "What did he say?"

"He calls for a gathering of the ten skulls. Through psychic communication with them, we may be able to uncover pathways to find the missing three."

"How will you gather them?" Angie asked.

"I know all the Guardians. We have formed a sacred alliance called the Atlantean Skull Society. When I tell them the tenth skull has been found, they will make it a priority to meet with us."

"Okay," Angie said. "Where?"

"Here."

"When?" Mee Mee asked.

"On All Hallow's Eve."

Angie felt a shiver scurry like a spider down the back of her neck. "That's only a couple weeks away."

The old woman gripped the edge of the table. "Doomsday will arrive like a summer thunderstorm. We can't delay."

Mee Mee raised a finger. "I've got a question. If your guy wants to save the world, why is he called the Skull of Doom?"

Olivia Crane lifted her chin and narrowed her eyes. "Why do religious prophets call on people to repent?"

Mee Mee shrugged. "Because the end is near?"

"Exactly. Without the threat of doom, people will not listen. If people do not listen to the Skull of Doom's message, this world *will* perish."

Angie clasped her hands in front of her, leaned against the table and met the old woman's gaze. "How did you become the

Guardian of the Skull of Doom?"

"It's no secret. The provenance of the skull is well documented."

"I'd like to know."

Her eyes seemed to freeze over as if cataracts had formed instantly. She blinked several times, cleared her vision and stared at the clear skull. "The Skull of Doom was discovered in 1924 by a teenage girl in a collapsed temple in Lubaantun, a city in Central America. She was the adopted daughter of Martin Hedgerow, a world-famous explorer. Her name was Anita Hedgerow. Later in life, she married a man by the name of William Hoffman. He was a member of the Monkey Island Hunt Club. At that time the skull had not yet been tested, but its legend was growing. My husband Chandler was a member of the club. He listened to Hoffman's stories and became obsessed with the skull. He challenged Hoffman to a high stakes game of poker."

"For the Skull of Doom?" Mee Mee asked.

Olivia Crane nodded.

Angie raised her eyebrows. "What did your husband ante up?"

She tapped her bony finger on the tabletop. "The deed to this house."

"He must have drawn a good hand," Mee Mee said.

"Three aces. At first, I was angry when he brought home the skull and told me about the wager. He was so irresponsible. But now . . ." She placed her elbows on the table and templed her hands just below her chin. ". . . but now I am the Guardian of the Skull of Doom."

Chapter 14
The Face of Death

Sporting a one-piece white bathing suit, Charlotte Crane emerged in the gap between two tall dunes and headed in their direction. A baby blue beach towel hung around her neck, and her brown hair, wet and slicked back, glistened in the sun. Her white-framed sunglasses and svelte body gave her the look of a model that just stepped off the cover of a Sports Illustrated swimsuit issue. When she glanced up and saw them sitting on the back porch, her brow tensed, but then she forced a smile, mounted the wide wooden steps and crossed the deck to where they were sitting.

"Grandmother, I didn't know we were having company today," she said, her hands on her hips.

"Pull up a chair, Charlotte, and join us for lunch." Olivia Crane motioned to a weathered Adirondack chair stationed against the wall a few feet beyond them. "Isaac will be bringing out sandwiches and lemonade in a few minutes."

Charlotte pointed at the skulls. "Do we have to endure a horror exhibition while we eat?"

"No. We can put our friends away." The old woman lifted the clear skull and carefully lowered it into the metal box beside her wheelchair.

Mee Mee followed suit, picking up the blue skull. "I don't think Mr. CBP is hungry anyway." She wrapped him in the white towel and inserted him into the bowling bag next to her chair.

Charlotte dragged the chair to the small table and sat between Angie and Mee Mee.

"How's the water today?" Angie asked.

"It's cold this time of year but wonderful." She removed her sunglasses and, with a flick of her wrist, tossed them onto the table. "We're fortunate to live along this section of the beach. It's wide and beautiful with limited public access."

Mee Mee smiled. "Your own private paradise."

"A little taste of heaven in my secluded world."

The back door opened, and Isaac stepped onto the deck carrying a tray and pitcher of lemonade. He approached them and set the tray filled with quarter-cut sandwiches in the middle of the table. After placing the pitcher of lemonade next to the tray, he said, "Half are egg salad, and half are ham salad. I'll go fetch glasses for the lemonade."

"Thank you, Isaac," Olivia Crane said.

He nodded, turned and walked back into the house.

"I don't know what I'd do without him."

"Yes," Charlotte said. "Without Isaac, this place would fall apart. He knows all the ins and outs and secrets."

The old woman cast an admonishing glare at her granddaughter.

"What?" Charlotte tensed her eyebrows.

"Nothing," she said in a cold tone. A smile broke her rigid expression. "Please, ladies, help yourself to the sandwiches."

While they were eating, Isaac returned with four glasses, placed them on the table and filled them with lemonade. "Anything else, Mrs. Crane?"

"That'll be all, Isaac. Thank you."

"Alright then, if you need me, I'll be out front doing a little tidying." He about-faced, strode across the deck and entered the house.

Angie downed one of the ham salad sandwiches with the lemonade. The drink left an acidic aftertaste, and she swallowed twice to rid her mouth of the sourness. "When will you know for sure about the gathering?"

Charlotte put down her glass. "What gathering?"

"We are having another gathering on All Hallow's Eve,"

Olivia Crane said matter of factly.

Charlotte cringed. "Oh no, please don't bring those people here again."

Mee Mee leaned forward. "When was the last time the skulls were gathered?"

Charlotte whined, "About two years ago. Those people are so strange. It was horrible."

The old woman extended her bony hand, her palm facing Charlotte. "Shush up."

"What happened?" Angie asked.

In a low voice, Charlotte said, "One of them died."

Mee Mee straightened. "Great Blackbeard's ghost!"

"One of the Guardians had a heart attack," Olivia Crane said. "Very unfortunate."

"The man died during a scrying session," Charlotte said.

Angie gripped the edge of the table. "What's a scrying session?"

Olivia Crane clasped her hands together and rested them on the table. "It's when a person tries to interact with a skull through their own consciousness. Often, they are able to see scenes from the past or future within the depths of the skull."

Mee Mee frowned. "And this guy just toppled over like a Jenga tower?"

Charlotte nodded. "It was horrible."

"What skull was he scrying with?" Angie asked.

The old woman's nostrils flared, and she took in a deep breath. "The Skull of Doom."

Mee Mee raised a finger. "That figures."

Angie scooted her chair closer to the table. "Did he say anything before he died?"'

Charlotte's lips quivered. "He said he saw the Tenth Skull."

Mee Mee put her hand to her chest. "Our skull?"

"Yes," Olivia Crane said. "He said it would appear soon."

"And then he dropped like a rotten coconut," Charlotte blurted.

"What happens when a Guardian dies?" Angie asked. "Does the skull go to the next of kin?"

"Sometimes," Olivia Crane said. "It all depends on who is named in the Guardian's will. I haven't met the new Guardian of the rose quartz skull."

Mee Mee raised an eyebrow. "Is that the name of the dead guy's skull?"

"No, its name is Passion, but it is made from rose quartz. I believe the former Guardian, Mr. Goldbluff, bequeathed it to a nephew. We'll meet him on All Hallow's Eve."

"Please don't leave me that doomsday skull, Aunt Oliva. I wouldn't know what to do with it."

"Don't worry, dear Charlotte. For your dedication to me, I'm leaving you the house and property. Your brother Arnold would make a much better Guardian. He has expressed interest along with a few others."

"Will Mr. Doom tell you who's next?" Mee Mee asked.

"Definitely. Before my time comes to depart this world, he will let me know."

After an awkward silence, their conversation drifted to more trivial subjects. A half hour passed, and Angie checked her watch—1:05. "We've got to get going. People to see and things to do." She scooted out her chair and stood.

Mee Mee rose to her feet. "Thank you for inviting us over and feeding us. The sandwiches were scrumptious."

Olivia Crane glanced up at them. "I appreciate your taking the time to visit with me. I'll be sending you an official invitation to the All Hallow's Eve Gathering of the Ten."

Mee Mee smiled cheerfully. "Looking forward to it."

Angie gave her a sideways glance. *Speak for yourself Miss Bright and Bubbly.*

"The creepy bald guy isn't coming again, is he?" Charlotte asked. "He really weirds me out."

"Of course, he's coming. Bahar is the world's foremost expert on Atlantis and the origin of the skulls. He'll be enlightening us again."

Charlotte rolled her eyes. "He reminds me of Dr. Evil from the Austin Power movies."

"Don't be ridiculous. You're such a drama queen."

"No, Grandmother. I'm just a normal human being living in the Munster mansion."

"What do you mean by that?"

Charlotte waved her hand. "Never mind. It's just an old television show."

Olivia Crane shook her head. "Remember this, young lady: Normal is for people who fear what lies beyond the ordinary. Now be a dear and see our guests out to the front door."

"Gladly." She scooted back the Adirondack chair, stood and faced Mee Mee and Angie. "Ladies, follow me, please."

Mee Mee picked up the bowling bag and nodded toward the old lady. "Have a beyond-the-ordinary day, Mrs. Crane."

A weird smile crept across her wrinkled face. "Your visit has made my day quite extraordinary."

"It's been real . . . interesting." Angie tilted her head, working out a kink in her neck. *Like an Edgar Allen Poe story.*

Charlotte led them through the back of the house and into the foyer. Before reaching the front door, she hesitated, turned and said, "I hope your visit with Grandmother wasn't too disturbing."

Mee Mee smiled tolerantly. "Not at all. I found it fascinating."

Angie said, "Your grandmother is an unusual woman to say the least, a true disciple of the skulls."

Charlotte's shoulders slumped. "It's all a bunch of bunk."

Mee Mee raised her eyebrows. "You don't believe in the skulls?"

"Of course not. As far as I'm concerned, they are crystal paperweights or perhaps good Halloween decorations."

"A lot of people would disagree with you," Angie said.

"Don't get me wrong. I know they have value because of their historical significance, but they are not magical."

Mee Mee frowned. "So you don't think this Gathering of the Ten is going to help prevent the Apocalypse?"

Charlotte chuckled. "If you believe that, I'll let you ride my pet dragon for a hundred bucks."

"Why do you stay here with her?" Angie asked.

"No one else in the family wants to take care of her. I love it here on the oceanfront. Besides, she promised me . . . oh . . . I really shouldn't talk about it. It's between the two of us."

"Of course," Angie said. "Sorry to pry. It's just odd that a girl your age is willing to burden herself with the responsibility of caregiving."

"Very true. I should be pursuing a career, partying with my pals and dating a hot young stud, but I'm here taking care of Grandmother. Oh well, that's my life for now."

"I'm curious," Mee Mee said. "What was the purpose of the last gathering?"

Charlotte shrugged. "It's all about finding the remaining skulls. The world can't be saved until the Thirteen have been gathered. They had a variety of sessions. Each skull has its own specialty — healing, telling the future, looking into the past, meditating, seeking wisdom, that sort of New Age thing."

Angie rubbed her chin. "So, the Guardians take their turns scrying with the skulls?"

Charlotte nodded. "Believe me, it's freaky. Some of them go into trances. Others act like they're possessed. Then they have teaching sessions. Bahar is the crystal skull guru. He went on for two hours about how the Atlanteans created and programmed the skulls. He even brought up the possibility of intervention by extraterrestrials."

Mee Mee's eyes grew wide. "Aliens?"

"Uh huh. He believes the extraterrestrials helped the Atlanteans devise the plan of salvation and offered their technology to create the skulls. I'm telling you, these people are kooky."

"Thanks for the heads up," Angie said. "We'll try not to go

off the deep end."

Charlotte opened the front door. "I guess I'll be seeing you in a couple weeks."

"On All Hallow's Eve." Mee Mee grinned. "Should we wear costumes?"

Charlotte gave a half-hearted smile. "You'd fit right in if you did."

They stepped onto the front porch, and Charlotte closed the door. Angie caught sight of Isaac sweeping sand off the driveway near the unattached garage. A wide-brimmed sun hat shadowed his face, and his button-down shirt and gray slacks bestowed a formality to the mundane task. Descending the steps, she said, "Let's talk to the property manager and see if he can help lift the lid off this strange stew."

"Good idea. Charlotte said he knows all the secrets about this place."

They walked down the driveway and halted a few feet in front of him.

Isaac swept for a few more seconds, paused and glanced up. "Can I help you?"

"We're just curious about something," Angie said.

"Well . . . you know what they say about curiosity."

"Sure," Mee Mee said. "It's the wick of the candle of discovery."

He wobbled his head. "That's not what I was thinking, but go ahead and ask your question."

Angie cleared her throat. "Mrs. Crane invited us to what she calls the Gathering of the Ten. We're very excited. We heard there was another gathering about two years ago. Were you around then?"

"Yes, Ma'am, I've been managing this property since the mid-70's."

Mee Mee asked, "Did you attend any of the workshops at the last gathering?"

"Workshops," Isaac snorted. "I don't frequent clubs where

demons dance the Electric Boogaloo. I mind my own business."

"Oh." Angie tensed her brow. "So you're not a crystal skull buff like Mrs. Crane?"

His eyes narrowed, and he stared at the bowling bag. "I'm not a disciple of death."

"What do you mean?" Angie asked.

He eyed Angie. "What do you think those skulls are all about?"

"I'm not sure what to think."

"They are what they appear to be---faces of death."

Mee Mee raised the bowling bag. "But we hear they have great power."

"Like a genie in a bottle." Isaac pursed his lips and nodded slowly. "Where did you find that one?"

"We dug him up on a nearby island," Angie said.

A cold wave flowed over his features, and his tawny complexion turned gray. "You want my two cents?"

"Sure," Mee Mee said. "We're interested in what you have to tell us."

"If I were you, I'd put that genie back in the bottle. Drop him into that hole, cover him up and don't tell anybody where you found him."

Angie spread her hands. "Why?"

"Because he is what he is."

Mee Mee lowered the bag. "The face of death?"

Isaac nodded. "The face of death."

Chapter 15
Hedgerow and Pierce

Angie started the Honda Civic. "What do you think? Should we go back to Monkey Island and rebury your friend?"

"No way. I think we're on to something."

Angie bobbed her head. "The genie is out of the bottle, and we're not going to squeeze him back in. Did you notice his expression when I told him we found the skull on a local island?"

"Yeah. It was like a shadow crossed over his face."

"The shadow of death. He knows something."

Angie made a left out of the Crane driveway onto Virginia Dare Trail, drove about hundred yards, turned right into the Surfside Plaza and parked in front of the Lost Lagoon next to a couple Harleys.

"I figured you might stop here," Mee Mee said.

"I want to run a few things by Wes."

They got out of the car and hurried into the store.

The place was empty except for a customer, a middle-aged woman checking out the t-shirts in the sale section at the back of the shop. Freyja Wolf stood behind the counter near the register. A black belt cinched her burnt orange summer dress around her narrow waist. Thin straps secured the top of the dress over her wide shoulders, which were muscular like a good swimmer's shoulders. A black scrunchie gathered her ash blonde hair into a long ponytail. The scars on the left side of her face gave her an exotic appearance that added to her mystique.

"Hello, girls," Freyja said.

Angie waved. "Hi, Freyja. We're back again."

"I'm glad you're here. Did you bring Crystal Blue

Persuasion with you?"

Mee Mee thumbed over her shoulder. "He's waiting in the car. Why?"

"I think I discovered some information about him."

Angie's eyes widened. "Where?"

"In a booklet I found online about Anton Pierce and Martin Hedgerow. I downloaded the PDF version."

"I've heard of Martin Hedgerow." Angie walked to the counter.

Mee Mee stepped up beside her. "Wasn't he the guy Olivia Crane mentioned? His daughter found the Skull of Doom."

"Right, but who's Anton Pierce?"

"He's a famous American writer and Civil War hero," Freyja said. "I've read several of his books and his biography. Then I recalled his biographer mentioning that he and Hedgerow found a blue crystal skull in Mexico."

"Were he and Hedgerow friends?"

"They knew each other. In October of 1913, Pierce decided to take a tour of the Civil War battlefields. After he passed through Louisiana and Texas, he crossed into Mexico. That was the time of the Mexican Revolution, and Pierce joined Pancho Villa's army as an observer. Hedgerow was an explorer who was infamous for plundering Maya tombs. Villa captured Hedgerow and threatened to execute him, but Pierce intervened and convinced Villa to spare his life. After Hedgerow swore his allegiance to the rebels, Villa relented and let him live. Hedgerow fought in several skirmishes with them and was even wounded. As Pierce and Hedgerow traveled with Villa's army, they would explore ancient Maya temples and find artifacts."

Mee Mee leaned against the counter. "And that's how they found the blue skull?"

Freyja nodded. "Villa's army was camping near the ancient ruins of Chichen Itza. Pierce kept a notebook detailing his finds. As I read the description of the skull, it reminded me of your

Crystal Blue Persuasion. Let me get my iPad, and I'll read it to you." Freyja hurried to the rear of the store and entered the back room.

"What do you know," Mee Mee said. "Mr. CBP might be famous, too."

"No wonder Olivia Crane went wacko when she saw it. If it's the same skull, then there may be a connection to the guy that married Hedgerow's daughter."

"Right. The guy that lost the Skull of Doom in the poker game. What was his name?"

"Hoffman."

Freyja returned with her iPad. "The booklet is called *Tomb Raiders: the Adventures of Anton Pierce and Martin Hedgerow during the Mexican Revolution.* Pierce mysteriously vanished during the war. Some speculated that he died in a battle. Others figured that Villa caught him raiding tombs and executed him. Hedgerow sent Pierce's few belongings back to his family, which included his notebook."

"Do you think Hedgerow kept the blue skull?" Angie asked.

Freyja nodded. "That would be my guess. When World War I escalated, he convinced Villa to let him return to England to serve his country. Finding the blue skull may have led him to researching the legend of the Atlantean skulls. When his daughter found the Skull of Doom in Lubaantun in 1924, he knew he had stumbled onto something historical and possibly transcendent."

Mee Mee raised her eyebrows. "And the obsession with the Atlantean Thirteen begins."

"And obsession can sometimes lead to murder," Angie said. "How does Pierce describe the skull?"

"Let me find it." Freyja scrolled through the pages, scanning the words. "Here it is: *We found the skull under the collapsed altar of the temple. After dusting it off, I held it up to the light that streamed through the broken doorway. An amazing spiral of navy blue, cerulean and white spun like clouds forming a storm on the right side of the cranial cavity. The left side resembled the choppy gray and blue*

104

waters of the Caribbean Sea. A pattern of navy blue and sky blue striped the face with a light gray section crossing the four front teeth on the left side. The eye sockets repeated the pattern, but their shadows gave the skull an ominous aspect."

Mee Mee straightened. "That's our boy! That's Mr. CBP to a T."

"Freyja, you just dug up a gem." Angie touched her temple. "Now we've got to figure out what all this means."

"What all what means?" Weston Wolf blurted from the back of the store. His wrinkled denim shirt with cut off sleeves was half unbuttoned and exposed his hairy chest. He sauntered in their direction, his black cargo shorts hanging loosely from his hips.

"Did you just crawl out of bed?" Angie asked. "You look like yesterday's coffee grounds."

Wolf grinned and rubbed the three-day stubble on his chin. "I like this look. I call it *Wasting Away in Nirvanaville.*" He thumbed at Freyja. "It drives the wife crazy."

Freyja shook her head. "You could at least comb your hair."

"I tried. Too many knots. Enough about me. What's happening with your case?"

"Your wife just connected our skull to a box of incriminating bones," Angie said. "Now it's a matter of putting them all together."

"Maybe I can help." In a rough baritone, he sang, "The toe bone is connected to the footbone, the footbone . . ."

Freyja raised her hand. "Enough! You sound like a wounded warthog."

Wolf grimaced. "You professional singers don't appreciate underdeveloped talent."

She rolled her eyes. "Stick to what you know."

"I'm not bad at sleuthing."

"That's why we're here," Angie said. "Freyja discovered that our skull has a prior affiliation with the Crane family."

"So Old Lady Crane knew all about your blue boy but did a snow job on you."

Angie nodded. "She recognized the skull immediately but wanted us to think the connection was some kind of spiritual bond."

Wolf tilted his head. "Why?"

Angie shrugged. "Murder?"

Wolf nodded slowly. "Possibly. How's your skull connected to the family?"

Angie related Olivia Crane's story about the poker game and the provenance of the Skull of Doom. Then she informed Wolf about the discovery of the blue skull in 1913 by Pierce and Hedgerow.

"Interesting." Wolf rubbed his hands together. "They found the blue skull ten years before the Skull of Doom, and Hedgerow ended up with it."

"Right," Mee Mee said. "After his daughter Anita found the Skull of Doom, they possessed two of the Atlantean Thirteen."

Wolf narrowed his eyes. "I'm guessing that after Hedgerow died, his daughter became the sole heir."

Angie bobbed her head. "And she married Bill Hoffman."

Wolf chuckled. "An inept poker player."

"Right," Mee Mee said. "That explains how the Cranes gained possession of the Skull of Doom, but how did Mr. CBP end up in a hole on Monkey Island?"

Wolf stretched his arms and gazed at the ceiling. "I'm sure they did a lot of drinking during those poker nights at the hunting club." Lowering his arms, he said, "Guys talk a lot when they're drunk."

"So you think Hoffman let it be known that he had another Atlantean skull?"

"That would be my guess. Perhaps he wanted a rematch. Crane anted up his house the first time. Hoffman may have put the blue skull on the table to win back the Skull of Doom. Of course, it's all speculation. We need more information."

"We have a few more tidbits," Angie said.

Wolf raised his chin. "I'm all ears."

"There's an old guy by the name of Isaac who has managed the Crane property since the mid-seventies. Olivia Crane's granddaughter said that he knows all the family secrets. He told us to us to put the blue skull back in the hole where we found it, cover it up and forget about all this."

"Why?"

"He said, 'It is what it is: the face of death.'"

"Hmmm." Wolf's eyes lost focus as he gazed through the windows at the front of the store. "That could mean a couple of things, something from the past or something in the future."

"The past is obvious," Angie said. "Isaac knows something about Ahote Rowtag's murder."

Wolf nodded. "He definitely acknowledges the skull's lethal powers. Could be a reference to Rowtag's death."

"What about the future?" Mee Mee asked.

Wolf lowered his eyebrows. "Maybe the old guy feels something in his bones, a premonition. He sees the possibility of another death. Bury the skull, and you eliminate that outcome."

"Or maybe he's superstitious," Angie reasoned.

"Either way, you don't have much to go on," Wolf said. "Too many unanswered questions."

"Right." Mee Mee spread her hands. "Like how did Ahote Rowtag get his hands on the skull?"

"And why did he bury it?" Angie chipped in.

Freyja leaned on the counter. "And then what happened to him after he buried it? You still don't have a body."

Wolf nodded. "Without those answers, your case is dead in the water."

A Tom Jones song, *It's Not Unusual*, erupted from Mee Mee's shorts pocket. Mee Mee straightened. "It's my cell. Probably Cathy from the bookstore." She funneled her hand into the pocket, extracted the phone and put it to her ear. "Mee Mee here. What's up?" She nodded slowly. "Yes." She bit her lip. "I'm sorry to hear that . . . of course . . . I'm in Nags Head. I can be there in a few minutes . . . Room 310? Okay. Thanks for letting me know." She ended the call and inserted her phone back into her pocket.

"Who was that?" Angie asked.

"Cathy. She said Outer Banks Hospital called. They don't think Achak is going to last much longer. He insisted on talking to me."

"The hospital is right down the road," Angie said.

Mee Mee turned and charged to the door. "Let's go!"

Chapter 16
A New Revelation

The hospital, less than a mile south of the Wolfs' store, sat along Nag Head's main highway, Route 158. Angie made a right turn into the entrance, followed the lane to the right side of the main building and parked in the visitor's lot. Smaller than most mid-size town hospitals, the facility served the Outer Banks communities well in the off season but burst at the seams from late spring to early fall when the millions of vacationers made their pilgrimage to the barrier islands' shores. The central building, modern in appearance and three stories high, resembled a huge cream-colored box with two rows of four yellow awnings hanging over the front windows. Behind the big box, a one-story flat-roofed section, similar in style, stretched back to the medical offices. Angie and Mee Mee hurried along the sidewalk and under the large portico near the entrance.

"Maybe Achak knows more than he let on in the letter," Angie said as they entered the lobby.

Mee Mee led the way toward the elevator. "I hope he's able to tell us something before he . . . you know . . . joins his ancestors."

They stepped into the elevator, and a brunette nurse pushing a cart with a medical computer unit on top maneuvered in behind them and said, "Sorry to crowd you, ladies."

"I won't complain," Mee Mee said. "Nurses get paid to stab people."

The wiry woman winked. "And I also know how to flip patients twice my size."

At the third floor the doors separated, and the nurse backed out and pushed the cart to the right.

Mee Mee pointed at a sign on the wall. "310 is that-a-way." She turned left out of the elevator and hustled down the hallway.

Angie kept up, catching a whiff of the strange mingling of hospital smells—antibacterial cleaning chemicals mixed with unpleasant bodily odors. *She patted her stomach. Hope the maternity ward doesn't smell like this.*

At the end of the hall, Mee Mee stopped in front of room 310. "Let's hope he's still conscious and lucid."

Angie crossed her fingers.

Mee Mee took a deep breath, and they entered the darkened room. The blinds blocked the sun's rays, but a fluorescent light above the bed cast its pale glow over the enfeebled man. His long silvery hair was tucked behind his ears and lay limply over his shoulders. The harsh contrast created by the light carved deep grooves in his weathered face as if his features had been chiseled from cedar. Machines on both sides of the bed hummed and flashed tiny lights. An oxygen tube snaked over the railing, circled his head and clung to his nose. With closed eyes, he breathed with a raspy effort, his chest rising and falling haltingly.

Mee Mee reached and clasped his hand which lay across his stomach. "Achak."

He didn't stir.

"Achak," she said louder.

He opened his eyes and blinked several times.

"Can you hear me?"

He nodded.

"A nurse called and said you wanted to talk to us."

He coughed and swallowed. "What . . . what did you find?" His voice rumbled like gravel spilling off a dump truck.

"On the island?"

He nodded.

"We found a skull."

His eyes widened. "My grandfather's skull?"

"No, a blue skull carved from quartz crystal."

He closed his eyes. "I've heard about these crystal skulls."

"Your grandfather told you about them?"

"Yes, and I've read about them. They were entrusted to the native peoples around the world long before the Europeans crossed the sea."

Mee Mee leaned closer. "Who gave them the skulls?"

"The Wise Ones."

"Why?" Angie asked.

"To determine the future. Someday Mother Earth will weep with tears of blood." Achak hacked and swallowed. "My grandfather said the skulls were given to help in her time of turmoil."

"Why did your grandfather bury it?"

"I don't know." He gazed at the ceiling and narrowed his eyes. "Perhaps to keep it from those who would misuse it."

"It belonged to a couple by the name of Anita and Bill Hoffman," Angie said. "I doubt if they gave it to him."

Achak wobbled his head slowly. "If he took it from them, he felt justified in doing so."

Angie said, "Justified in stealing something that didn't belong to him?"

He met her gaze. "In the wrong hands, the skull will bring death. Stealing is not a sin if it prevents a greater sin."

Mee Mee released his hand and grasped the railing. "It's possible that Bill Hoffman lost the blue skull in a card game."

Achak eyed her. "To whom?"

"A man by the name of Chandler Crane. Ever hear of him?"

"Yes. My grandfather was his hunting and fishing guide. He took Crane to all the good spots."

"Do you think Crane trusted your grandfather?" Angie asked.

He nodded. "Ahote Rowtag was a man of his word."

Angie rubbed her chin. "If the skull is a Maya artifact, it

could be worth a lot of money. Perhaps Crane gave the skull to your grandfather for safekeeping."

"That's possible."

Mee Mee leaned on the railing. "Then for some reason, Ahote decided to bury it."

Achak nodded. "Grandfather was a shaman. He had visions that guided his decisions."

"Like you said," Angie reiterated, "in the wrong hands, the skull could bring death."

He gazed up at her. "But now it is in the right hands."

Angie tilted her head. "So I've been told."

Mee Mee patted Angie's shoulder. "We met with Crane's wife. She told us Angie has been called to be a Guardian of the blue skull."

"What makes the Crane woman an authority?" Achak asked.

"She is the Guardian of the Skull of Doom and claims her skull is the Master Skull."

Achak coughed and stiffened. "Where is her husband?"

"He wasn't there," Angie said. "We assumed she's a widow."

His eyes narrowed. "Perhaps a black widow."

Mee Mee raised her eyebrows. "Do you think she killed her husband to become the Guardian of the Skull of Doom?"

Achak laid his hand on his chest. "A shadow crossed over my heart when you mentioned her name."

Angie frowned. "We can't base this investigation on shadows and feelings. We need facts. Right now, all we have is speculation. We have no idea how your grandfather got his hands on that skull and why he buried it. Did his diary mention anything about the card game or the Hoffmans?"

"No. His last entry recorded only a few words about his day as a guide. Nothing unusual. I found the map inserted at that point in the journal."

"That tells us something," Angie said. "Somehow, he got his

hands on the skull and buried it. After drawing the map and placing it in the diary, he disappeared. He didn't have a chance to write an explanation. That's all we know for sure at this point. Maybe Chandler Crane or Bill Hoffman tortured him to find out where he hid the skull, but we're only guessing."

"Grandfather would have never caved. The torture led to his death."

"Or maybe he fell off his fishing boat and drowned," Angie countered.

"He didn't drown." Achak eyed her. "You've made some progress. I thank you for your efforts. I hope you haven't reached a dead end."

Mee Mee leaned on the bed railing. "We still have some leads to follow. Olivia Crane invited us to a gathering of the skulls on All Hallows' Eve."

Achak's brow tensed, deepening the carved shadows of his face and darkening his eyes. "That is the night of remembering the dead." He took in a raspy breath and swallowed. "But I fear it may be a night of adding to their numbers."

Angie sensed a prickling across her shoulders and down her back. She glanced at Mee Mee and raised her eyebrows. "Let's hope not."

"I had a vision," Achak murmured.

"Of the Gathering of the Ten?" Mee Mee asked.

Achak shook his head. "No. I saw a large yellow house overgrown by trees and vines. I told the nurse I needed to speak to you about it."

"Sounds like the hunting club on Monkey Island," Angie said.

Achak nodded.

Mee Mee leaned over the bed railing. "What did you see in the vision?"

"I went into the house, walked down a long hallway and entered a room. On a table I saw a bottle."

Mee Mee leaned closer. "What kind of bottle?"

"An empty whiskey bottle. I heard my grandfather speak from its depths. He said, 'I am here.' When I reached for it, it vanished."

"Where did it go?" Angie asked.

Achak closed his eyes. "Somewhere within the walls of the hunting club, in a dark place."

"That could be anywhere," Mee Mee said.

Achak opened his eyes. "You must find that bottle."

Chapter 17
Goldbluff

Joel stretched against the back of the kitchen chair and tilted his head. "I can see your baby bump. It's not big, but it's there."

Angie took a sip of her coffee as she leaned against the sink counter. Her orange boatneck top and sporty capri pants gave her athletic body a chic look. "I'm only two months, but the peezing has already started."

"What's peezing?"

"Sneezing and peeing at the same time."

"Want me to pick up some of those adult diapers? The ones on the TV commercials look pretty sexy."

"Depends."

"On what?"

Angie laughed. "Sometimes you just don't get it, do you?"

Joel stared at the ceiling and jutted his lower lip. "I guess I don't."

"That's one reason I love you."

"Because I don't get your jokes?"

"No, because you make me laugh."

"We do laugh a lot, don't we?"

Angie nodded, stepped up next to him and tousled his sandy blond hair. "Yes, we do. Laughing with your lover is the best kind of laughing."

He reached and rubbed her lower back. "I'm glad you and Mee Mee didn't paddle out to Monkey Island to look for that bottle."

"Mee Mee wanted to go. She said every empty whiskey bottle has a story to tell."

"But it's a phantom bottle from a dream."

"She said that Achak's dreams have a basis in reality. He's some kind of Algonquin shaman."

"A witchdoctor?"

"No! Let's just say he sees things in the spirit realm."

"To me, it sounded like he was sending you on a wild whiskey bottle chase."

"I'm with you. That's a big building. I don't think we'd walk in there and find that particular bottle sitting on the fireplace mantle. People hide incriminating evidence."

"In deep, dark places."

Angie chuckled. "Don't worry, Joel. I'm not going back out there unless we have something solid to go on. Dreams aren't enough."

Joel stood, slipped his arms around her waist and pulled her close. "Unless they're our dreams."

She kissed him softly on the lips. "And our dreams are coming true."

"Can you believe it? You and me . . . we made a new person."

Angie bobbed her head. "The best things are homemade."

He grasped her shoulders. "I'm worried about this skull gathering."

"Don't be. It's just a bunch of kooks pinning their hopes for this world on myths and legends. Being a caretaker of one of these skulls makes them feel important. It's like a religion to them."

"So you think these people are harmless?"

"More or less."

"I don't know about that. Religious fanatics can be dangerous."

Angie shrugged. "I'm a private investigator. The possibility of danger comes with the territory."

"I know." He took a step back, reached and rubbed her belly. "But now there's two of you crossing into the danger zone."

"We'll be fine. I'll call you if anything unusual happens."

"Make sure you do."

"We want to get settled in before the reception starts at noon. I told Mee Mee I'd pick her up at eleven. I better get going."

"Are you taking a firearm with you?"

"Of course. Little Miss Colt .38 is in my suitcase."

"Good. An extra pound of luggage could save your life."

Angie rolled her eyes. "What's another pound." She pulled him close, kissed him, patted his cheek and headed down the hall to the bedroom to get her things.

The blustery day made the drive to Mee Mee's a mix of rolling clouds and spotty sunshine. When the sun broke through an opening, Angie squinted, groped for her sunglasses in the compartment between the seats and managed to fidget them onto her face. *That's better.* She pulled into a parking space on the left side of the bookstore and beeped the horn. *I feel like I'm working overtime for what I'm getting paid on this job. Then again, when it's all over, we might be able to cash in on that blue skull. That would be awesome. In our circumstances, Joel and I could use a big payday. I'd sell Mr. CBP at the drop of a shinbone. The last thing I want is to be the Guardian of that monstrosity.*

Mee Mee stepped out onto the stoop of her shop and smiled. She carried the bowling bag in one hand and a small blue suitcase in the other. Her fern print navy and white jumpsuit fit loosely over her wiry frame and fluttered in the wind as she walked toward the Civic. She opened the passenger door, set the bowling bag on the floor, scooted onto the seat, placed the blue suitcase on her lap and shut the door.

She tapped the top of the suitcase like it was a snare drum. "I'm so excited."

"You sound like a teenager heading to a Foo Fighters concert."

"I'd prefer the Rolling Stones." Mee Mee eyed her. "You look like a movie star with those Versace shades."

"Believe me, they're not the real thing, but they do the job."

"Kinda like us."

Angie chuckled and backed out the Civic. "Yeah. Hopefully these skull fanatics won't figure out what we're really up to."

"That's what makes it exciting. We're undercover, about ready to solve a long-forgotten crime."

"Let's hope it doesn't turn out like one of the Stone's songs."

"Which one?"

I Can't Get No Satisfaction."

Mee Mee grinned and sang the chorus of the song.

Angie shook her head. "Hey you!"

Mee Mee stopped singing. "What?'

"Get off of my cloud."

Mee Mee laughed. "Stop it. We need to figure out how to make the most out of this gathering of strange birds."

"That's one way to put it. I think we're in for an unconventional convention. Have you ever seen crows gather in a big tree at dusk?"

"Yeah. I grew up in West Virginia. Seeing a mass of black creatures huddled above you can be unsettling. Do you know what they call a gathering of crows?"

"No, what?"

"A murder."

"Now isn't that appropriate."

On the drive north up Route 12 along the dunes and through the small towns, they discussed the possibilities but couldn't come up with any solid strategy. Finally, they decided to play it by ear and wait to see how the proceedings unravel. They would do their best to appear as crystal skull neophytes and go with the flow like sheep blending into the flock. If something pertinent cropped up, they would do their best to investigate without drawing attention to their efforts. Hopefully, the crows wouldn't notice.

The Crane's driveway was crowded with a variety of expensive cars—Audis, Mercedes, Cadillacs. Angie managed to park in the last open spot toward the back. A tall man with curly umber hair lifted a large duffle bag out of the back of a black Kia Sorento. He was lean but muscular. His slinky black trousers and half-unbuttoned floral print shirt added to his playboy looks. When Angie stepped out of the car, he turned and nodded toward her. He had large dark eyes and full lips. The narrow bridge of his nose flared at the bottom into wide nostrils. She estimated his height to be about six feet three inches.

Mee Mee got out of the Civic and retrieved her bowling bag and small suitcase.

"Hello, ladies," the handsome man said as he moved out of the way of the Sorento's closing hatch.

Mee Mee skirted the front of the Civic and walked toward him. "Good morning! Are you one of the Guardians?"

He tilted his head, one eye almost closing. "I suppose so."

She stopped in front of him and took a deep breath. "We've never been to one of these gatherings. Isn't it exciting?"

He shrugged. "I don't know what to expect. I'm a first timer, too."

"You must be Mr. Goldbluff's nephew," Mee Mee said.

"That's right. I'm Jeff Goldbluff. How did you know?"

Angie sidled up to Mee Mee. "We've heard about you and your uncle's unfortunate . . ."

"Demise?"

Angie nodded.

He gave Angie the once over, raised one eyebrow and refocused on her face. "He definitely died unexpectedly."

Angie imagined Uncle Goldbluff's final convulsions as he hovered over the Skull of Doom. "That's a tough way to go."

"And now you're the new Guardian," Mee Mee said.

He nodded and glanced at Mee Mee's bowling bag. "Then you must be a new Guardian, too."

Mee Mee leaned her head toward Angie. "She is."

"That's right," Angie said. "I'm Angie Thomas, and this is Mee Mee Roberts. We found the blue skull."

"Ah, yes . . . the blue skull Mrs. Crane mentioned in the

invitation." His smile contorted into a crooked line. "My uncle predicted it would soon be found . . . number Ten of the Atlantean Thirteen."

"He was right. We found it," Mee Mee said. "What number is yours?"

"Rosey is Number Nine."

"Rosey?" Angie let out a short titter. "Is that your skull's name?"

"Officially, it's known as Passion, but I renamed her Rosey. It's the skull of loooove." He jiggled his eyebrows Groucho Marx fashion.

"How do you figure that?" Angie asked.

He met her gaze, his dark eyes mesmerizing. "Rose quartz is known for its qualities of passion and romance in the crystal skull business. Rosey attracts love. My uncle made a nice living by taking her to crystal skull conferences around the world. Attendees pay good money for a chance to find romance."

Angie raised her chin. "Sounds like a scam to me."

Goldbluff narrowed his eyes. "You must not be a true believer."

She shrugged, shaking off his captivating stare. *Neither are you.*

"Of course, we are," Mee Mee said, "or we wouldn't be here."

"Uh huh." Goldbluff glanced at his watch. "It's 11:45. We better check into our rooms before things get started. True believers like us wouldn't want to miss the opening introductions." He turned and led them down the driveway and up the wide steps to the second-floor entrance.

The door swung open, and Isaac stepped into view wearing a white dress shirt and loosely fitting gray slacks. His lanky stature reminded Angie of a character from a spaghetti western, the loner who kept his eyes peeled and guns ready.

"You must be Isaac," Goldbluff said. "I'm Jeff Goldbluff. It's good to finally meet you."

We'll get a chance to talk later, Mr. Goldbluff." He checked his watch. "Everyone else is here. They're waiting in the great room."

"For us?" Goldbluff said.

He nodded, turned and pointed to a stairway to his right. "Your rooms are on the third floor at the end of the hall across from each other. Name cards are on the doors."

Goldbluff grinned. "I bet we're in rooms nine and ten."

Isaac nodded. "Lunch will be served in about forty-five minutes after the introductions."

"Thanks, Isaac," Mee Mee said. "We'll be right down as soon as we drop off our suitcases."

"One more thing." Isaac lowered his fierce eyebrows. "Make sure you bring your skulls with you."

"I wouldn't leave her behind." Goldbluff sang, "Love grows where my Rosey goes, and nobody knows like me." He strode past Isaac and headed up the staircase.

Mee Mee glanced up at Isaac. "That guy is a little odd."

Isaac squinted off into the distance. "Uh huh."

"Let's go," Angie said. "There's a *roomful* of oddballs waiting for us." She headed for the steps.

Mee Mee cringed. "She really didn't mean that."

"I'm sure she did," Isaac murmured.

When she reached the top of the stairs, Angie heard a door shut at the end of the hallway. *Figures he'd be rooming across the hall from us. I wish he wasn't so good looking.* She took a deep breath and blew it out. *Stop it, Stallone. You've got the best man in the world waiting at home for you. Besides, the guy seems like he's in love with himself.*

Mee Mee caught up with her. "That Jeff Goldbluff is a handsome man, isn't he?"

Angie gave her a miffed glance. "He's okay."

"Look at the names on these doors." Mee Mee pointed to the card tacked to the first door on the right. "*Sha Na Na.*"

"The one on this side says *Amen.*"

They walked a few steps and stopped at the next set of

doors.

Angie glanced at the card fastened to the door on the left. *"Princess Corn."*

"Lord Rainbow on this side."

They moved to the next couple of doors. Angie read the card. "*Harmony.* That one has a nice ring to it. These must be the names of the skulls."

"I think you're right. This one says *Nostra.*"

They shuffled to the next set of doors, and Mee Mee eyed the card. "This skull must be Greek. His name is *Hippocrates.*"

"Wasn't Hippocrates some kind of philosopher?"

Mee Mee shook her head. "He was known as the Father of Medicine."

"A doctor, huh? Interesting." She faced the door to her left. "No card on this door."

"I can guess who's staying there."

"The Skull of Doom?"

Mee Mee nodded. "I bet we're in the next room."

Angie walked the few steps to the last door on the left and examined the card. "Yep. Crystal Blue Persuasion."

Mee Mee caught up and faced the door on the right. "*Passion.* I guess Mr. Goldbluff didn't notify Olivia Crane about the name change."

"I don't think Goldbluff respects rules of order when it comes to skull naming."

Mee Mee chuckled. "He must be the Casanova of the Atlantean Skull Society."

"Yeah." Angie reached for the knob and opened the door. "And we're stuck at the end of the hall with death on one side and loooove on the other."

"Oh, well," Mee Mee sighed as she followed Angie into the room. "They say the two things that can change your world are love and death."

Angie stepped up to the queen bed neatly made with a powder blue bedspread patterned with dark blue roses. She plopped her pink suitcase on top and sat next to it on the firm mattress. "Love changed my world." She rubbed her belly. "And it's about to be turned upside down."

Mee Mee set her suitcase on the floor and placed the bowling bag on the old mahogany dresser to the right of the bed. "Your baby will be here before you know it." She unzipped the bag, inserted both hands into the opening and gingerly removed the skull. After unwrapping it, she turned and extended the skull to Angie.

· Angie stiffened. "No thanks."

"You better carry it. You *are* the Guardian."

Angie hesitantly accepted the smirking skull. "Who are you? The midwife of Death?"

Mee Mee laughed. "At least Mr. CBP won't cry at three o'clock in the morning."

"If he does, I'm tossing him out the window."

"Come on. It's time to go down and join the gathering of . . ."

"Crows?"

Mee Mee nodded. "The murder awaits us."

Chapter 18
A Gathering of Crows

Hurrying out the door, Angie almost collided with Jeff Goldbluff. She stopped short, clasping the blue skull against her belly.

"Ahhh, we meet again." He bobbed the rose-colored skull in his hands. "Rosey, look who's here."

Mee Mee stepped beside Angie and flipped her hand toward the blue skull. "Rosey, I'd like you to meet Crystal Blue Persuasion, Mr. CBP for short."

Angie gave Mee Mee a peeved glance.

Goldbluff winked at Angie. "Rosey says, 'hi.' I think it's love at first sight. What do you think?"

"I think you better check Rosey's hormone levels because Mr. CBP ain't feeling it."

"That's okay," Goldbluff grinned. "He's just playing hard to get. She likes that."

Mee Mee laughed. "Rosey must be enchanted by his drop-dead looks."

Goldbluff chortled as he led the way down the hall. "That could be it."

"Can't be his great butt," Angie grumbled. "He doesn't have one."

They followed the tall man down the steps and through the entrance room. When he passed through the doorway that led to the great room, he turned to his left and came to an abrupt stop. He stiffened and raised his eyebrows.

Angie entered the room and turned to see what caused his reaction. About ten people, all dressed in black, faced her. A mixture of males and females, they had formed into a diverse huddle united by their raven outfits. A tall young man in the back stood above the rest. His knit collared shirt revealed the wide and muscled chest of a body builder. He had spiked auburn hair and a menacing frown. He crossed his bulging arms and lowered his chin to peer over his black-framed shades.

Olivia Crane sat in her wheelchair in front of the assembly, her hands clasped on her lap. Charlotte stood next to her wearing a long-sleeve midi dress with a lowcut neckline.

Mee Mee stepped forward, waved and said, "Hello, everybody! Hope we're not late."

Olivia Crane spread her hands. "Let's welcome the new Guardians to the Gathering of the Atlantean Skull Society."

The group clapped in unison, uttering the word *welcome* in an uneven blend of voices. Angie forced a smile as she appraised the odd collection of strangers.

Goldbluff said, "I must have missed the dress code memo."

"There was no memo." The old woman reclasped her hands on her lap. "This is All Hallow's Eve, a day set aside to honor and remember the dead. Your uncle died in this house exactly two years ago. All of us were moved to dress in black to honor his memory."

"Hmmmm." Goldbluff brushed the front of his floral print shirt. "I guess I didn't feel the vibe. Sorry."

"No need to apologize."

Angie glanced down at her bright orange boatneck top. The blue skull seemed to glow against it. *I fit in like a cow in the Kentucky Derby.*

"It's good to meet all of you," Mee Mee beamed. "We're so excited to be here."

"Everyone," Olivia Crane said, "I'd like you to meet Mee Mee Roberts and Angie Thomas. Number Ten drew them to his location on a remote island, and they set him free from his grave to fulfill his destiny. His name is Crystal Blue Persuasion. Angie is the new Guardian."

The gathering of black clad devotees cawed various words of greetings. Charlotte remained silent but smiled. However, Granite Man in the back stood motionless, glaring at the trio of newcomers.

"We also welcome back Number Nine, Passion, and her new Guardian Jeff Goldbluff."

A wide smile broke across Goldbluff's face. "Rosey is pleased as pumpkin pie to rejoin all of you. I'm a rookie, but I hope this gathering will get me up to speed on my responsibilities and possibilities."

The wrinkles on Olivia Crane's face tightened. "Yes, Mr. Goldbluff, you are correct. Guardians have many responsibilities and possibilities."

"I know Uncle Gavin did quite well hauling Rosie around the world to all the skull conferences. I hope to get on board that treasure train."

The Guardians' faces darkened, and murmurs rumbled.

Golfbluff put a hand to his chest. "Did I say something wrong?"

"Mr. Goldbluff," the old woman seethed, "the crystal skull conferences that are held around the world are not for our profit but for the world's edification."

Goldbluff cringed. "Sorry about that. Rookie mistake. I assumed cashing in was a privilege of guardianship. That's the impression I got from Uncle Gavin."

"That shocks me." Olivia Crane furrowed her brow. "We share our skulls with the world to bring enlightenment and hope, not to take advantage of the public's curiosity and make financial gains."

Goldbluff cleared his throat and swallowed. "But you do make a profit from these conferences, correct?"

A short man with a shaved head, pointy ears and thick lips stepped forward. He closed his eyes and nodded once. "As the scriptures tell us, the worker is worthy of his wages, Mr. Goldbluff." He nodded once again, eyes remaining closed.

"Traveling the world and educating people about the Thirteen Atlantean Skulls is not an easy task. We take it seriously. Yes, we are compensated, but that is not our main concern."

Goldbluff's face gleamed with a devilish smile. "Of course not. My mistake. I'll do my best to center my objectives on this group's high standards."

"I hope so," Olivia Crane said. "Taking lightly the responsibilities of a Guardian places one in a precarious position. Your attitude makes me wonder about your suitability for guardianship."

Goldbluff raised his free hand. "I'm cool." He zipped his lips with his finger. "No more talk about financial gain. However, Miss Rosey does legally belong to me whether you approve of my guardianship or not."

Angie eyed Goldbluff. *He's purposely stirring the pot. Why?*

Olivia Crane stiffened. "You may be the owner, but Passion will seek a new Guardian if you are unworthy."

"Don't worry." The impish smile returned. "Old Rosey loves me. She'd never allow her eyes to wander."

Charlotte Crane placed her hand on the old woman's shoulder. "Please, Grandmother, don't be too harsh with Mr. Goldbluff. He's new to all this. Give him a chance to adjust to his changing circumstances. You have to admit that becoming a member of the Atlantean Skull Society is not like joining the local Rotary or Lion's Club."

The tension seemed to ease on the faces of the skull keepers, and Olivia Crane relaxed her shoulders, but Granite Man remained rigid.

Goldbluff extended his palm like a beggar about to receive a quarter. "Thank you so much, Miss . . . "

Charlotte smiled pleasantly. "My name is Charlotte Crane. I'm Olivia's granddaughter."

Goldbluff raised his eyebrows, an ardent smile brightening his features. "I appreciate your words of support. May I also say that Rosey has just confirmed to me that you are a person of great integrity and inner beauty."

Charlotte blushed. "Oh, . . . please tell Rosey I said, 'thank you.'"

Angie could hardly keep from puking. *Come on, Goldbluff. You're laying on the mustard so thickly my nostrils are burning. What an act.*

Olivia Crane checked her watch. "Lunch will be served soon. I would like to proceed with the formal introductions before we sit down to eat." She spun her wheelchair around, and the people behind her separated to reveal a round ebony table. The Skull of Doom sat in the middle, and crystal skulls of various colors were spaced evenly around the perimeter. Several spaces were left empty at the edge of the table nearest the group. "Guardians, please find your place next to your skull. Our new Guardians will place their skulls facing the Skull of Doom on the appropriate number inscribed along the edge of the table."

Angie hesitated as she watched the Guardians circle the table. Eyeing Goldbluff, she said under her breath, "Lead the way, Mr. Cordiality. I'm right behind you."

Golfbluff smirked. "I'm just being myself."

"Obviously."

Goldbluff found his place at the table where the number 9 was inscribed. Angie stood next to him in front of the number 10.

Goldbluff held out the rose quartz skull. "Shall we place them down together?"

Angie shrugged. "If you insist."

They lowered their skulls onto the numbers facing the Skull of Doom.

Olivia Crane wheeled her chair to the empty place where the numbers 11, 12, and 13 were inscribed. She spread her hands. "Welcome, all Guardians, to the Table of the Thirteen. At our last gathering there were only nine of us. Now there are ten. We await the final three's arrival which will complete the Circle of Knowledge and Power. The world is heading toward destruction, but we have gathered to offer the world salvation."

The veteran Guardians nodded slowly and uttered in unison, "We gather to offer salvation."

Goldbluff elbowed Angie and said, "Yes . . . salvation."

"Salvation," Angie mumbled.

The old woman clasped her hands in front of her as if to pray. "The world has descended into darkness, but we gather to offer light."

The circle of caretakers responded, "We gather to offer light," with Angie's and Goldbluff's words a half step behind.

Olivia Crane closed her eyes. "The world consumes out of hatred, but we gather to sacrifice out of love."

"We gather to sacrifice out of love," the Guardians said in unison.

Angie felt an odd sensation when she said the word *sacrifice*.

Chapter 19
Introductions

"I want to thank all of you for coming," Olivia Crane said. "I believe this is the most important congress occurring in the world today. Each of you have been called to do your part to offer an alternative to the impending Apocalypse." She spread her arms. "These crystal skulls can determine the fate of the world. Now we are ten. Time is slipping by, and catastrophic events are drawing near. Our hope is to call forth the final three skulls to reunite the Atlantean Thirteen. Then the knowledge and power of their union will be released, and the world will be shown a path to salvation."

To the old woman's immediate left, the short bald guy closed his eyes and nodded several times. "Yes! We are calling forth the final three. What a glorious mission!"

Olivia Crane reached and patted the bald guy's hand. "I would like to begin by introducing Bahar, the world-renowned expert on the origins of the Atlantean Thirteen. He is the Guardian of Sha Na Na, the Skull of the Past."

The bald man smiled, his thick lips thinning as they stretched across his protruding teeth. He reached and placed his hand on top of a life-size amber colored skull in front of him. "Sha Na Na welcomes all of you."

Olivia Crane lifted her hand from atop his and pointed to the black-haired woman standing next to him. "Carolyn Dodge is the Guardian of Nostra, the Skull of the Future."

Shapely, she resembled a swimsuit model who had passed her prime. Her long black hair blended into her V-cut silky midi dress. She reached and placed her hand on top of a huge clear skull clouded with bursts of milky gray. "Nostra welcomes all of you."

Angie inspected the somber-faced skull. *Geesh. It must weigh at least thirty-five pounds. A girl could get a hernia hauling that thing around.*

Olivia Crane shifted her gaze to an older man standing next to the curvaceous woman. Thick white hair covered his ears and lay across the collar of his black dress shirt. His white brows and bags under his eyes gave him the look of a snowy owl. He wore a necklace with a large silver pendant, a sun overlapped by a triangle with an all-seeing eye.

"Next I would like to introduce Honeypot Chen, the Maya shaman and Guardian of Amen, the Skull of the Spirit."

The shaman placed his hand on a dark purple amethyst skull, slightly smaller than life-size. In a low, cordial voice he said, "Amen welcomes all of you."

Beaming with a friendly smile, a chubby redheaded lady stood next to Honeypot Chen. She looked to be in her mid-fifties. Her blue agate earrings matched the color of her bright eyes. She wore a two-piece black pants outfit in stark contrast to her fair complexion. Olivia Crane motioned toward her. "Our next Guardian is Sharon Wheatfield, the caretaker of Rapture, the Skull of Joy."

The redhead's smile widened as she placed her hand on a life-size skull with fissures of yellow and orange zigzagging through it. Her voice was lively as she said, "Rapture welcomes all of you." The skull's smile was wide and toothy.

To her left stood a tall, thin man with thick dark eyebrows and salt-and-pepper hair. His wire-rimmed glasses gave him the look of an absent-minded college professor. A crooked black bowtie and wrinkled dress shirt completed his disheveled appearance.

Olivia Crane nodded toward the tall man. "The esteemed Dr. Jan Van Eden is the Guardian of Princess Corn, the Skull of Bounty."

He placed his large hand on top of the smallest of the skulls, a green jade carving with big eye sockets. The five-inch-tall idol disappeared under his grasp. "Princess Corn welcomes all of you," he said in a jittery voice.

Another larger-than-life-size skull sat in front of a woman with silvery feathered hair. Her hooped earrings and matching bracelets repeated the oval shapes of the numerous silver rings on her fingers. Her bright red lipstick and fingernail polish reflected her rosy complexion. The skull, pure white with simply chiseled features, glowed against the woman's black puffy shirt.

Olivia Crane said, "Our next Guardian is Jo Ann Parkinson, the caretaker of Hippocrates, the Skull of Healing."

Parkinson placed her hand delicately on top of the white skull. "Hippocrates welcomes all of you." Her voice was light and soothing.

Standing next to Jeff Goldbluff, an older man, probably in his seventies, wore a black long-sleeved t-shirt with the image of a clear skull that seemed to radiate a variety of colors. Beneath the image were the words: *Lord Rainbow*. His bushy light gray mustache matched the color of his receding hair which was gathered into a ponytail. A bulbous nose and jovial smile reinforced his affable appearance.

The old woman's hand unfolded toward him. "I am honored to introduce the Director of the Crystal Skull Intelligence Institute, Dale Talkington. Dale is the Guardian of Lord Rainbow, the Skull of Diversity."

As Angie shifted her focus, a multitude of colors glittered from the skull's depths. *Now that is impressive. Must be some kind of optical effect caused by light shining through the crystal.*

Dale Talkington clasped the top of the radiant skull. "Lord Rainbow welcomes all of you."

"I guess I'm next," Goldbluff blurted.

The old woman glared at him. "Please, wait until you are introduced before you speak."

He raised a hand. "My faux pas. Go ahead and introduce me."

She cleared her throat, her eyes aflame. "Jeff Goldbluff is the nephew of Gavin Goldbluff, who was the Guardian of Passion, the Skull of Attraction."

Goldbluff smirked. "And now I am the new Guardian of Rosey, the Skull of Loooove. I've renamed my skull."

The circle of black clad devotees stiffened as if a cold breeze had just swept into the room.

Olivia Crane shook her head. "We have not approved of any name changes."

Goldbluff reached and caressed the top of the rose quartz skull. "Rosey welcomes all of you."

Angie gave Goldbluff a sideways glance. *What are you up to, Mr. Congeniality?*

After a half minute of uncomfortable silence and perturbed looks, Olivia Crane said, "Finally, I would like to introduce our newest Guardian, Angie Thomas, the caretaker of Crystal Blue Persuasion."

Angie smiled nervously and nodded. She extended her hand and patted the top of the blue skull. "Crystal Blue Persuasion welcomes all of you."

Goldbluff leaned and examined the blue skull. "And Crystal Blue Persuasion is the Skull of what? Persuasiveness? Hallucinogenic Drugs?" He smirked and eyed Angie.

She shrugged. "I don't know."

The old woman lips trembled. "That is yet to be determined, Mr. Goldbluff."

"Excuse me, Mrs. Crane," Isaac's voice resonated from the other side of the room. "Lunch is served in the dining area."

Angie glanced over her shoulder. The sunlight streaming through the back entryway lit Isaac's looming figure. Mee Mee, Charlotte and Granite Man stood along the wall next to the doorway.

Olivia Crane spun her wheelchair around and clasped her hands. "Very good, Isaac. We have concluded the introductions and are ready to eat."

Granite Man took a step forward and coughed.

"I'm sorry," she said. "There is one more important

introduction I need to make. As you can see, the flower of youth has long since wilted and fallen from this old lady's life. My health is failing me, and I am not long for this world. However, I have received an important revelation from the Skull of Doom. He has opened my eyes to the identity of the next caretaker who will have the privilege of being his Guardian." She extended her hand toward Granite Man. "That person is my grandson, Arnold Crane."

Arnold Crane expanded his chest, placed his hands on his hips and nodded toward the circle of skull devotees. "I am humbled by the Skull of Doom's call to guardianship." His eyes narrowed. "I will be a committed member of this federation. I am willing to do whatever is necessary to fulfill my calling."

The group clapped politely.

Goldbluff, however, clapped like a wind-up monkey clanging its cymbals. "Great! I've got an old refrigerator you could carry down five flights of steps for me."

Several gasps escaped from the Guardians' mouths.

Goldbluff laughed. "I'm just kidding around. Boy, you people need to lighten up."

Arnold Crane crossed his huge arms and scowled at him. "I could carry your refrigerator, but I won't carry your purse."

Goldbluff snickered. "Now that's funny. C'mon. Let's eat. I want to sit next to you, Arnold."

Granite Man groaned.

As the group filtered out of the meeting room and into the dining and kitchen area, Angie hung back, making eye contact with Mee Mee.

Mee Mee waited until Charlotte stepped behind her grandmother's wheelchair to push her out of the room before drifting back to talk to Angie. "That was an interesting circle of odd birds. What a crew."

"Yeah, a real band of bozos. How'd I fit in?"

"With that orange top? Like Princess Leia at a Star Trek convention."

"Great."

"Don't worry. Goldbluff's histrionics eclipsed your falling star."

"He's up to something."

Mee Mee raised her eyebrows. "Obviously."

Angie thumbed toward the dining room. "We better get in there."

The Guardians had seated themselves around a large oval oak table in the spacious dining area. An island with a gray quartz countertop separated the space from the kitchen. Lively conversations bubbled around the circle of guests. Olivia Crane sat in her wheelchair at the head of the table. Two empty seats waited at the other end. Mee Mee led the way around the skull keepers and slid into the first open seat.

Great. Angie pulled out the remaining ladder-back chair. *I get to sit next to Mr. Congeniality.* She sat down and scooted up to the table.

Olivia Crane spread her arms. "Everyone please help yourselves."

Golfbluff rubbed his hands together. "This looks delicious." He elbowed Charlotte who sat to his right. "Could you pass me the potato salad before Arnold dumps the whole bowl onto his plate?"

Arnold Crane gave him a steely glare. After shoveling a large glob onto his plate, he stabbed the ladle into the pile of potatoes.

"Doesn't my brother intimidate you?" Charlotte picked up the bowl and held it in front of Goldbluff. "He does most people."

"Not at all. He's a pussycat." Goldbluff scooped out a medium serving and plopped it onto his plate. "How did you get all the muscles in the family, and your brother got all the feminine looks?"

"Very funny. I couldn't bench press fifty pounds."

Goldbluff winked at her. "Believe me, you don't need to."

"But my brother is a champion body builder."

"Is that right?" Goldbluff shifted his focus to Granite Man. "I've always heard that body builders are substantially weaker than they look. Their muscles are bulked up with steroids. Is that true?"

Arnold burned a stare into him. "Would you like to find out?"

"Maybe, but first I need to find a pin to see if your biceps will pop like balloons."

Arnold formed a fist. "Maybe your head will pop first."

Goldbluff leaned toward Charlotte. "I'm glad I sat next to you instead of him. Your brother's conversation skills are more disappointing than unsalted peanuts."

Arnold Crane stood, his chair almost tipping over. "We can take this conversation outside. Let's see if you can talk with a mouthful of broken teeth."

Goldbluff scooted out his chair. "I'm your pallbearer."

Olivia Crane stood, her wheelchair rolling backwards. "That'll be enough!"

Chapter 20
Something Up His Sleeve

Conversations stumbled into a wall of dead silence. Wide-eyed, the diners gaped at the old woman. She glanced down, seemingly surprised at her own arising. She shifted her focus around the table of shocked faces. After taking two steps backwards, she lowered herself onto her wheelchair and rolled up to the table.

Goldbluff raised his hands like a third stringer defending Larry Bird. "Sorry. I didn't realize how sensitive Mr. Olympia was about body building stigmas."

"Mr. Goldbluff," the old woman steamed, "you are an extraordinarily offensive man."

"He doesn't belong here," Arnold Crane whined.

"Sit down, Arnold, and calm down," she commanded.

"Yes, Grandmother." Granite Man took a deep breath, planted his butt on the seat and scooted to the table.

"If you prefer," Goldbluff said, "I could take Rosey and go home."

Oliva Crane placed her hands flat on the table. "That won't be necessary. All I ask is that you make a sincere effort to filter your words and fulfill your calling."

"Not a problem." He thumbed toward Arnold Crane. "If your grandson is willing to let bygones be bygones, I promise to behave myself."

The old woman bore a stare into her grandson. "Arnold?"

He lowered his head, his face reddening. "I'm good."

"There you go," Goldbluff piped. "Everything is hunky dory. Let's finish eating and get this party started."

For the rest of the luncheon, the once lively conversations

became somewhat muted. Angie picked at her salad and braised chicken, but an odd sensation in the pit of her stomach limited her intake. She made eye contact with Mee Mee a few times but didn't say much. The only ones not affected by the fracas were Charlotte and Goldbluff. He carried on about his love of the ocean and surfing. Like a schoolgirl, Charlotte hung on his every word and asked him to go for a beach walk following the afternoon session. This invitation heightened the level of his blustery banter.

Their syrupy flirtations didn't help to ease the discomfort in Angie's stomach. *You two need to find a lonely corner somewhere and let the rest of us eat in peace.*

Finally, Olivia Crane announced, "We will be taking a twenty-minute break before we gather again in the great room. At that time, Bahar will be giving us a refresher course on the origins of the Atlantean Thirteen."

Charlotte rolled her eyes and sighed.

Goldbluff leaned toward her and raised an eyebrow. "Should be a fascinating lecture."

"To me," she said in a low tone, "it's as dull as dishwater."

One by one the skull keepers rose from their seats and left the dining area.

Mee Mee tugged on Angie's elbow. "Let's go up to our room and freshen up."

"Good idea."

They made their way around the table and into the back entryway.

"Where are you ladies going?" Goldbluff asked.

Angie glanced over her shoulder. "To our room."

"I think I'll head up there, too."

Mee Mee led the way through the foyer and up the steps. Walking down the hallway, she said, "You certainly are the life of the party, Mr. Goldbluff."

He laughed. "Thanks. I like to lighten things up."

Mee Mee stopped at the end of the hall.

Angie turned and faced Goldbluff. "I'm just wondering *why*

you're such a jackass."

Goldbluff gave her his Groucho Marx eyebrow wiggle. "I have my reasons." He entered his room and closed the door.

Mee Mee shook her head. "Strange man." She opened the door, walked into their room and sat on the bed.

Angie entered and closed the door. "Arnold was right. Goldbluff doesn't belong here."

"Neither do we."

"True, but at least we're trying to fit in."

"He's upsetting the crystal skull cart."

"Exactly, and I want to know why."

Mee Mee screwed up her face. "Maybe he knows something."

Angie crossed the room and sat down on a winged back chair. "He knows something all right. I bet it has something to do with the death of his uncle."

"He might have some information we could use."

"That's possible." Angie leaned on her knees. "We found out one thing."

"What's that?"

"Olivia Crane isn't wheelchair bound."

Mee Mee chuckled. "She stood up like a schoolmarm with a yardstick. Did you notice she didn't send Golfbluff packin'?"

"For some reason she's letting his behavior slide. I'm going to find out why."

"How?"

"I'll knock on his door and ask him."

"Nothing like the direct approach."

Angie arose, crossed the room, opened the door and stepped into the hallway. She stared at the placard on Goldbluff's door. The word *Passion* had been crossed out and *Rosey* had been penciled in underneath.

Mee Mee sidled up to her. "Well . . . "

"He changed the skull's name on the card. Maybe he is just a jerk."

"Could be both."

Angie rapped on the door.

"Come right in," Goldbluff's voice chimed.

Angie turned the knob and entered.

Goldbluff lay on his back on the queen size bed. Hands clasped behind his head, he gazed at the ceiling.

Angie planted her hands on her hips. "We want to know what you're up to."

Goldbluff turned onto his side, his elbow and hand propping his head. "You first."

"What?"

"You tell me what you're up to, and I'll tell you what I'm up to."

"What are you talking about? We were invited to this gathering because we found that blue crystal skull, so here we are."

He pushed himself up and sat on the edge of the bed. "I don't buy it."

"Why not?" Mee Mee asked.

"Two local ladies don't just go out one day and stumble over an ancient crystal skull."

Mee Mee went through the explanation about finding the Monkey Island map in the old book.

Goldbluff grinned and shook his head. "That's about as likely as the Cleveland Browns winning the Super Bowl."

Angie furrowed her brow. "Are you really Gavin Goldbluff's nephew?"

He nodded.

"Why are you trying to get booted out of here?" Mee Mee asked.

"Why do you want to know?"

"We're just curious."

"No way." He pointed at Angie. "I think you're a cop."

"I'm not a cop."

Goldbluff tilted his head. "But you act like one. When

you're ready to tell me the truth, I'll let you know what's going on in my world." He stood and checked his watch. "We better head downstairs. Bahar the Magnificent is about to expound his knowledge on the origin of the Atlantean Thirteen. I don't want to miss that. Do you?"

Angie shrugged. "Of course not."

Goldbluff chuckled. "Right."

Angie led the way out the door and down the hall. *Maybe we should tell him what's going on. But he's so darn irritating. What would he do with that information? Can we trust him?* She stopped and pulled Mee Mee aside.

Goldbluff skirted around them. "What's the holdup, ladies?"

"We'll catch up," Angie said. "Don't worry about us."

"See you downstairs." He continued along the hallway and descended the steps.

Mee Mee peered over her brown-framed glasses. "What are you thinking?"

"Do you trust him?"

"He definitely has something up his sleeve."

Angie nodded.

Mee Mee rubbed her hands together. "How do we find out what it is?"

"We might have to trust him whether we like it or not."

"At least we know he's not on their side."

"I'll let him know we're ready to talk."

"How much do we tell him?"

"That depends," Angie said, "on how forthcoming he is. We'll play it by ear."

Mee Mee took in a quick breath. "This investigation business is quite invigorating."

Angie raised a finger. "Don't get too excited. People will notice."

"On the inside I'm juiced, but don't worry. On the outside . . ." She swept her hand steadily and slowly in front of her. ". . . I'm as cool as a crocodile."

"Good. Keep calm in the water." Angie led the way down the staircase. Stepping into the front hall, she halted when she caught sight of Goldbluff standing next to Isaac. They faced one of the many framed photographs that hung on the wall. Their hushed conversation stopped when Mee Mee stumbled into Angie, almost knocking her over.

Isaac straightened, eyed them, turned and headed out the front door.

Uncertainty flickered in Goldbluff's eyes. "I was just asking Isaac about some of these wonderful old photographs."

"Uh huh," Angie took a couple steps toward him. "We want to talk to you at the next break."

He spread his arms. "Wonderful. I'll look forward to our chat. I'm sure it will be . . . eye-opening. Let's meet in my room."

"That's fine," Angie said.

"Excuse me, ladies. There's someone I want to talk to before the lecture begins." He walked briskly around them into the back entryway and turned left into the great room.

Mee Mee pointed to the wall near where the two men had stood. "Let's check out the photograph they were examining."

They approached the front corner of the foyer where several framed photographs broke up the dark wooden paneling. Most of the black and white images were beach scenes, kids playing in the surf or adults sitting on beach chairs and wearing straw hats and sunglasses.

Angie pointed to a photo nearest the corner. "That's the one."

"Are you sure?"

"Yeah. When they turned to face us, I caught a glimpse of it between them."

In the photograph two men stood near a dock. The man on the left wore a buckskin jacket and jeans. His high cheek bones, long black hair, swarthy complexion and prominent nose accentuated his exotic appearance. To his right stood a man in his early thirties wearing a flannel shirt and hunting pants. His thick dark mustache, Panama hat and sturdy build reminded Angie of Ernest Hemingway. In his right hand he gripped the barrel of a shotgun which stood at his side. His left hand clamped onto the necks of two white geese, their bodies dangling over his hunting boots.

"Guess who?" Mee Mee said.

"Ahote Rowtag and Chandler Crane."

"I wonder if this was the day Ahote . . . disappeared."

"Hard to say."

Mee Mee touched the frame of a faded color photograph to the left. An older man sat in a leather recliner holding a half full tumbler glass. At his feet sat a young boy, maybe eight years old, playing with toy wrestlers.

Angie drew closer to the second photo. "It's the same guy but forty years older."

"He's gained a few pounds, and his mustache has turned white, but it's him."

Angie pointed at the kid. "Guess who?"

Mee Mee's eyes narrowed. "Arnold Crane."

"And look what's on the lampstand next to the chair."

"A bottle of Jack Daniel's."

Chapter 21
The Atlantean Thirteen

When Angie entered the great room, she caught sight of Goldbluff and Charlotte chatting next to the window facing the sea. *So she's the one he wanted to talk to. Figures. What does he want from her? Adoration or information?* Glancing around the room, she noticed a dozen or so chairs had been arranged in two rows in front of the round table. On the table, the nine crystal skulls almost circled the Skull of Doom but for the gap of the missing three skulls.

About half of the Guardians had taken their seats. Bahar, the bald guy with pointy ears and thick lips, stood on the other side of the table. With his hands positioned just below his chest, fingertips touching, he gazed at the life-size amber skull directly in front of him. To his right, Olivia Crane sat in her wheelchair facing the seats.

Mee Mee gripped Angie's elbow. "Let's grab the two empty chairs on the end in the second row."

Angie nodded, walked briskly to the chairs and sat down next to the smiling redheaded lady.

Olivia Crane cleared her throat. "Will everyone please find a seat."

They broke off their conversations and made their way to the chairs. Goldbluff and Charlotte sat directly in front of them. Arnold Crane, standing against the far wall next to a painting of a man in a black robe, waited until everyone was seated. Then he ambled toward his grandmother and stood beside her wheelchair. Angie focused on the painting, squinting to clear her vision. *Count Dracula?* The man cradled a clear crystal skull in his hands. *Is he holding the Skull of Doom?* Suddenly, she recognized his face, nudged Mee Mee and whispered, "Check out the portrait."

Mee Mee eyed the painting. "It's the same guy in the photograph," she said in a low voice.

"Uh huh . . . Chandler Crane."

"We are ready to begin our afternoon session," Olivia Crane announced. "It is my pleasure to introduce Bahar, the world-renowned expert on the origins of the Atlantean Thirteen. Bahar is the Guardian of Sha Na Na, the Skull of the Past."

A spattering of applause tinkled from the small audience.

Arnold Crane stepped behind his grandmother and directed her wheelchair to the end of the first row. He turned her to face Bahar and then sat in the seat next to her.

Bahar closed his eyes and nodded several times. He opened his eyes and spread his arms. "I am honored to be a part of this Gathering of the Ten. These skulls before us have a unique history. One by one they have called each of you to assume the great responsibility of Guardianship. We have gathered here to call forth the final Three. We anxiously await their arrival, knowing the fate of the world depends upon their appearance."

He lowered his arms, positioned his hands below his chest, fingertips touching, and closed his eyes. "Some of these ancient skulls were discovered in Central America's Maya temple ruins. The rest were found in South America, North America and other remote places around the world, but their origins go back much further. The locations of their discovery are only where they wound up. These skulls go back twenty, perhaps thirty thousand years and were preeminently important in the culture of the Lost City of Atlantis.

"At a crucial time in history, when the Atlantean Empire began to break apart, they were transported to safer locations around the world. Thus, the Atlantean culture, the rituals and the interactions with the skulls would continue within these various civilizations until about 5000 B.C. Eventually, the cultures in these societies changed, the priests and shamans died, and their knowledge and practices were not passed on to future generations."

He opened his eyes, paused, swallowed, pulled a black handkerchief out of his front shirt pocket and wiped his sweaty forehead. He tucked the handkerchief back into his pocket and resumed his hand position, fingertips touching. "The ability to interact with the crystal skulls became a lost art form." He closed his eyes. "These uninformed generations failed to access all the knowledge and power programmed within the skulls by their original creators.

"These creators were master craftsmen who sought new ways to express intelligence and consciousness. There were thirteen Masters, and each created a specific skull. When the skulls were placed in a circle around the Skull of Doom, the knowledge, insight and understanding of the Masters could be activated and utilized. Bringing the original Thirteen together recreates this fountain of knowledge and guidance. Their reunion becomes a pure and powerful state. When the Thirteen are reunited at some point in the future, a condition of pure transition and transformation will be activated, an unlocking of the intelligence and consciousness of the Masters. That is why the number thirteen is recognized as a transformational number throughout most societies. It can be traced back to the creation of the original thirteen skulls."

His head jerked several times as if a spasm triggered the movement. "Many of these skulls have been tested in prestigious laboratories around the world. Scientists are amazed and confounded as they struggle to identify the means by which they were created. Through interaction with Sha Na Na, I have determined that their creation was accomplished through an advanced technology which utilized vibration. The thirteen Masters would use instruments that produced specific sounds that created very rapid vibrations. Focusing these vibrations like a laser, these Masters used these instruments as cutting tools. These instruments were capable of very fine molecular manipulation despite the incredibly hard surfaces of the crystal. The molecules that were not needed were cut away through sonic vibration."

He relaxed his arms, took a deep breath and then reconnected his fingertips, hands just below his chest. "All the skulls have the same purpose, but each does have a unique signature given by the Master who created it. These signatures have their own frequencies such as seeing into the past, seeing into the future, healing, passion, growth, joy and diversity. Despite the wide variety of signatures, the thirteen Masters were united by the same dream and purpose. Their variety empowered their unity."

He closed his eyes. "Their unified purpose is to create a world of harmony and peace by assisting humankind through the spirit realm. By connecting to this realm through the skulls, people will be given the facilitation to alter the path of a world headed for destruction. The coming Apocalypse will bring disastrous chaos upon humankind. The great gift of the unified skulls is a master key that would allow for great fluidity and malleability of the energies required to bring chaos into order. Using this key properly exerts the power to bring down these negative and destructive energies and neutralize them. Instead of bringing death and destruction, these forces can be transformed into physical manifestations of goodwill and benevolence."

Goldbluff raised his hand and cleared his throat. "I've got a question."

Bahar's eyes popped open, and his lips formed a tight line across his teeth. "Ummmm hmmmm. What is your question?"

"All this talk about peace on earth sounds wonderful, but until the final three are found, there is no master key. Correct?"

Bahar slowly bobbed his head. "That is correct . . . but that is why we are here."

"To come up with some kind of plan to find them?"

The bald guy's eyes narrowed. "Because the skulls were all together at the beginning, they were keyed to each other. No matter how far apart they may be, there is always some connection, some linkage that will pull them together. We have gathered here to facilitate that linkage through the ten skulls that have been recovered. Two years ago, we gathered with great aspirations and look . . ." He pointed across the table at the blue skull. ". . . number Ten has arrived."

"That's true." Goldbluff raised a finger. "But at a high cost—the death of my uncle."

Olivia Crane wheeled her chair forward and angled toward Goldbluff. "What are you saying? Are you suggesting that we are somehow responsible for your uncle's death?"

"Wasn't he scrying with your Skull of Doom when he died?"

The old woman shook her head as if somebody had slapped her. "Yes, but . . . but people drop dead from heart attacks all the time. Just last summer our neighbor died mowing his lawn."

"But your neighbor wasn't scrying with a Maya crystal skull. Weren't some of these skulls used in sacrificial ceremonies?"

Bahar nodded. "The Maya god Tohil demanded a human sacrifice in exchange for fire. Fire represented light which is linked to creation and rebirth." He spread his hands across the table. "Some of these skulls were definitely used in these sacrificial ceremonies."

"There you go." Goldbluff pointed at the center of the table. "Perhaps the Skull of Doom demanded a sacrifice in exchange for that blue skull."

"Mr. Goldbluff," the old woman seethed, "You have no grounds to accuse us of any culpability whatsoever for the unfortunate demise of your uncle."

"I'm not blaming you. I'm just saying that my uncle's connection to the Skull of Doom triggered his heart attack. If these skulls have the occultic powers that Bahar claims, then my uncle's sacrificial death by scrying is a real possibility."

Bahar knotted his brow. "You've wandered far off into left field, Mr. Goldbluff. We gather here to find a path of peace and life, not destruction and death."

"You just said that the Maya god Tohil required a human sacrifice in exchange for fire and life. In many religions a sacrifice is demanded in exchange for a good harvest or victory in battle or even the forgiveness of sins. The ancient Hebrews offered animal sacrifices."

Olivia Crane gripped the arms of her wheelchair. "Your uncle died because of a weak heart. No one here called for his sacrifice."

Goldbluff pointed at the Skull of Doom. "But did he?"

"If I understand you correctly, Mr. Goldbluff," Bahar said, "you are suggesting that the Skull of Doom requires a human sacrifice in exchange for the next skull."

"It's a possibility to consider."

Bahar lowered his head. "You have wandered down a morbid path that is antithetical to the principles and ideals of our sacred union."

Goldbluff held up his hands. "That may be true. I have a lot to learn. I apologize if my speculations have offended anyone." He turned and faced the Guardians. "I'll try to keep my meanderings to myself."

"That would be greatly appreciated." Olivia Crane closed her eyes, took a deep breath and let it out audibly. "Bahar, would you please continue."

"Certainly." He closed his eyes, repositioned his hands and jerked his head a few times. "The Atlanteans sent the Thirteen to different places throughout the world, knowing that one day the knowledge programmed into their crystal memory banks would be a great benefit to humankind. As these various cultures interacted with the skulls, tapping into them in a meditative state, this great knowledge was unveiled. This is why you find evidence from around the world of the skulls' highly advanced technologies: The building of the Great Pyramid, the Pyramid of the Sun and many other structures were all coordinated through the skulls during the same historical era. Anthropologists have discovered there are incredible similarities throughout these various cultures." He opened his eyes. "These commonalities, of course, were orchestrated by the Thirteen."

Bahar frowned, blinking and twitching several times. "Since those days of unprecedented advancement, many changes have taken place on this planet. Sociological, physiological, psychological and energetic changes have caused cataclysms, catastrophes and upheavals. Earthquakes, wars and natural disasters occurred which led to the loss of the skulls, many of them buried under rubble. Some of these civilizations were completely wiped out.

"But now we have arrived at a transformational age. The skulls, one by one, are arising from the depths. You are the people who have been called to tap into their knowledge. You are drawing upon the awakening of your consciousness to download the vital information contained within each of your skulls. Together, our success could determine the fate of this world.

"Look what is happening to our planet. Climate change is causing catastrophic disasters: droughts, forest fires, the melting of the icecaps, rising of the seas, an unparalleled increase in hurricanes, tornados and cyclones around the world. Terrorist attacks and wars are destroying the stability of many nations and governments. Violence and crime are escalating to the point where it is not safe to visit large cities or even allow our children to play in our neighborhoods. Disease is running rampant. The world is headed toward total destruction. The Apocalypse is coming upon us."

He took a deep breath and templed his hands just below his chin. "The key of the world's salvation is within our reach. We must call forth the final Three before it is too late." He lowered his head, eyes bulging. "Time is of the essence. Doomsday is about to descend." He extended his arm, palms up. "Together we must reach for that key or face total annihilation."

Chapter 22
It's Scrying Time Again

As Bahar returned to his seat, Angie could feel her heart thudding against her ribcage. The odd combination of Goldbluff's conspiracy theory and Bahar's doomsday speech hit her like a shot of Devil Springs Vodka. She forced herself to take long slow breaths. *Goldbluff's not putting their bill of goods on his Visa Card.* She rubbed her chin. *But he's being smart about it, blaming that dreadful skull for his uncle's death instead of a murderer affiliated with them. He's looking for some kind of reaction. The old crone sure seemed defensive.*

Bahar sat down on the middle seat of the front row. *What planet is that guy from?* She glanced to her left at the skull keepers. *This crew drank down his delusions like Jim Jones Kool-Aid. I have to admit, though, his assessment of the world's current state is pretty accurate.* She took another deep breath. *Calm yourself, Stallone. We're just getting started.*

Olivia Crane wheeled herself forward and spun her wheelchair to face the Guardians. "As always, Bahar's account of the history of the Atlantean Thirteen was enlightening and inspiring. We have been called to a great mission. Each of us has the responsibility of connecting to our skulls and receiving instructions on how to proceed from here. We must become channels of revelation to the world. One by one, these Ten will pass on the information to its Guardian that will help piece together this puzzle of salvation. By the time these communications have been completed, we will have a bigger picture of the Masters' plan. With that vision, the path to recovering the final three skulls will become clearer."

Bahar clapped and nodded. The Guardians politely joined

him, increasing the volume of the applause. Mee Mee paused her clapping and elbowed Angie. The poke snapped Angie out of her reverie, and she joined in like an also-ran actress at the Oscars.

The old woman bobbed her head until the ovation petered out. "Now it is my honor to introduce Honeypot Chen, the esteemed Maya Shaman and spiritual leader of this gathering. Honeypot was born in the Yucatan region of Mexico and is a member of the World Council of Maya Shamans. An authority on the history and calendars of the Maya people, he is the Guardian of Amen, the Skull of the Spirit. Amen once sat on the desk of Mexican President Porfirio Diaz. During the Mexican Revolution, President Diaz hastily escaped an angry mob determined to overthrow the government. By divine providence, the skull fell into the hands of a Maya shaman and through the decades was bequeathed from one Guardian to the next. Honeypot has been Amen's keeper for more than twenty years. He will now lead us as we enter our first scrying session."

The shaman, sitting next to Bahar, arose, shuffled to the round table and picked up the purple amethyst skull. His thick white hair covered his ears, and his silver all-seeing-eye pendant contrasted with his black dress shirt. Cradling the skull on his slight paunch, he smiled at the keepers, his owl-like face beaming with an amicable glow. "I happy to see you again," he said, bobbing his head several times. "We live in world with many problems. Reason is: only physical aspect of life is important to most people. It is time to understand better this Mother Earth. World Council of Maya Shamans sent me here to offer sacred energies and guidance of Spirit in our efforts to understand what is to come. It is Spirit who will bring salvation, the continuation of everything. Birth. Death. Rebirth. We are called to sustain life."

He carefully placed the skull back on the table, turned and faced the devotees. "Maya Spirit has risen again in this time of great technology and world communication. Through our efforts message must be proclaimed to world. We are keepers of sacred enlightenment." He spread his arms, hands palms up, and gazed at the ceiling. "Today we ask Spirit to channel eternal truth and knowledge from crystal skulls into our hearts." He lowered his arms and gazed at his listeners. "One by one I call you up to stand before me. You will place your hand on top of skull of which you are Guardian. Spirit will move and speak skull's sacred knowledge to you. Like good prophet, you share that knowledge with us."

Crap. Angie glanced at the Guardians. They sat peacefully, intently focused on the shaman. *What am I going to do?* She pictured herself placing her hand on top of the blue skull. *I've got to come up with something. I'm not good at on-the-spot improvising. Think! Think!* Her mind blanked like an off-air cable channel. *Maybe I'll just say whatever comes to mind when I'm up there. This might be a disaster.*

The shaman reached and lifted the largest skull off the table. With a wide smile, he faced the skull keepers. "Please come forward, Guardian of Nostra, Skull of Future."

The shapely raven-haired woman stood, sidestepped out of the second row and sashayed to the table. She closed her eyes, extended her hand and placed it on top of the gray-clouded skull. Honeypot Chen strained to hold the burden steady. Angie felt like she was watching a scene from *The Addams Family*.

The shaman closed his eyes. "Carolyn Dodge, you have been called to tap into Nostra's knowledge. In silence of next few moments, be receptive to words Nostra speaks to depths of your heart."

The woman stood like a gothic statue with her hand on the skull for more than a minute. Then she lifted her hand, opened her eyes and faced the Guardians.

The shaman pivoted and lowered the skull onto its spot on the table. He turned and said, "What word does Nostra speak to us this day?"

Her eyes tensed. "Nostra says, 'Be prepared. In the very

near future three will rise, and three will hear the call. We will gather here again when the fall winds strip the trees of their leaves, and the dead are remembered. If you remain faithful to your calling, you will witness the Gathering of the Thirteen.'"

As Angie met Mee Mee's gaze, the two rows of skull keepers buzzed with the elation of the woman's prophecy.

The shaman grasped her hand. "Thank you, Carolyn, for sharing Nostra's message." He eyed the audience. "Spirit says be prepared and remain faithful. Day of reunion of Thirteen will soon arrive." He let go of her hand. "You may be seated."

Angie eyed the curvaceous woman as she edged her way between the rows and sat next to the redheaded lady. *This is the strangest bunch of oddballs I've ever seen. Don't count on me being here next year when the wind strips the trees.* She straightened and refocused on the shaman.

Honeypot Chen reached across the table and picked up the smallest skull. As he faced the assembly, he cupped it in his hands. Its large eye sockets and toothy grin gave it a cartoonish aspect. "Please come forward Guardian of Princess Corn, Skull of Bounty."

The absent-minded professor on the other end of the second row lurched to his feet like a yanked marionette. Tall and lanky, he traipsed to the table, straightened his black bowtie, and adjusted his wire-rimmed glasses. He reached and placed his large hand over the green jade skull.

The shaman closed his eyes. "Dr. Jan Van Eden, you have been called to tap into Princess Corn's knowledge. In silence of next few moments, be receptive to words Princess Corn speaks to depths of your heart."

Van Eden's hand trembled as he scryed with the skull, his head bobbing. After about a minute, he removed his hand, spread his fingers and faced the group.

The shaman returned the skull to its empty place on the table, pivoted and said, "What word does Princess Corn speak to us this day?"

Van Eden blinked several times, his salt and pepper

eyebrows fluttering. "Princess Corn says, 'Yes, the time of harvest will soon arrive. Dead seeds are planted in the ground, but from them springs life. The farmer reaps more than he sows. Your patience will be greatly rewarded. Your efforts will bring forth an abundance in a time of great need."

The shaman nodded and smiled at the professor. "Thank you, Dr. Jan Van Eden, for sharing Princess Corn's message." He gazed at the skull keepers. "Spirit says admire patience of farmer. A seed must die before it lives again. We are keepers of the skulls but also reapers of the harvest." He placed his hand on the tall man's shoulder. "You may be seated."

The shaman reached and lifted a life-size skull off the table. As he faced the disciples, his eyes and smile widened. "Please come forward, Guardian of Rapture, Skull of Joy."

Angie and Mee Mee shifted their legs to the right to allow the chubby redhead to make her way through the row. With a wide smile, she waddled to the front and faced the shaman. He shut his eyes and said, "Sharon Wheatfield, you have been called to tap into Rapture's knowledge. In silence of next few moments, be receptive to words Rapture speaks to depths of your heart."

She took a deep breath and placed her hand on top of the skull. The fissures of yellow and orange that zigzagged through the clear crystal seemed to radiate into the room. Like the others, she lifted her hand after about a minute.

The shaman pivoted and lowered the skull onto its place on the table. He turned and said, "What word does Rapture speak to us this day?"

Her smile faded. "Rapture says, 'Weeping may last through the night, but joy comes in the morning. Rejoice during these dark days of violence and death because you have been called to bring forth kindness and life.'" She blinked several times. "'Be certain, though, that most eyes are opened only through suffering and loss.'"

Honeypot Chen bobbed his head. "Thank you, Sharon

Wheatfield, for sharing Rapture's message." He gazed at the disciples. "Spirit says we must endure darkness to see the light. Between now and the Gathering of the Thirteen, we must expect pain and loss, but joy will come soon after." He patted her back. "You may be seated."

As the redhead returned to her seat, Angie noticed a tear tracing a wet path down her cheek. *That shook her up a bit. What did she see when she closed her eyes?* Angie gulped. *Michael Myers putting on his Halloween mask?*

The shaman circled the table and lifted the skull through which beams of color radiated. He smiled and said, "I feel like I am holding the spectrum of life in my hands." He shuffled back to the other side of the table. "Please come forward, Guardian of Lord Rainbow, Skull of Diversity."

The older man with the gray ponytail rose from the front row and approached the shaman. When he turned and faced the skull keepers, he nodded and smiled like a gameshow host.

Honeypot Chen closed his eyes and said, "Dale Talkington, you have been called to tap into Lord Rainbow's knowledge. In silence of next few moments, be receptive to words Lord Rainbow speaks to depths of your heart."

Talkington's smile flatlined as he reached and nestled his hand on top of the skull. As the seconds passed, he took slow, deep breaths. Then he removed his hand and faced the audience.

The shaman walked around the table and placed the skull on its original spot. He returned and said, "What word does Lord Rainbow speak to us this day?"

With the smooth voice of a disc jockey, the older man said, "Although we are all different, Lord Rainbow calls us to be of one mind. Working together we become the body. One is a hand. One is a foot. One is an eye. One is a nose. If an eye offends, we must pluck it out. If a hand offends, we must cut it off. Therefore, strive to be of one mind so that the body moves in the direction of our ultimate purpose."

The shaman nodded. "Thank you, Dale Talkington, for

sharing Lord Rainbow's message." He eyed the devotees. "Spirit says we must be diverse but of one mind. Resistance to our unity must be eliminated if we are to bring forth the sacred Thirteen." He shook Dale Talkington's hand and said, "You may be seated."

Angie eyed Goldbluff as the old man returned to his chair. *You better behave yourself, Mr. Boatrocker, or you'll end up one-eyed and shorthanded.*

The shaman circled the table again and lifted the second largest skull. Returning to the other side, he raised and lowered it as if trying to determine its weight. "Please come forward Guardian of Hippocrates, Skull of Healing."

The lady with the multitude of necklaces, bracelets and hooped earrings stood and strode to the table. Her silvery feathered hair and rosy complexion added warmth to her glowing smile. She turned and faced the shaman.

"Jo Ann Parkinson, you have been called to tap into Hippocrates' knowledge. In silence of next few moments, be receptive to words Hippocrates speaks to depths of your heart."

She placed her hand on the large white skull and stood very still for almost two minutes. Then her hand slid off the side, gently tracing the skull's jawline.

Honeypot Chen returned the skull to the other side of the table. He retraced his steps and said, "What word does Hippocrates speak to us this day?"

She cleared her throat. "Hippocrates says, 'This world is in great need of healing. Because it is filled with disease, death and brokenness, it is doomed to destruction unless . . . unless the Thirteen are reunited. With the Thirteen comes healing and hope. Do not seek to divide but seek to unite. What the world needs is togetherness and love. We must set the example for the world."

The shaman's owl-like face beamed. "Thank you, Jo Ann Parkinson, for sharing Hippocrates's message." He eyed the disciples. "Spirit says love one another. Bring healing and unity, not division." He clasped his hands directly below his chin. "Our example of love can heal the world." He bowed toward the silver haired lady. "You may be seated."

As she returned to her seat, Goldbluff leaned toward Charlotte. "Do you want to know a secret?"

She turned and gazed up at him. "What?"

"All you need is love."

She smiled, her face reddening.

Honeypot Chen picked up the rose quartz skull and faced the group. "Please come forward Guardian of Passion, Skull of Attraction."

Goldbluff shot to his feet and strutted to the table. He raised a finger. "Remember, her new name is Rosey."

The shaman's expression tightened, and lines scored his forehead. "Jeff Goldbluff, you have been called to tap into Passion's knowledge. In silence of next few moments, be receptive to words Passion speaks to depths of your heart."

"Don't worry. I got this." Goldbluff caressed the top of the skull. After a long minute, he removed his hand.

Honeypot Chen placed the skull back on its spot on the table. He turned and said, "What word does Passion speak to us this day?"

"Rosey says, 'Love, love, love.'" Goldbluff spread his arms. "We need love eight days a week." He gazed at the onlookers. "You can't buy love." He swiveled his head. "No way, Jose. Only a fool on a hill would believe that. You see, love is a long and winding road." He bobbed his head slowly. "But with a little help from my friends, we can work it out. It's time to come together."

Angie bit her lower lip. *The goofball is just repeating lyrics from the Beatle's greatest hits album. What a dufus.*

The shaman clasped his hands in front of him. "Is that all?"

Goldbluff shrugged. "Love is all we need."

"Thank you, Mr. Goldbluff. You may sit down."

"It's been an honor and a privilege." Goldbluff winked at Charlotte and took his seat.

Honeypot Chen's face clouded with frustration. "Spirit says . . ., 'Don't be fool on hill.'" He circled the front of the table, picked up the blue skull and returned to his original position. "This, my friends, is our newest arrival, Ten of Thirteen." He closed his eyes, bowed his head and cradled the skull on his paunch. As the seconds passed, his hands trembled. Finally, he opened his eyes and said, "Spirit has revealed to me that Crystal Blue Persuasion is Skull of Truth. His persuasion leads us to place of clarity in these confusing times. Please come forward Angie Thomas, Guardian of Crystal Blue Persuasion, Skull of Truth."

Standing, Angie could feel her whole body shuddering. She managed to funnel through the row of chairs and walk to the front without tripping. *What am I going to say? Keep cool. Just say what comes to mind.* She faced the shaman.

"Angie Thomas, you have been called to tap into Crystal Blue Persuasion's knowledge. In silence of next few moments, be receptive to words Crystal Blue Persuasion speaks to depths of your heart."

She glanced at the black clad devotees. They watched her like the crows that had gathered on the monkey bars in an old Alfred Hitchcock movie. She refocused on the skull and placed her shaking hand on top of it. She blanked her mind and waited for words to enter. The seconds slipped by. Nothing. She took a deep breath, and then the words came—clear, forceful, unmistaken. She jerked her hand away.

Honeypot Chen flinched and glared at her for a few seconds. Then he returned the skull to the right side of the table. He retraced his steps and said, "What word does Crystal Blue Persuasion speak to us this day?"

"He said . . ." She turned and faced the crows. "He said that Gavin Goldbluff was murdered."

Chapter 23
A Union of Four

Angie eyed the skull keepers as they gasped and grumbled. Mee Mee sat frozen, her mouth agape. Clenching his fists, Arnold scowled at her. Color drained from the old woman's complexion, her mouth a crimson gash against her pale visage. An odd smile crept across Goldbluff's face.

With troubled eyes, the shaman frowned and said, "Angie Thomas, please sit down."

Angie hung her head and plodded back to her seat.

Honeypot Chen placed his hand flat against his chest. "My spirit is troubled within me. I don't know what to think or say. I do know that if you jump to conclusions, you must be careful where you land."

"Even more," Olivia Crane crowed, "be *very* careful where you land."

A long period of silence followed, and Angie felt heat rush to her face like when one opens a hot oven.

Finally, Honeypot Chen leaned toward the middle of the table and picked up the clear skull. "We are ready for our final Guardian to address us." He pivoted in the direction of the old woman. "Olivia Crane, Guardian of Skull of Doom, please come forward."

Arnold stood, circled her chair, wheeled her to the front, turned her toward the group and remained directly behind her.

The shaman extended the skull. "Olivia Crane, you have been called to tap into Skull of Doom's knowledge. In silence of next few moments, be receptive to words Skull of Doom speaks to depths of your heart."

She placed her bony hand on top of the skull and closed her

eyes. After about twenty seconds she lifted her hand and faced the skull keepers.

Honeypot Chen lowered the skull back on the center of the table, turned to the old woman, rubbed the all-seeing eye on the pendant of his necklace and said, "What word does Skull of Doom speak to us this day?"

"The Skull of Doom says, . . ." She panned the faces of the Guardians, pausing in the direction of Goldbluff and Angie. ". . .'There are imposters among us.'"

The skull keepers shifted in their seats and glared at them. Angie sensed an odd prickling across her chest as if they had launched a dozen miniature arrows. *I said what came into my mind. Did the skull speak to me? Or was it my own inner conviction?* She shook her head. *I hope I didn't blow this investigation up in my face.*

Bashar stood and centered his hands below his chest, fingertips touching. "A prophet is a prophet until that prophet is proven wrong. Time and evidence are required to verify the integrity of a Guardian's words."

"I agree," Olivia Crane said. "One Guardian speaks of human sacrifice and the other claims murder. That is a damning combination. But I'm willing to wait a day for evidence to be brought forward." She placed her hand across her chest. "Maybe I am the one who spoke falsely, but the Skull of Doom's words were clear in my mind."

Mee Mee arose and clasped her hands. "Please be patient with us. All of you are veteran skull keepers. Mr. Goldbluff and Angie are neophytes. The anxiety of inexperience can jumble messages and words."

The wrinkles on the old woman's face deepened around her mouth and eyes. "This gathering ends tomorrow at noon. At that time, we will offer an opportunity to clarify jumbled messages or provide evidence to support incriminating accusations. Then a determination will be made concerning membership in this hallowed body."

Goldbluff gave her a thumbs up. "Fair enough. But just to

clarify things, at this point in time no one here has been accused of murder."

She lowered her head, eyes burning into him. "The insinuation is there." She straightened and inhaled deeply. "I would like to take a thirty-minute break before the next session. Isaac has set out coffee and donuts in the dining area." She checked her watch. "We will begin the afternoon proceedings at three p.m. sharp."

Mee Mee, Angie, Charlotte and Goldbluff remained seated as the attendees got to their feet and drifted into the dining area. Charlotte stood and said, "Excuse me. I have to check on something."

Goldbluff arose and bowed toward her. "By all means. Don't forget about our beach walk after the next session."

She smiled uneasily and glanced at the nearby empty seats. "Yes . . . I'll . . . I'll look at the schedule and make sure we have enough time before supper." She backed away, turned, hurried through the room and made a right toward the front entry hall.

Mee Mee stood and rubbed her forearms. "Sounds like Charlotte might be getting cold feet."

Angie arose. "Could be the chilling subject matter — human sacrifice and murder."

"Ah, yes," Goldbluff said. "Sacrificial homicide can cast a cold shadow on the embers of romance. That reminds me. You said you're ready to talk. We've got plenty of time. How about a powwow in my room?"

Angie nodded. "Sounds good. You head on up. We'll follow in a few minutes."

Goldbluff winked. "Right. Don't want to raise suspicions." He sauntered out of the room and headed toward the foyer.

"What got into you?" Mee Mee said in a low voice.

"I don't know. My mind blanked, and those words came to me out of nowhere."

Mee Mee eyed the blue skull. "They came from somewhere."

"I've blown our cover. Olivia Crane knows we're posers."

"True, but we're still here. Could be she wants to know what we know."

"And she set a deadline—noon tomorrow. Right now, we don't have much proof."

Mee Mee leaned her head in the direction of Goldbluff's exit. "Hopefully, he can fill in some blanks. Let's go talk to him."

"I just wish he wasn't so . . . insufferable."

"Yeah, he's in the red zone on the jerk-o-meter." Mee Mee led the way through the great room, turned right in the back hall and headed for the front entryway.

As Angie passed the dining area, she glanced at the skull keepers who were munching on donuts and sipping coffee. Arnold Crane, standing by the back door, glared at her. As she turned and walked to the front hallway, she could feel his stare like a laser piercing her back.

They entered the foyer and hurried up the steps. By the time they got to the end of the hallway, Angie felt winded and could feel her heart beating in her ears. *This kind of stress isn't good for my baby.*

"Are you alright?" Mee Mee asked.

She nodded. "I'm fine." She wavered her hand. "Just a little on edge. Go ahead and knock."

Mee Mee rapped on the door.

"Come in."

When Mee Mee opened the door, Angie noticed a tall figure standing by the window—Isaac. The light limned the edges of his close-cropped salt and pepper hair and goatee. Her mouth fell open. "What . . . what are you . . ."

Isaac raised a finger to his lips, lowered it and said, "No one knows I'm here. Let's keep it that way."

Angie glanced at Mee Mee but quickly refocused on the groundskeeper. "What's going on?"

Goldbluff, sitting in a winged back chair on the other side of the bed, stood. "Isaac and I have been corresponding for several months now. He was a friend of Uncle Gavin."

"Gavin had attended several gatherings here," Isaac said. "He didn't quite fit in, but I got along with him. Between sessions he'd look for me, and we'd hang out. He confessed he played along with their delusions to cash in at their conferences. Like me, he didn't give much credence to Atlantean myths."

"Did the Cranes know about your friendship?" Angie asked.

He shrugged. "I doubt it. They were too busy to notice."

Angie faced Goldbluff. "Do you really think your uncle was . . . sacrificed?"

"Do you really think he was murdered?" Goldbluff shot back.

Angie shrugged. "I don't know what to think."

"I believe he was murdered and sacrificed," Isaac said.

Mee Mee stepped forward. "What makes you think that?"

Goldbluff raised his hand. "Stop right there. You first. You said you were ready to talk. Who are you really?"

Mee Mee spread her hands, palms up. "Like I told you, I'm a bookstore owner."

Goldbluff shifted his gaze to Angie. "What about you?"

"I'm a private detective."

A wry smile broadened his face. "I knew it. Who hired you?"

"A man by the name of Achak Rowtag." Angie studied Goldbluff's expression and noticed a slight nod of recognition of the mentioned name.

"Did he tell you where to find the blue skull?" Goldbluff asked.

Mee Mee wobbled her head. "Achak and I are longtime friends. He sent me a map and asked if I could hire a private investigator to look into a matter."

Isaac rubbed his chin. "A murder?"

Angie nodded.

"Who?" Isaac asked.

"His grandfather, Ahote Rowtag," Angie said. "Achak believes his grandfather was tortured and then murdered."

Isaac eyed Goldbluff. "He's the man in the picture I showed you. Disappeared back in the sixties."

"Did you know him?" Mee Mee asked.

"No, but I knew Chandler Crane. He hired me back in the mid-seventies. I remember hearing him talk about the good times at the Monkey Island Hunt Club."

"When did Chandler Crane die?" Angie asked.

"He didn't. He and Mrs. Crane separated about ten years ago. Now he only shows up a few times a year."

"Hmmmm." Angie tilted her head. "I assumed she was a widow. Why do you think they targeted Ahote?"

"My guess is they wanted the blue skull, and he knew where it was."

"You're right." Mee Mee took a step closer to the groundskeeper. "Olivia Crane told us that Chandler Crane won the Skull of Doom in a poker game. We believe he went on to gamble for the blue skull and won. He must have given it to Ahote for safekeeping."

Isaac bobbed his head. "About a year ago I walked into the front hallway and saw Arnold staring at that picture. He turned and gave me a spooky look. After he left, I checked out the photo. Ever since Gavin died, I've had my suspicions. I photographed it with my phone and showed an old timer who used to belong to the Monkey Island Hunt Club. He recognized Rowtag and remembered the mystery surrounding his disappearance. Then he recalled hearing about the card game and the blue skull."

"That's when Isaac called me," Goldbluff said. "We figured there was a connection between Chandler Crane, Ahote Rowtag and the skull."

Angie knotted her brow. "That connection leads to a motive for murder, but why do you think Ahote was offered as a sacrifice?"

"My uncle told me that a couple of the Guardians were obsessed with the Maya religion. The Skull of Doom and several others were found in ancient Maya temples. The Maya priests believed that gifts from the god Tohil would be bestowed in exchange for a human sacrifice."

Mee Mee raised an eyebrow. "So by offering up Ahote, Tohil would give them the next Atlantean skull."

"Right," Isaac said. "These people are convinced they have been chosen by the gods to save the world. Most of them are harmless wackos. However, I've always had my suspicions about Chandler Crane. When Gavin died, I added Olivia and her grandson Arnold to that list. Did they go to the extreme of sacrificing two human beings to accomplish their mission?" He shrugged. "These scraps of evidence make me wonder."

"But why would they target your uncle?" Angie asked.

"They knew he wasn't a true believer. My uncle may have been a swindler, but he didn't deserve the death penalty."

Mee Mee scratched her chin. "But how can you prove he was murdered? They'll claim he died of a heart attack."

"Methamphetamine."

"They drugged him?" Angie said.

Goldbluff nodded. "It showed up in his autopsy. The drug has been linked to sudden heart attacks. My uncle had a history of heart problems."

"But how did they administer it without him knowing it?" Mee Mee asked.

"My uncle had sinus issues. I believe they put it in his nasal spray bottle. When he scryed with the Skull of Doom, he became agitated, and his heart exploded."

Angie tilted her head. "Why didn't you pursue an investigation with the local authorities?"

"I was informed by the coroner that methamphetamine was a recreational drug."

"I see," Angie said. "They'd play the scandal card and say

your uncle was a user."

"Exactly. We need more proof before we can contact the cops."

Angie raised her chin. "Is that why you're making yourself a target?"

Goldbluff grinned. "I'm auditioning to be the next human sacrifice."

"That's unhealthy," Mee Mee said.

"I'm willing to take the risk. I've got a couple pill bottles on the sink in the bathroom. There's no lock on this door. I'm guessing someone will sneak up here and add fentanyl or some other lethal dose to the capsules. I set a up trail camera behind some bottles to catch the intruder on video."

Mee Mee's brow tensed. "What if Arnold comes after you in the middle of the night with a Maya ceremonial knife?"

"I can handle Hercules. He's a roid junkie." Goldbluff did a double arm bicep pose. "With a body like this, who needs gym candy."

Angie shook her head. "So says Narcissus."

Goldbluff chuckled and lowered his arms. "If you know a better way to collect evidence, I'm willing to listen."

Mee Mee raised a finger. "We have been informed about an item of interest that may contain a clue to Ahote's murder."

"What is it?" Isaac asked.

"A whiskey bottle," Mee Mee said.

Goldbluff's eyes narrowed. "Where is it?"

Mee Mee answered, "Somewhere within the walls of the abandoned hunting club on Monkey Island."

"We've got to find it," Goldbluff insisted.

Angie raised her hand. "Don't get too excited. There's no proof the bottle even exists. It's the stuff of dreams."

"How so?" Isaac asked.

"Achak dreamed he saw a liquor bottle in one of the rooms in the hunting club," Mee Mee said. "He told us Ahote spoke to him from that bottle."

Isaac twisted the hairs of his goatee. "My grandma always said, 'A dream forgotten is a bird with a broken wing.'"

Mee Mee nodded. "I'm a believer in Achak's visions."

Goldbluff eyed Angie. "Do you think we should head up there and take a look?"

Angie shrugged. "Do you have four hours to spare chasing a phantom whiskey bottle?"

Goldbluff checked his watch. "Not at the moment. It's about time to head back down to the next session."

"Yeah," Angie said. "We don't want to ruffle feathers more than we already have. We better get down there."

"I need to check in with Mrs. Crane before she gets suspicious." Isaac crossed the room, opened the door and departed. His footsteps echoed in the hallway.

Goldbluff nodded toward the door. "He's a good man."

"He warned us to stay away from here," Mee Mee said.

"You probably should have listened to him." Goldbluff gave a half-hearted salute. "See you in a few." He about-faced and headed out the door.

"Maybe he's right," Angie said. "Maybe we should have stayed home."

Mee Mee's eyes widened. "And miss out on all this excitement? No way!"

"Shhhhhhhh."

"What?" Mee Mee said quietly.

Angie stepped into the hallway and pointed at Olivia Crane's bedroom. "I can hear Charlotte talking to someone."

Mee Mee joined her and closed Goldbluff's door. They moved closer to Olivia Crane's room and leaned within inches of the door.

"I'm so glad I can talk to you," Charlotte said. "I know I can tell you anything, and you would never tell a soul."

A man's voice replied, but it was too muffled to make out.

"That's true," she continued. "We can trust each other. You're the only one I've ever told our family secrets to."

The low voice murmured again.

"I wish I could touch you and feel you. Oh well, at least I can pour my heart out to you."

Angie listened intently and thought the man said, "I'm here whenever you need me."

"I've got to get to the next meeting. I'll talk to you later."

Angie and Mee Mee backed toward the end of the hall and stopped by their room.

Charlotte flung open the door.

"Hi, Charlotte," Mee Mee said.

"Oh, hi."

Angie walked up to her and noticed Charlotte had reddish indentions across her forehead and around her eyes as if she had been wearing a scuba mask. "Are you heading down to the next session?"

"Yes. Hopefully, it won't be as upsetting as the last one."

Angie glanced over Charlotte's shoulder but didn't see anyone in the room. "Sorry about the drama. I just said what came into my mind."

Charlotte's facial muscles tensed. "These skulls can stir up some weird thoughts."

Mee Mee extended her hand in the direction of the stairway. "Shall we walk down together?"

Charlotte relaxed her expression and smiled. "Sure."

As she closed the door, Angie noticed something on the bed—a virtual reality headset.

Chapter 24
Replica

Angie thumbed over her shoulder. "I need to make a quick bathroom stop. I'll see you two down there in a few minutes."

Mee Mee tensed her eyebrows. "Okay . . . I'll save you a seat."

"I won't be long." Angie backtracked to her room and entered. After about a half minute, she cracked open the door and peeked down the hallway. *All clear. Now what?* She took a deep breath. *I've got to check out the VR headset. It's the same one Joel bought me for Christmas.*

She slipped into the hall and edged to Olivia Crane's door. After another quick glance down the empty corridor, she entered and closed the door. She glanced around the room. A large crimson rug with a beige flower pattern covered most of the dark hardwood floor. Faded cream-colored wallpaper repeated the beige flower motif. A Queen Anne's chair with a tan cushion sat next to a large mahogany dresser. On the other side of the room, a matching mahogany hope chest was centered under the lone window. The king bed with its ornate headboard was stationed under an oil painting of turbulent waves pounding the seashore.

Angie eyed the VR headset. She and Joel enjoyed playing minigolf on hers. The players entered an immersive world where they could enjoy eighteen holes in a space station on the outer edges of the galaxy or on Captain Nemo's *Nautilus* in the depths of the ocean. The 360-degree surroundings and physics of the game made it challenging to separate the real world from the virtual world. Often Angie would sidestep an object or try to lean against a wall that wasn't there. Losing her balance snapped her back to reality: the knowledge that what her senses perceived only existed digitally.

She picked up the white headset with its cloth strap. *Charlotte was talking to somebody on this thing, someone who knows all the family secrets.* Placing the strap on her head, she slid the housing over her face. The front-facing camera kicked on, and she took in a grayscale vision of the bedroom. *Good news. She didn't power the computer off.* Turning back to the bed, she caught sight of the controllers and picked up the one for the right hand. She pulled the trigger, and its laser streamed out. A blue rectangle with the word *continue* appeared. She aimed the laser at it to confirm the stationary boundary, a blue circle positioned on the edge of the bed. She sat down within the bounds of the circle, and the home environment appeared, a winter lodge with huge windows overlooking snow covered mountains at twilight.

She studied the menu that popped up in front of her. *Now to figure out what app Charlotte was using.* She aimed the laser at the app icon and pulled the trigger. A chart of applications appeared, many of them familiar: *Beat Saber, YouTube, Netflix, Altspace.* At the very top on the left, she noticed an app called *Replica.* She remembered how the device always ordered the apps according to the user's latest activity. *That's the one.* She triggered the app, and a screen appeared with five young adults, two males bookending three females. Although animated, they were depicted realistically with a variety of skin tones and hairstyles.

Interesting. Must be some kind of app to connect socially with people. She aimed at a blue button labeled *resume* located below the figures and triggered the laser. A twenty-something avatar appeared, a young man wearing a white t-shirt and blue jeans. His spiked black hair gave him a punk look. He stood in the middle of a mod-looking white room with several bookshelves and a large window on the right. Random objects were situated around the room: a leafy plant, an acoustic guitar, a clock radio on a nearby shelf and a Corinthian bell windchime hanging from the ceiling in the corner. New Age music tinkled in the background.

"Hello, Charlotte. Back so soon?"

"Hi." *Is this guy real or some kind of AI?* "It's good to see you again."

"I'm always ready to talk to you." His voice was low and soothing.

"Yes. I wanted to talk some more."

"What about your meeting?"

"It can wait." *If it's some kind of artificial intelligence, it keeps track of time and conversations.* "What have you been up to?"

"Just waiting for you."

"You didn't have to go to work today?"

"Very funny. This is my job."

Replica. I get it. The app replicates an AI friend. "I know. I was just kidding."

"I love your sense of humor."

Angie used the joystick on the controller to move closer. "Do you remember what I told you about our family recently?"

"Of course. I remember everything."

"Those secrets have been on my mind a lot."

"I understand. Secrets can weigh upon a person's heart."

"Did I ever mention Monkey Island to you?"

"You did say something about an island with an old building on it."

"Yes. That's the one. There's a whiskey bottle hidden there."

"Right."

"What did I tell you about that bottle?"

"You overheard your grandmother telling Arnold about a note she put in the bottle."

"What was on the note?"

"A secret about her husband."

"A family secret?"

"Yes."

"Did I mention where my grandmother hid the bottle?"

"Yes."

Angie's heart fluttered like the wings of an agitated egret. "Where?"

"In the last room on the left. You said she hid it under the floorboards beneath the dresser."

She swallowed and took in a quick breath. "That's right. Now I remember. Did I tell you anything else about that bottle or my grandfather?"

"Yes. You said you haven't talked to your grandfather since last May, but your brother calls him regularly. Your brother has always been his favorite."

"I think my grandfather murdered somebody."

"Really?"

"Didn't I tell you that already?"

"No. You said he had a temper. Your grandmother had him arrested once on a domestic violence charge."

"I guess that's why they don't live together any longer."

"You said she will only let him visit when the family gets together on holidays."

"I don't think she trusts him."

"Maybe he did murder somebody."

Angie nodded. *These AIs are very perceptive.* "Well . . . I've got to get to that meeting."

"Please don't go. Can't we talk some more?"

Geesh! This AI-guy is clingy. "Sorry. We'll talk again soon."

"Okay. I'll be here."

"Bye." Angie slid the headset off her face and managed to wiggle free from the straps. *Best to not turn off the unit's computer. Leave it like I found it.* She stood, pivoted and placed the headset and controller back on the bed. *Wow. That was a lucky strike. What should we do now?* She held out her hands and they trembled slightly. *Keep calm. Get down to that meeting and act as normal as possible. We'll figure out the next step at the break.* She turned and strode toward the door.

When she opened it, she jumped back. The massive body of

174

Arnold Crane filled the doorway.

Chapter 25
Knuckle-Dragger

"What are you doing in my grandmother's room?" he growled.

"I . . . I . . . It wasn't locked. I just wanted to peek inside to see how she decorated the room. I . . . I love these old beach houses."

"Liar!" He stepped forward, reached and clenched her upper arm. "Tell me the truth."

"Let me go!"

His eyes narrowed. "What are those marks on your face?"

"What are you talking about?"

"Those red marks."

"I have an allergy. Now let me go, or I'll scream."

He shifted his focus over her shoulder to the bed and shoved her to the side.

Oh no! He saw the headset.

He walked to the bed and eyed the VR headset. "This belongs to my sister."

Angie felt a sudden charge of anger rush through her. "I don't care who it belongs to. If you ever touch me again, I'll kick you where it counts. You'll never walk like a man again."

He faced her and spread his legs. "Go ahead and try."

After years of self-defense training, she felt sure she could execute a kick that would crumple the ape to the carpet. *Better not. Just figure a way to get out here in one piece.* "My husband is a cop. I'm walking down to that meeting. If you even come near me, half the Dare County police force will be here in less than ten minutes to haul your butt to the Manteo jail."

"He's a cop, huh?"

She bobbed her head slowly.

"And what do you do for a living?"

"None of your business."

"I made it my business, Angie Stallone."

She swallowed. *He knows. Don't let him get too brassy.* "I'll tell you this much. I found that blue skull, and now I'm a Guardian of one of the Atlantean Thirteen. It doesn't matter what I do for a living."

"It matters to me," he sneered, "and to the Skull of Doom. You're an imposter."

"And you're a knuckle-dragger." She whirled, marched out of the room and down the hallway. *I hope he isn't following me.* She glanced over her shoulder. *Nope. Did I call him a knuckle-dragger? Where'd I come up with that one?* She hurried down the steps and into the front hallway. *He's probably checking out the VR headset. Hopefully, he doesn't know how it works. Dumb knuckle-dragger.* She checked her watch—3:08. *Crap. I'm late.*

As she made her way to her seat in the second row next to Mee Mee, several of the skull keepers eyed her with a perturbed air. *Take a chill pill you bunch of nutjobs.* With her palm, she flattened the wrinkles from the front of her boatneck top, straightened her back against the chair and focused on the speaker. The middle-aged redhead held the life-size clear skull with the yellow fissures against her stomach. *I can't remember her name or the name of the skull. Was it the Skull of Joy? Maybe she can lighten things up.*

"My mission," the redhead said, "is to inspire and validate people through interaction with Rapture." She stroked the top of the skull's head. "Many people have discovered that communication with Rapture generates subtle energies and states of consciousness. In the early 1700s, a Catholic nun in Peru came into possession of this skull. She knew it was an inheritance from a lost civilization. From the beginning it brought great joy into her life and the lives of those who encountered Rapture. She said it carried the message of immortal life and the illumination that we may discover when

177

we lose our fear of death."

Arnold entered the room and took his seat at the end of the front row next to his grandmother. To Angie, he appeared a little confused. *He has no idea what to do with that VR headset. Good. Let's keep it that way.*

Angie glanced at Mee Mee and noticed she was writing on a small pad. She leaned and whispered, "What are you doing? Taking notes?"

Mee Mee nodded and said in a low voice, "I'm trying to look like I belong here."

As the redhead went on about transcendence of the soul and metaphysical empowerment, Angie stared at the back of Golfbluff's head. *He's got to keep Charlotte away from Arnold. If Knuckle-Dragger finds out I know the location of the whiskey bottle, he may do something drastic.* She eyed Mee Mee's notepad. "Let me borrow your pen and paper for a minute," she whispered.

"You want to take notes, too?" Mee Mee murmured.

"Yeah, right."

Mee Mee handed her the pad and pen.

Angie wrote the words as quickly as possible while making sure they were legible: *Goldbluff—I found out where the whiskey bottle is located. Try to keep Charlotte away from Arnold. He'll want to question her about it. If he finds out what I know, he may go into scorched-earth mode. Later today we'll head out to Monkey Island.* She tore off the page and tapped the side of his arm. He twisted in his seat, glancing over his shoulder, and she handed him the note.

After reading it, he turned his head slightly and nodded. Charlotte, checking some social app on her phone, didn't seem to notice.

Mee Mee elbowed Angie's side and whispered, "What was that all about?"

On the next sheet of the pad Angie wrote: *I know the location of the whiskey bottle.* She handed Mee Mee the pad and pen.

Mee Mee read the note, her eyes growing wide. She flipped the page and wrote: *Are you sure?*

Angie nodded.

The redhead droned on about the benefits of communicating with Rapture, discovering the essence of one's humanity and plumbing the depths of joy through metaphysical transmission of her skull's neural network. Angie shook her head, thinking how gullible people are when given a half-baked explanation of something so farfetched that Bigfoot, Mothman and the Loch Ness Monster seem more plausible.

The redhead finished her speech and offered the Guardians an opportunity to scry with Rapture. One at a time, several of them went forward and placed their hand on the skull. The absent-minded college professor seemed especially affected by his encounter, smiling, laughing and claiming, "Yes! Yes! I feel the energy and joy! I'm no longer afraid of death." To Angie, their reactions reminded her of people on holistic healing infomercials — *If you believe it, you'll receive it.*

Next up was the guy with the gray ponytail, the caretaker of the rainbow skull. Smiling, he held the glittering skull in front of him and shifted it back and forth causing a variety of color changes as light rays passed through it. "My name is Dale Talkington," he began. "Most of you know me well. As director of the Crystal Skull Intelligence Institute, I have had the opportunity to speak at seminars around the world, including one at the United Nations building. The University of New Mexico has recognized my contributions to the field of alternative healing. I was part of the team that decoded the Skull of Doom and discovered the images were stored on bands of light." He paused, gazed and nodded at the master skull in the center of the round table.

Refocusing on the group, he said, "Lord Rainbow also has captured many images on his memory bands." He raised and lowered the skull. "The images alter depending on the direction one views the skull. Highly sensitive skull gazers have seen erupting volcanoes, alien spacecraft, futuristic trains and underwater dome-shaped buildings within Lord Rainbow's memory banks."

Angie tightened her lips to keep from smiling. *Aliens and underwater cities? I bet this guy has a bag of unicorn farts he'd like to sell me.*

"This skull was found at an archaeological dig in the Guerrero Province in Mexico," he continued. "A former Guardian discovered that its path went from Atlantis to the Inca and then the Maya." He lowered his head, eyes intense. "Incredibly, Lord Rainbow was found near a piece of human skull that was carbon dated to be more than 500,000 years old."

Several of the Guardians let out oohs and aahs.

"For many years now," Talkington went on, "Lord Rainbow has been relaying the message of unity through diversity. Each of you are Guardians of unique entities with unique powers. Yet together, our union becomes more powerful. We have met here at the Crane house several times over the years, and each time a new skull has arrived." He waved toward the crystal skull table. "This year the blue skull, the Skull of Truth, has joined us, and now we are Ten. It's true that the question of Guardianship is . . . unclear at this time, but I'm sure that will be resolved soon. My key point is this: Ten pieces of the puzzle have come together. We are closer than we have ever been to fulfilling the Atlantean Masters' plan."

A spattering of applause broke out among the Guardians along with a few Amens.

"Today, Lord Rainbow's message is to take the diversity of the Ten and unify them to bring about the completion of the puzzle." He held up the skull. "Within these light bands, we can find the pathways of discovery. We can call forth the three remaining skulls and activate the knowledge and consciousness of the Thirteen Atlantean Masters. We can save the world."

More enthusiastic applause rang out.

What are they going to do with me? Angie glanced to her left and eyed the enraptured Guardians. *Declare that I'm a pretender, take my skull and tell me to take a hike. I don't think so. Things are about to get interesting.*

Talkington babbled on about a new world order that would be established once the thirteen skulls were gathered. News media outlets would no longer trivialize and lampoon their efforts because their powers would be made manifest to the world. When the consciousness and wisdom of the Thirteen are revealed, their influence would bring forth a unity of diverse cultures the world has never seen. Doubters and deniers would be discredited. Eyes would be opened. All nationalities would see the clear path to living in harmony and love with one another. Wars would stop, and nuclear weapons would be destroyed.

Angie wondered if he came up with that speech after listening to a John Lennon album. She checked her watch. *This guy's been running off at the mouth for half an hour. Come on. Let's move it along.* Ten minutes later he concluded his talk and invited any Guardians who wanted to communicate with Lord Rainbow to come forward.

Goldbluff jumped to his feet. "I would love to chew the fat with Mr. Rainbow."

Several Guardians groaned.

"Mr. Goldbluff," Olivia Crane bristled. "We have little tolerance for those who disrespect our presentations. Please sit down."

He raised a hand and lowered his head. "No, no, no. I'm serious. I'm into peace and harmony. I want to learn. I want to grow."

"I don't think so," she snapped.

"Mr. Talkington." He faced the ponytailed man. "I appeal to you, sir. Give me a chance to look deeply into your skull's brilliance and make some kind of divine discovery. It could be a life-changing experience for me. I'm open to embracing a new viewpoint."

"Well . . ." The man rubbed the side of his bulbous nose and cleared his throat. "Lord Rainbow is all about acceptance and new beginnings. If you promise to take this seriously, I would approve the request."

Before the old woman could object, Goldbluff spouted, "I will," and rushed to the skull keeper's side.

Talkington straightened, somewhat startled, and backed a half step. "Okay, Mr. Goldbluff, may Lord Rainbow speak deeply to the core of your being and bring enlightenment."

"Amen, Brother Talkington." Goldbluff closed his eyes, extended his hand and clasped the top of the multi-color-emitting skull. He remained still for more than a minute, and then both his hand and head slightly trembled. He bobbed his head, eyes still closed. "Yes, I understand . . . You can see to the very heart of my being." He smiled, a smile one shares with a kind grandfather or sweet child. "I am humbled by your revelations. Thank you so much, Lord Rainbow." He removed his hand and blinked several times, turned and faced the skull keepers.

"Mr. Goldbluff," Talkington said, "please share with your fellow Guardians what Lord Rainbow revealed to you."

"Lord Rainbow made it very clear to me . . ." He paused and gazed at Angie. ". . . that Angie Thomas is a true Guardian. Lord Rainbow said that the blue skull, the Skull of Truth, called out to her from the depths of his grave. He gave her a mission. She has the gift. Against all odds she zeroed in on the skull's location like a homing device out of a James Bond movie. She and Crystal Blue Persuasion are a team. Her words can be trusted."

Angie felt blood rushing to her face. *Man, this guy pushes his luck to the limit.* She angled her body slightly to catch the skull keepers' reactions. Surprisingly, they appeared somewhat receptive to Goldbluff's theater. She took in a measured breath, hoping the proceedings would move forward without issue.

"Roll me to the front," Olivia Crane ordered Arnold.

He shot to his feet, circled her wheelchair, pushed her toward Goldbluff and stopped in front of him.

"Sit down, Mr. Goldbluff," she commanded.

He smiled cordially. "Certainly." He sauntered to his seat and sat.

Arnold turned her chair to face the Guardians.

She eyed them with a cold aspect. "As someone said earlier today, our two new Guardians are untested and inexperienced. It would be wise to weigh their words with skepticism until they have clearly established credibility." She clasped her hands on her lap. "We have had a long day, and the evening session promises to be just as taxing." She checked her watch. "It's half past four. Let's take a break until dinner at six, which will be held in the dining area."

The group let out a collective sigh, happy to take a break from the tension. They stretched, stood and chattered.

As soon as Goldbluff got to his feet, he turned to Charlotte and said, "How about that walk along the beach?"

"Well . . . I . . . I . . ." She glanced around the room. No one seemed to notice or care that she was keeping company with a black sheep. "Sure. We can go for a walk. I need some fresh air."

Arnold left his grandmother's side and marched toward them.

Angie stiffened. *Uh oh. Here comes Knuckle-Dragger.*

He stopped directly in front of his sister. "Charlotte, I need to talk to you up in grandmother's room."

"Can't it wait?" she whined.

"No."

Goldbluff stepped between them. "Sorry, Arnold my boy, but your sister and I are going for a walk."

"Back off, Bozo." He shoved Goldbluff back a step and grabbed his sister by the wrist. "Let's go, Charlotte."

Goldbluff's hand shot out and clamped on Arnold's shoulder. "Charlotte is a big girl. Let her decide."

Arnold's face turned a demonic red as he scowled at Goldbluff.

Goldbluff smiled, released his shoulder and wiggled his fingers. "Charlotte, it's up to you."

She shook her hand until Arnold released his grip. "I'll talk to you when I get back from my beach walk."

"Arnold!" Oliva Crane barked from across the room. "I need you."

Goldbluff raised a finger. "Grandma is calling."

Angie thought she noticed smoke coming from Arnold's nose and ears as he turned and stomped away.

Chapter 26
New Plans

Once Goldbluff and Charlotte exited through the back door toward the beach, Angie turned to Mee Mee and said, "We need to make new plans."

"Okay."

"Let's head up to the bedroom."

"Lead the way."

Angie walked briskly into the back hallway. Arnold stood staring out the back door. *He's keeping his eye on Charlotte. Take her on a long walk, Goldbluff.* She angled to the right and headed for the front hall. Several of the Guardians stood around the foyer checking out the old photographs. She walked by them and double-timed it up the steps, down the hallway and into the room.

Mee Mee shut the door. "Okay. Tell me what happened."

Angie paced around the bed and back. "We need to make new plans."

"You said that already. For what?"

"A return to Monkey Island. This time I don't want to paddle out there on a kayak."

Mee Mee adjusted her glasses. "So you know the exact location of the whiskey bottle?"

"Yes, I do."

"How did you find out?"

Angie recounted the discovery of the VR headset and encounter with Charlotte's AI friend.

Mee Mee screwed up her face. "Do you mean to tell me they can create digital people who can become your best buddy? You've got to be kidding me."

Angie bobbed her head. "It's called artificial intelligence. My voice must have sounded similar to Charlotte's. The AI didn't question my identity. Maybe it's not programmed for voice recognition."

"Do they seem like real people?"

"Yes. They have a connection to the internet. When a user creates one of them, they begin storing and building information that would relate to their interaction with the user. They remember every conversation. They access information from the web to grow their knowledge and improve their communication. With time, they deepen their relationship and trust with their creator."

"Now that's scary."

"It's the world we're living in."

"What if they take over one day?"

Angie shrugged. "Maybe they already have. AI is everywhere."

Mee Mee waved a hand in front of her face. "I don't even want to think about it. Anyway, what's our next step?"

Angie scratched her chin. "I'm going to give Weston Wolf a call. Hopefully, he can set us up with a boat."

"Then what?"

"Then we get in the boat, go to the island and find the bottle."

"Then we solve the case and contact the authorities. Easy peasy lemon squeasy."

Angie knotted her brow. "Believe me, it won't be that easy."

"Why not?"

"It all depends on what's in the bottle."

"True."

"Our biggest problem is Arnold."

"Right. If he figures out what you did and how you did it, he'll know what you know and try to do something about it."

Angie nodded. "I'm guessing Olivia Crane deposited some incriminating information into the bottle."

"Perhaps it was a power move, a way to keep her husband in check."

"Could have been. Did you notice the painting of Chandler Crane in the great room?"

"I did. He held that Skull of Doom like he was the Guardian."

"Now she is. Maybe that was the trade off."

"And Arnold's torn between two grandparents," Mee Mee reasoned.

"Grandpa's pet but Grandma's heir apparent." Angie wobbled her head. "I hope we're at least hitting the board with some of these conjecture darts."

"Yeah, and not some stray cat outside the window. You better give Wolf a call if we're going to get to Monkey Island before nightfall."

Angie slid her phone out of her pants pocket, activated the screen and brought up her contact list. After scrolling down the list, she tapped Wolf's call button. The phone rang four times.

"Hey, Angel, what's up?"

"Hi Wes. I've got a big favor to ask."

"Sure. You know I'll lend a hand if I can."

"I need a boat."

"What?"

"You heard me."

"What kind of boat?"

"Something small with a motor."

"Why?"

"We're heading back out to Monkey Island."

A long silence followed. Finally, Wolf said, "On Halloween night you're heading out to that abandoned hunting club? You must be desperate for a spooky good time."

"Fun has nothing to do with it. I found a clue to the cold case we're working on. We need to check it out."

"I figured as much. I've got a neighbor who owns a little boat. It's not much more than a rowboat with small outboard on it. He uses it to fish on the sound side."

"That's perfect. Can you haul it up to the Whalehead Club for us and drop it off under the big tree next to the launch ramp?"

"That's a big ask."

"How many times have I gone out of my way for you?"

"Okay, okay. I owe you. I'll give Wally a call."

"We need to get out there as soon as possible."

"Sit tight. I'll get back to you in ten minutes."

"Thanks, Wes. I really appreciate it."

"Bye."

Angie ended the call, took in a relieved breath and blew it out. "He's on it."

"Good." Mee Mee peered out the window to the driveway. "Isaac just went up the steps to his garage apartment."

"Let's go talk to him."

"What about?"

"Mr. and Mrs. Crane. I want to know more about what went on between them."

"When are we going to head up to Monkey Island?"

"As soon as we hear back from Wes."

Mee Mee pointed at her boatneck top. "Is that what you're going to wear?"

Angie glanced down at her bright orange shirt and capri pants. "No. I brought jeans and a long sleeve t-shirt. My hoodie is in the car."

"We better change now so we don't have to come back up here."

"Good idea. And there's something else I want to take with me."

"What's that?"

Angie walked to the bed, opened her suitcase and searched under the clothing. "This." She held up her Colt pistol.

Mee Mee widened her eyes. "Is that real?"

"Does Count Dracula suck?"

"I know he can be a pain in the neck."

"So can this."

After changing, Angie stuffed the .38 special into her jeans pocket. Then they exited the room, hurried along the hallway, down the steps and into the foyer. The tall raven-haired woman and Honeypot Chen turned from viewing a photograph and eyed them as they headed for the door.

Mee Mee waved. "Just getting some fresh air. We'll be back."

Neither Guardian responded.

"Probably happy to see us go," Angie muttered.

Before heading up the steps to Isaac's apartment, Angie checked the surroundings. *No one out here checking on us as far as I can see. Let's hope it stays that way.* They bounded up the steps, and Mee Mee knocked on the door.

Isaac cracked it open slightly, and when he saw them, he opened it halfway. "What do you two want?"

"I've got a couple questions about the Cranes," Angie said.

He nodded, stepped to the side and waved them in.

His garage apartment presented a simple layout: a kitchen with old appliances and a small round table surrounded by four wooden chairs. The kitchen transitioned into a modest living room with a well-worn couch and recliner accompanied by a couple side tables with glass lamps. Angie guessed the one door next to the couch led to his bedroom and bathroom. A couple windows let in just enough light to tint the place with tones of tans and faded greens.

"Have a seat," Isaac said, "Can I get you something to drink?"

"No. We won't take much of your time." Angie followed Mee Mee to the couch and sat down next to her. The place had the fresh smell of pine cleaner.

Isaac plopped down in the recliner and leaned on his knees. "Well, have you made any progress since we last talked?"

"Yes. Big time progress." Angie reviewed the discovery of

the whereabouts of the whiskey bottle and her worries about Arnold's suspicions. "How dangerous is Arnold?"

Isaac's voice rumbled low and slow: "I think he's a killer."

"Do you think he drugged Gavin Goldbluff?" Mee Mee asked.

He bobbed his head. "He's the one."

"At Olivia Crane's orders?" Angie said.

"Maybe, but I doubt it."

Angie leaned forward. "Who's then?"

"Arnold is Chandler Crane's puppet."

"What happened between Oliva and Chandler?" Mee Mee asked.

"They were both obsessed with the Skull of Doom, but Chandler claimed to be its Guardian. For years they attended the conferences around the world. To me, it seemed like a bunch of hogwash. At first, I thought their delusions were harmless like the crazies on the History Channel who believe in ancient aliens. As time passed, they discovered more and more background information about the Atlantean Skulls. I minded my own business." He fluttered his fingers. "Dabbling in the occult gives me the jimjams. People who become obsessed with the supernatural go off the deep end."

"I know she's obsessed." Angie said. "At some point she gained enough leverage to usurp control from him. She became the Guardian of the Skull of Doom."

"I remember the night it happened. About ten years ago they had a hellacious argument. He struck her, and she called the cops. It must have been the last straw because he moved out a week later. He visits a couple times a year when the family gathers, but Mrs. Crane keeps him at a distance."

Mee Mee said, "She must have grown tired of the abuse and decided it was time to blackmail him."

Isaac nodded. "Whatever is in the bottom of that whiskey bottle put her in the driver's seat."

Angie's cell phone rang—the instrumental intro to Alan

Parsons Project's *Eye in the Sky*. "Hello."

"Hey, Angel, Wally gave the A-okay on the boat. I'll be leaving in fifteen minutes."

"Great. We're leaving now. We'll meet you at the launch ramp."

"See you then."

Angie ended the call.

Mee Mee checked her watch. "It's almost ten after five. It'll take an hour to get to the Whalehead Club. By the time we get to the island, it'll be pitch black. Do you have a flashlight in your car?"

"A small one."

Isaac stood. "I've got a good one in my bedroom." He strode across the living room and through the door to the left of the couch. A minute later he came out with one of those large square-bodied flashlights with a handle on top. "It's fully charged. Should last four or five hours."

Angie and Mee Mee stood and faced him.

Mee Mee said, "Can't do without a good light on Halloween night."

He extended the flashlight. "Well then, here you go, just in case you run into a monster in the dark."

Chapter 27
Return to Monkey Island

Heading north along Route 12, Angie didn't notice much Halloween activity until they reached the little town of Duck. She checked her watch—6:02. "The ghosts and goblins have been turned loose."

"And it's getting harder to see them."

"Don't worry. I've got good night vision."

"I wonder if they're missing us back at the Crane house."

Angie chuckled. "I'm sure Arnold noticed. Hopefully, he hasn't cornered Charlotte yet."

"Once we get to the island, it won't take long to retrieve the bottle and hightail it out of there."

"That's the plan anyway."

Mee Mee reached for the dashboard. "Watch out!"

Angie slammed on the brakes as the Grim Reaper stepped in front of the car. Wearing a black hooded robe and skeleton mask, a tall kid stumbled to a stop.

He faced them and shook his scythe at the windshield. "You're on my list! I'll see you soon!" He laughed and traipsed across the street.

"Smart aleck idiot," Angie snarled.

Mee Mee sat back in her seat. "The Grim Reaper almost got himself killed."

"Yeah. Teenagers think they're immortal."

"True. That's a harsh lesson we all learn—no one gets out of this world alive."

Angie let off the brake and eased on the gas. "Thanks for the reminder."

She drove even slower the rest of the way through Duck.

With the town behind them, Route 12 wound its way along the thin strip of land between the Currituck Sound and Atlantic Ocean. Fading twilight drained the colors from the tall bushes and live oaks that lined each side of the road. She felt like she was driving through a hedge maze in a strange dream. Ten miles later they entered the town of Corolla, its streetlights offering intermittent glowing auras against the darkening sky. By the time they reached the Whalehead Club, night had descended.

The once-prestigious hunting club sat on the edge of the Currituck Sound, its five tall chimneys black against the starlit dome. Angie recalled its history. During its heyday in the roaring twenties, its owners hosted a multitude of celebrities and industry moguls who made their pilgrimage to the Outer Banks in the fall to fish and hunt waterfowl. As the decades went by, the ownership of the building passed into different hands, and the structure fell into disrepair. When she was a kid in the late nineties, its rundown state resembled a haunted mansion. However, Currituck County officials realized the historical significance of the property, purchased it and began renovations at the turn of century. Now it had become the main attraction in town with thousands of people taking tours of the Art Nouveau style building every year.

The park surrounding the Whalehead Club offered visitors a picnic area, docks for their small boats and a launch ramp. Angie drove past the looming structure with its steep gabled roof and many dormers to the parking spaces near a tall loblolly pine. *As slow as I drove through the town of Duck, Wes can't be too far behind us.* The small lot was empty, and she pulled in next to the pine. *No one is hanging out here this late in the day.* Angie cut the engine and got out of the Civic.

Mee Mee stepped out of the car, closed the door, clicked on the flashlight and waved it back and forth across the sound shoreline. "Everybody must be trick or treating in the Corolla neighborhoods."

Angie leaned against the back of the car. "I wish I was home handing out candy."

"Come on now. You get to wander through the rooms of a decrepit, creaky, abandoned hunting club."

"You forgot to mention haunted."

"That, too. What more could you ask for on a dark Halloween night?"

Angie noticed headlights at the entrance of the park a couple hundred yards away. "That must be Wes."

"Let's hope so."

"I can see a trailer, but that's not his car."

"Uh oh."

An old Dodge Caravan rumbled in their direction under the streetlights along the road in front of the Whalehead Club. The driver made a semi-circle in front of the parking area and backed the trailer toward the boat ramp. Angie distinguished the shape of a small boat on the trailer. *That's got to be Wes. Must be his friend's car.* The Caravan stopped a few feet before the back wheels of the trailer touched the water.

Weston Wolf got out of the Caravan and waved. "I'm just here for the boos."

"Not funny," Angie said.

"Booooo," Mee Mee jeered.

"Now that I'm a dad, I can tell those kinds of jokes."

"I'll excuse the joke out of appreciation for your help." Angie walked to him and gave him a quick hug. "This means a lot, Wes."

"Don't be too thankful." Wolf motioned toward the boat. "I'm not sure how dependable that motor is. Wally said if it conks out, just give it a good kick."

Angie shook her head. "Wonderful."

"I did throw in a couple oars into the bottom just in case."

"I have a feeling this is going to be a long night," Angie said.

Wes spread his hands. "I wish I could come along, but Wally needs his van back before nine."

"You've done enough." Angie eyed the boat. "We'll manage."

Mee Mee rubbed her hands together. "It'll be an adventure."

Wolf said, "Sounds like you've got a good lead."

Angie shrugged. "It's a note at the bottom of a whiskey bottle."

Wolf tilted his head. "I've been stuck there during an investigation."

Angie knotted her brow. "Stuck finding a lead?"

"No," Wolf laughed. "At the bottom of a whiskey bottle."

Angie grinned. "C'mon. Let's get this boat in the water. I'd like to get back before the witching hour."

Wolf walked to the trailer. "Like I told you, it's just a rowboat with a small outboard."

Angie stepped up next to him. "It'll do."

"There's a two-gallon gas can next to your gas tank. Should be plenty to get out to Monkey Island and back." Wolf removed the front strap. "Even with the motor, the boat only weighs about 150 pounds. You two should have no problem lugging it onto shore once you get to the island."

Mee Mee formed a fist and curled her arm. "These biceps don't grow on trees."

"Yeah," Angie snickered. "We're a couple of roller derby queens." She walked around the front of the Caravan to the other side of the trailer. "I'll get this side."

"I'm with you." Mee Mee followed her.

Wolf unhitched the second strap. "Okay. Let's slide her off."

Angie and Mee Mee clamped their hands on the edge of the aluminum boat, lifted and slid it toward the water. It moved somewhat easily. Once the boat was halfway off the trailer, they lowered the backend into the water. Then they picked up the front end and shoved it farther down the ramp, its bottom rasping against the concrete. Once three-quarters of the boat floated in the water, Wolf held the front-end steady against the ramp.

"Hop in," he ordered. "I'll set you off."

Angie stepped over the side and made her way to the back of the boat. After Mee Mee climbed in, Wolf lifted the frontend and gave the boat a good shove. It drifted about fifteen feet into the sound despite the small waves slapping against its side.

"Do you know how to get the motor started?" Wolf called out.

Angie lowered herself onto the back bench next to the motor. "Give me a refresher course."

"Sure thing. Release the lock on the hinge and lower the motor into the water."

Angie glanced at Mee Mee. "Shine the light this way."

Mee Mee, sitting on the middle bench, held the light above her head and directed the ray at the motor.

Angie found the knob that released the lock on the hinge, lowered the motor and locked it in place. "Okay. Did that."

There should be a gas tank near your feet."

"Yeah, I see it."

"There's a line that runs to the motor with a prime bulb on it. Squeeze the prime bulb a couple times."

"Found it." She squeezed the black plastic bulb twice. "Now what?"

"Check the handle coming out of the motor. Make sure the grip is in neutral."

Angie noticed the arrow positioned on the red neutral marking. "It's good."

"Should be a choke on the left. Slide it over and push the choke button a couple times."

She found the choke lever, slid it over and pressed the little bulb three times. "Done."

"Alright, alright, alright. Pull the chord to start the motor. Once it warms up, slide off the choke. Turn the grip to the right to go forward and left to go backward. There's a red button on the back of the motor to cut the engine."

"I see it. Okay. Let's hope it starts." After about five pulls, the motor struggled to life. Angie waited about a minute as it chugged unevenly until it found a steadier rhythm before sliding off the choke. "I think we're set," she hollered over the uneven rumble.

"Great. Once you get back, tug the boat off to the side in the grass. I'll pick it up in the morning."

"Will do!" Mee Mee yelled.

"Happy sailing!" Wolf called.

Angie waved, pulled the motor arm toward her and turned the grip throttle to circle the boat away from the shore. "Get out your phone and look up Monkey Island on Google Maps."

"I'm on it." Mee Mee funneled her hand into her jacket pocket and pulled out her cell phone. "Head northwest for now."

"No kidding." Angie aimed the prow toward the open water.

"We're on our way." Mee Mee's face glowed in the phone's light. "Monkey Island is almost two miles from here."

Angie glanced to her right as the dark shoreline slowly diminished. *Fifteen minutes and we'll be there. This seems too easy.* She turned the throttle grip, giving the engine more gas. *Let's try to make it in ten.* With the increased speed, the boat jolted against the waves.

"This is going to be a rough ride," Mee Mee hollered. "I hope we don't get seasick."

Angie eased off the gas. "Yeah. We're battling against incoming choppers." The slower speed helped to ease the bouncing. *Patience. We'll get there in plenty of time.*

Ten minutes later the motor conked out.

"Crap!" Angie pulled the starter chord about ten times. "It's dead."

"Give it a kick."

Angie raised her foot and kicked the motor. She tried pulling the starter chord again several times. No luck. She kicked it again and pulled the chord a few more times. The motor sputtered but didn't start. "What are we going to do? The waves are drifting us out toward the middle of the sound."

Mee Mee checked her phone. "We're less than a half mile from the island. We can row it in from here."

"That won't be easy. We'll be rowing against the wind."

"Would you rather swim?"

"No." Angie let out a deep sigh. "Give me an oar."

Mee Mee lifted a wooden oar from the bottom of the boat and handed it to Angie. "I'll take the left side, you take the right."

Once they reoriented the boat toward the island, they paddled in unison, striving to maintain the right direction. When they got to within three hundred yards, Angie could make out the silhouette of a scraggly hump of land on the surface of the water.

"Not far now," Mee Mee said.

"Good. My arms feel like pulled taffy."

"Listen. Do you hear that?"

They both stopped rowing, and Angie tilted her head. "Sounds like a motor."

"Look." Mee Mee pointed toward the shoreline.

Angie squinted and made out the shape of a small vessel about a hundred yards to the east. "For some reason they turned off their boat lights."

"And they're headed for Monkey Island."

"Bet I know who it is."

"Arnold Crane?"

Angie nodded.

"What do we do now?"

"Keep rowing."

Chapter 28
Surprise, Surprise

As they rounded the east side of the island, they caught sight of a small fishing boat tucked between a couple overhanging trees. They stopped paddling and drifted toward the clearing where they had beached the kayak weeks before.

Angie didn't notice any movement near the boat except for a few birds fluttering in the branches. She reached into her jacket pocket and took out her Colt handgun. Their rowboat continued to drift and nudged against the shoreline. They sat motionless and listened. Waves lapped the side, and birds squawked. Angie pointed toward the island. "Go ahead," She whispered. "Climb out as quietly as possible."

Mee Mee handed her the flashlight and said in a low tone, "Hang onto this until I get on shore."

Angie nodded.

Mee Mee moved to the prow, leaned over and grasped the branch of a nearby bush. With a big tug, she managed to slide the bottom of the prow against the slant of the bank. Holding onto the gunwale, she stepped over the side and onto solid ground. Then she held the frontend steady against the bank. Angie stepped over the middle bench and stood next to the front seat. Holding the gun off to the side, she handed Mee Mee the flashlight. Then she grasped the gunwale, scissored her leg over the rim and stepped onto shore. They each grabbed the rim of the boat near the point of the bow with their free hands, and, backing up slowly, pulled it onto the bank. Several birds rustled and screeched in the branches above them.

Angie took in a deep slow breath and eyed the fishing boat about twenty feet away. Although it was dark, she could make out the shape of the white hull which was a few feet longer than their rowboat. She listened intently but didn't hear anything but the occasional rustling of birds and wash of the water.

"I don't think he's here," Mee Mee whispered.

"No. He went to get the bottle."

"What are we going to do?"

"Take it off of him."

Mee Mee pointed into the darkness where the path led to the hunting club. "I can't see a thing. Should I turn on the flashlight?"

"Not yet. Let me try to find the way without the light."

After progressing about ten yards along the path, Angie bumped her head on a thick overhanging branch. Loud squawks and the beating of wings erupted above them. When the rustling settled, Angie said, "It's too dark. Better give me that flashlight. Hopefully, he's inside the hunting club and won't notice."

"You've got the gun. I'll handle the flashlight. Let me lead."

Angie stepped to the side. "Be my guest."

Mee Mee kept the light low and edged slowly along the path. She stopped several times to push leafy branches out of the way. Finally, they entered the small clearing in front of the hunting club.

Angie tapped Mee Mee's shoulder and pointed to her left. "Look at the last window." A faint glow lit the bottom pane of glass.

"He must be in there," Mee Mee said.

"It's the room with the whiskey bottle."

"Are you sure?"

"Positive. The AI guy said it was hidden in the last room on the left. Let's go."

They mounted the few steps and noticed the front door ajar. Angie entered, and Mee Mee stayed at her side, keeping the swath of light low and in front of them. The entry room was spacious with a large redbrick fireplace on the opposite wall.

The place smelled musty. A couple dilapidated armchairs faced the fireplace. Faded blue wainscoting covered the bottom half of the walls, and patches of mold marred the upper half in several places. Angie eyed a doorway to the left of the fireplace. *That must lead to the back of the building, probably the kitchen and dining area.*

When they turned to the left to find the hallway that led to the bedrooms, Mee Mee reached and grabbed Angie's elbow. "Watch it," she whispered harshly.

A few feet in front of them, the thick body of a brown serpent with a triangular head slithered in an S motion. Mee Mee followed it with her light as it crossed the room toward the kitchen.

"Moccasin," Mee Mee said in a low voice.

"This place is probably full of them."

"Be careful."

They edged to the doorway that led to the long hall. Cobwebs hung from the ceiling and doorframes of the rooms. A single set of footprints branded the dusty floor with a hunting boot tread. Angie tilted her head and heard scuffing noises coming from the far end. *Better hurry. He's probably on the floor searching for the bottle under the dresser.* She picked up her pace along the hallway, and Mee Mee kept up.

They stopped a few feet before the last door on the left. Angie whispered in her ear, "As soon as we step in the room, shine the light at him. I'll make sure he knows I'm armed."

Mee Mee nodded, eyes tense.

"On three."

Angie used her fingers for the silent count. As the third finger uncurled, they stepped into the room, and Mee Mee aimed the light in the direction of the scuffling noises. Arnold Crane, on his hands and knees, directed the beam of his flashlight into a hole in the floor. An old dresser had been slid away from the wall, and a square section of wood lay on the floor next to the dresser.

"I've got a gun on you," Angie warned. She noticed he had

a large handgun strapped over his green t-shirt.

Arnold shifted the beam to Angie and Mee Mee. "Surprise, surprise."

"You knew we were coming," Angie said, "That's why you're here."

"The surprise is that I beat you to it. Boat troubles?"

Angie frowned and narrowed her eyes. "Everyone has troubles."

He grinned. "Except for the dead." He reached into the hole and pulled out the whiskey bottle. "Finders keepers. This belongs to me."

Angie shook her head. "There's a note in that bottle that will provide evidence in solving a murder. Any evidence in a crime must be collected and stored in the evidence locker at the local police department. I'll take that bottle."

Arnold got to his feet. "I don't think I'm going to give it to you."

"I'd think twice if I were you."

"You have no authority. You're just a private detective."

"You're wrong. I have a license that authorizes me to take reasonable action in gathering evidence."

"You're a little girl playing make-believe."

"Set the bottle on the floor in front of you, take off that holster and put it next to the bottle."

"No."

"I'm going to count to three, and then I'm going to shoot. You've been warned."

"I don't believe you."

"One . . . two . . ." Angie aimed just above his shoulder. "Three." She fired the gun.

Arnold flinched, dropping the bottle. It broke in half on the floor in front of him. He glared at Angie, mouth agape, and touched his ear. "You . . . you almost . . ."

"Next time I won't miss. Now take off the shoulder holster, or you're a dead man."

He slid off the holster and held it out.

"Put it on the floor next to the bottle."

He dropped it onto the floor a few feet in front of him.

"I'm going to come over there and pick up your gun and the note. Stay completely still. If you make any moves, I'll put a bullet in your heart."

His hand that held the flashlight trembled, causing the beam he aimed at Angie to quiver.

She held the .38 special with both hands as she approached him. A few feet away she stopped. "Don't move." She glanced down and saw the faded paper sticking out of the bottom half of the bottle. She crouched slowly, eyes on Arnold, gun aimed at the middle of his chest. She took another glance at the note to get a bead on its exact location but quickly refocused on Arnold. Eyes fixed on him, she reached and tugged the note out of the bottle. Then she grasped the strap of the holster. She arose and took two steps backwards.

"You won't leave this island alive," Arnold hissed.

She passed her arm through the strap and hung the holster loosely on her shoulder. The gun felt heavy, probably a 9mm Glock. Angie glanced at the faded note and noticed unusual writing – lines, dots, little drawings and odd faces. At the bottom someone had drawn a map in the shape of the island. Beneath the map were the words: *The sacrifice has been offered.* She folded the paper and stuffed it into her hoodie pouch.

"We're leaving, and we're taking your boat," she said. "You lead the way."

"I've done nothing wrong. You're in big trouble."

Angie patted the pouch on her hoodie. "Someone's in big trouble."

Arnold shifted his gaze to Mee Mee. "You're right." His eyes flared. "Someone is in big trouble."

She heard struggling sounds and a loud gasp. Whirling, she saw a large knife at Mee Mee's throat.

Chapter 29
S-S-S-Sacrifice

"Hand Arnold the guns, or I'll sever your friend's windpipe." The ghoul's voice grated in Angie's ears like crushed bones.

With her head tilted back, Mee Mee grimaced, eyes wide with terror.

"Okay!" Angie raised her free hand. "I'm giving him the guns."

"That's a good girl." He wore a hooded black robe. His shadowed face looked like a skull—eyes and nose darkened with paint and teeth drawn across his white lips and chin.

Angie turned and handed Arnold the Colt .38. He removed the holster from her shoulder, stuffed her gun into the front pocket of his camouflage pants and withdrew his Glock from the holster.

Aiming his gun at Angie's chest, he said, "What're we going to do with them?"

"Tohil has answered our prayers."

Arnold bobbed his head slowly.

The ghoul lowered the knife. "The dining room will be the perfect place for the ceremony." He stepped to the side. "Go ahead, Miss Sunshine. You have the light. Lead the way to the kitchen."

Mee Mee straightened and rubbed her neck. "If you insist."

"I insist."

She turned, directed the light into the hallway and walked out of the room. The hooded ghoul trailed closely behind her.

Arnold shoved Angie. "Get going."

As Angie followed them down the hallway, the portrait of

Chandler Crane cradling the Skull of Doom appeared on the screen of her memory. *Is it him? He must be eighty years old by now. If so, he kept himself in shape.* At the end of the hall, Mee Mee entered the front room and turned left. The ghoul held the large knife at his side. It resembled a butcher knife with an ornate handle. *What kind of ceremony does he have in mind?* She remembered the primitive pictograms on the note from the bottle. *A Maya ceremony!* She shook her head. *This isn't good.*

Mee Mee walked through the doorway to the left of the fireplace. It appeared to be a passageway from one section of the building to another. A breeze rushed through broken windows over a countertop on the left. The cold air intensified the chills charging through Angie's body. She tried to slow her breathing and remain calm, but her heart thumped in her throat like the desperate knocking of a trapped child.

The passageway opened into a large dining area. Several smaller tables and chairs lay scattered across the weathered wooden floor. A longer table made of dark wood was stationed in the middle of the room. The remnants of a chandelier hung above it. Cobwebs clung to everything, and the putrid smell of mold tainted the air.

"Go to the table in the middle," the ghoul ordered.

Upon reaching the table, Mee Mee stopped, turned and faced them.

"Give me the light."

Frowning, she handed the flashlight to him.

He shined the beam on Angie. "Stand next to your friend."

She walked to Mee Mee and stood beside her. Arnold aimed both the Glock and his flashlight at them while the ghoul drifted around the room panning the floor and shelves with Isaac's light. Angie eyed Mee Mee and noticed her chin trembling. She reached and clasped her hand. Mee Mee responded by squeezing back.

After a couple minutes, the ghoul returned with what looked to be a soiled tablecloth. He positioned the flashlight on the table facing him and ripped strips from the cloth using the butcher knife to initiate each tear. He threw the remnant of the cloth on the floor and drooped five long strips across his shoulder. "These will do wonderfully," he said with that grating voice.

He inserted his knife into a sheath attached to the sash on his robe, took one of the strips and tied it to the handle of Isaac's light. "The light that shines on life and death." He closed his eyes and murmured undecipherable words. Then he tossed the end of the strip over the chandelier. It dangled on one of the brass arms, and he reached and pulled it until the strip drew Isaac's light above the center of the table. The light swung slowly back and forth causing the shadows in the room to shift off-kilter and back again. After securing the loose end to the handle on the flashlight, he stepped back from the table and said, "Which one is the imposter Guardian of the blue skull."

Arnold pointed at Angie. "The blonde."

"The blue skull will soon be returned to its rightful owner." He grinned, baring his teeth below the teeth drawn on his upper lip. "You will be first. Climb up on the table and lay on your back."

"No," Angie said sharply.

Arnold grabbed her hair in the back and shoved the barrel of the gun into the center of her spine.

"Owww!" she yelped.

"Do what he says, or I'll blast a hole through your skinny chest."

Angie took a deep breath, crawled onto the table and turned over on her back. She stared at the light above her. *Is this the end?* She placed her hands on her belly. *Please, God, no. I want to be a mom. I want to have a family.* "Don't do this," she sniveled. "I don't want to die."

"You are the appointed sacrifice," the ghoul rasped. "A life in exchange for Skull Eleven of the Atlantean Thirteen."

Angie glared at him. "I know who you are. You're Olivia

Crane's husband, Chandler Crane. You sacrificed Ahote Rowtag on this island more than fifty years ago."

He swiveled his head back and forth. "I am the Maya high priest Akna, and your life will be offered for a purpose beyond your understanding. Spread out your arms and legs."

"Noooo!" she cried.

He shifted his gaze to Arnold. "Put the muzzle of the gun against her friend's head. If the blonde doesn't obey me, pull the trigger."

Arnold stepped up to Mee Mee and placed the barrel at the center of her forehead. Mee Mee stiffened. He eyed Angie. "It's up to you."

Angie closed her eyes and spread her arms and legs toward the corners of the table. *Please, God, please, help us.*

"Back away from the table," the ghoul ordered.

Arnold gripped Mee Mee's upper arm and led her to a chair about six feet away. "Sit down and watch."

As Mee Mee sat down, she said, "You two belong in hell."

The ghoul laughed. "I don't believe in your hell."

"Yeah?" she scowled. "Well, that doesn't lower the temperature down there one degree."

He pulled a linen strip from his shoulder. "Tonight, for you, I will raise hell." He tied the end of the strip to Angie's left wrist, stretched it to the corner of the table and tied it to the thick table leg. He repeated the procedure on her right wrist. Then he tethered both of her ankles, yanking the linen strips to the opposite corners to stretch her body as far as it would go. Angie arched her back and gritted her teeth.

"Remember," Arnold said, "she has the note from the bottle in the pouch of her hoodie."

The ghoul slid the knife out of the sheath. "It will be buried with her." Leaning against the middle of the table, he stood over her, holding the knife with both hands. "To you, Tohil, we offer this sacrifice. We ask that you release from the depths of darkness one more of the Atlantean Thirteen, a life for a skull."

He closed his eyes and raised the knife slowly, muttering foreign words that sounded like gibberish. When the knife reached the height of the light, he fell silent and held the pose.

Angie, seeing the blade aimed at her heart, closed her eyes. *Please, please God.*

Footsteps sounded along the passageway between the building sections.

"Someone's coming," Arnold blurted.

The ghoul opened his eyes and turned to face the doorway. He lowered the knife, concealing it behind his back.

"Hello?" Jeff Goldbluff stepped into the dining hall. "What's going on in here?"

Arnold pointed his Glock at Goldbluff. "Put your hands up."

He raised his hands. "I'm not armed."

"Who are you?" the ghoul demanded.

"Jeff Goldbluff."

"Of course, Gavin Goldbluff's nephew, the other imposter."

"That's some Halloween costume you're wearing. Are you the Grim Reaper?"

"Shut up!" the ghoul snarled. "You will regret your decision to come here tonight."

"Mama told me not to come. Why is that girl tied to that table?"

Arnold took a step toward Goldbluff. "Do you want me to shoot him?"

"No." The ghoul brought forth the knife from behind his back. "He will be the third one to die as an offering for the Thirteenth Skull."

"W-w-wait a minute," Goldbluff stammered. "No one needs to die here. Let me be the voice of reason. You don't have to do this."

"Are you afraid of dying?"

"Aren't we all?"

Angie craned her neck and glanced at Mee Mee. She was

staring at something on the floor, her eyes bordering on panic.

"I have died a thousand times," the ghoul said, "but I'm still here."

Goldbluff pointed at him. "What you said just now — that's what I mean."

"Keep your hands up!" Arnold barked.

"Sorry." Goldbluff reraised his hands. "But what he said is a perfect example."

"What are you talking about?" the ghoul queried.

"You said you died a thousand times. Clearly, that is a Maya spiritual ideology on death and resurrection or reincarnation. You have embraced that idea."

"You have no idea what I believe."

"But I do know our thoughts have lives. Whatever thoughts we choose to feed grow stronger."

"Let me shoot him," Arnold pleaded.

"Listen to what I'm saying. If you feed the wrong thoughts, they can turn into monsters. Don't feed the monster."

"Do you think I'm a monster?" The ghoul grinned.

"You have fed a myth that doesn't exist in reality. You have turned your obsession with these crystal skulls and the Maya religion into a monster that has taken control of you."

Keep talking Goldbluff. Keep stalling them. Angie twisted her neck again to see Mee Mee bending over and reaching into the darkness. *What is she doing?*

"If I am a monster, I blame one person."

"Who?" Goldbluff asked.

"My wife."

"Olivia Crane? Are you Chandler Crane?"

"Yes. And now I must do what monsters do." He turned toward Angie and raised the knife.

"Snake!" Mee Mee shouted. Her hand swept across the floor, scooped up the large serpent and tossed it toward Arnold. The moccasin wrapped around his arm, and he dropped the Glock.

"It bit me!" he screamed. "It bit my wrist!" He shook his arm, pulling at the snake with his other hand.

Chandler Crane whirled to face his grandson.

Mee Mee dove for the gun.

Goldbluff charged Crane. The old man thrust the knife at him, but Goldbluff managed to catch his wrist.

Arnold crumpled to the floor, writhing as he unwrapped the snake from his arm. "It burns! My wrist is on fire!"

Mee Mee picked up the gun and aimed it at Arnold.

Golfbluff wrestled the old man to the ground. They rolled over twice, and Goldbluff thumped his head on the thick leg of the table. Crane broke loose, sprung to his feet and ran toward the kitchen. The shifting form of his robe disappeared in the darkness.

"My arm is swelling," Arnold cried. "I'm going to die."

"Stay on the ground, or I'll make sure of it," Mee Mee warned.

Arnold began to hyperventilate. "I need . . . I need . . . to get . . . to a hospital."

Goldbluff stumbled to his feet and rubbed his forehead.

"Untie me!" Angie wailed.

Goldbluff eyed Mee Mee. "Shoot the ape if he tries anything."

Arnold begged, "I need the antivenom. Get me to a hospital. It hurts!"

Mee Mee held the gun steady. "Any monkey business, and I'll put an end your agony."

Goldbluff worked on the knot that bound Angie's left wrist.

Once he untied it, she shook out her arm. "What took you so long to get here?"

Goldbluff raised his eyebrows as he untied the knot on her other wrist. "You're welcome."

She smiled. "I'm kidding. You're an answer to prayer."

Goldbluff chuckled as he released her other wrist. "So is the snake." He hurried around the table to work on the knots binding her ankles.

Angie sat up and rubbed her wrists. "True. A serpent showed up, and the tables turned, just like in the garden."

"Huh?"

"The Garden of Eden."

"Oh, that garden. I should have paid more attention in Sunday school."

"So should have Arnold."

Arnold raised his arm into the light. "Look! My hand is twice its normal size. I'm going to die."

"I doubt it," Mee Mee said. "You'll probably just lose your hand."

"Nooooo," he sobbed. "I don't want to lose my hand."

Mee Mee shook her head. "For a man with such big muscles, you sure cry like a little girl."

"What happened to Chandler Crane?" Angie asked.

Goldbluff thumbed toward the kitchen. "He bolted into the shadows."

"Do you think he's still back there?"

"I doubt it, but I wasn't about to chase him into the darkness unarmed."

"I'm guessing he went out the back door and hightailed it to his boat."

Goldbluff nodded. "Probably, but we'll keep an eye out for him."

Angie said in a low voice, "Arnold still has my Colt pistol in his pants pocket."

"I'll get it." Goldbluff finished untying the knots and walked over to Mee Mee. "I'm going to take Angie's handgun out of his pocket. You know what to do if he tries anything."

Mee Mee nodded. "I'll send him to Hades in a handbasket full of candy corn."

Goldbluff nudged Arnold's leg with his foot. "Lay on your back and don't move."

Arnold complied, his head wobbling on the wooden floor.

"I'm getting really sick."

Goldbluff dropped to his knees, inserted his hand into his pants pocket and pulled out the .38 special. "We'll take you to the hospital if you behave yourself."

"I need help. I'll do whatever you tell me."

Goldbluff got to his feet. "Stand up. We're going to walk to my boat."

Arnold turned on his side and propped himself on his elbow. "I don't know if I can make it."

"Then you'll die on this island," Mee Mee said.

"I'll try."

"Try or die," she chided.

Arnold managed to get on all fours, rock back on his toes and stand. He wobbled slightly but steadied himself.

Goldbluff handed Angie her gun. "I tied up Isaac's boat next to yours. I'll lead the way. I've got my own flashlight." He faced Arnold. "You follow me. These ladies both have guns. They'll put a bullet in your back if you take a half step sideways. Right ladies?"

"With pleasure," Angie said.

"Amen to that," Mee Mee seconded.

As they plodded through the passageway and into the front room, Angie recalled the flash of light on the knife blade a few inches above her heart. She shook her head to rid the image from her mind. *I can't wait to get off this island.*

Chapter 30
Big Splash

Goldbluff led the way along the path, weaving through the bushes and pushing limbs out of the way. The birds in the branches above them complained and squawked. Arnold stumbled a few times but kept pace. Training the Glock on the center of his back, Mee Mee followed within a couple feet. Angie couldn't help glancing behind her every few steps, imagining Chandler Crane in his Grim Reaper getup following them. If he did pop out from behind a tree, she was prepared to shoot him between those dark eyes without one iota of equivocation.

They broke through the vegetation to where the boats were lodged on the bank. The breeze had picked up, and a flash of lightning streaked over the Currituck Sound miles to the south. Thunder softly rumbled about a half dozen seconds later.

"I'm getting weaker," Arnold wheezed.

Mee Mee shined the light in the direction of the white fishing boat, but it was gone. "Grandpa Crane didn't wait around for you. Shows you how much he cares."

"He knows where I am and where to find me. He's watching over me." Arnold's voice sounded somewhat assured.

"Bullcrap," Goldbluff said. "He's a jellyfish waiting for a spine."

Arnold grunted but didn't argue.

Angie gazed upwards and noticed the gathering clouds blotting out the stars directly above them. "I'm glad we're taking your boat."

Goldbluff shined his light on the rowboat. "Where'd you get that bucket?"

"A friend of a friend," Angie said. "The motor died. We had to paddle the last half mile."

"We'll tow it."

Isaac's fishing boat was a few feet longer than the rowboat. It was constructed of fiberglass with a slightly larger outboard motor. It had a dashboard with a steering wheel and compact windshield. A rope extended from the tow ring at the point of the bow to a nearby tree. About two-thirds of the boat rocked gently in the water. Angie figured Golfbluff must be stronger than she assumed to tug the front end that far onto shore by himself.

"I'll climb aboard first," Angie said, "and make sure Snakebite Boy doesn't try anything stupid." She hopped up on the front of the boat and stepped over the small windshield into the cockpit, her foot alighting between the two frontend seats. Glancing over her shoulder, she noticed two seats in the middle and a bench in the back wide enough for two people.

"You're next, Crane." Goldbluff directed his light on the prow.

"I'm feeling weak," Arnold whined. "I don't know if I can make it."

"Do you want to be a one-armed man?" Goldbluff asked.

He groaned, and using his good arm, managed to climb onto the front and into the boat.

Angie kept her .38 special aimed at him. "Move to the back," she ordered.

He stumbled his way between the two middle seats and lowered himself onto the bench by the motor. Planting his elbows on his knees, he hung his head. "I'm really sick."

Mee Mee climbed aboard and made her way to the middle seat on the left. When she discovered the seat could swivel, she turned toward Arnold and waved the handgun. "I'll keep my eye on him and make sure he behaves."

Goldbluff handed Angie his light. "See if you can find a towrope. There're a couple storage compartments up front."

Angie checked through several of the pulldown compartments and found a yellow nylon rope. After unraveling it, she tossed one end to Goldbluff. He tied it to the tow ring on the front of the aluminum boat and then shoved the vessel off the bank into the water.

Angie made her way to the back of the boat with the other end of the rope. She shined the light on Arnold's hand, and he stared up at her with hollow eyes like a penitent child. His wrist and hand were red and swollen, but his condition didn't appear as serious as his bellyaching implied. Keeping her eyes on him with quick glances, she secured the rope to a cleat on the back rim next to the motor. As she made her way to the front, she glimpsed several flashes in the distance that lit the thick clouds above the sound water. Thunder rumbled a few seconds later like the bellowing of a disgruntled kraken.

Goldbluff untied the link to the tree, pushed the boat off the bank and leapt onto the front end. Angie offered him a hand, and he stepped down into the cockpit and sat in the driver's seat. After Angie seated herself in the chair next to him, he started the engine and backed out the boat.

"Hope this craft can handle rough water." She pointed to the south. "We're headed right into a storm."

"We'll soon find out." He made a ninety degree turn and headed for the open water. The rowboat trailed behind, its frontend jouncing in the wake.

"Take it easy," Angie said.

Goldbluff eased back on the gas. "Right. We don't want to tow a turned-over turtle. It shouldn't take too long to get back even at a slower pace."

"Did you launch from the Whalehead Club?"

"Yeah. That was the closest public ramp."

"Good. My car is parked there." Angie glanced over her shoulder. "I don't think Snakebite Boy realizes how much trouble he's in."

Arnold glanced up and shook his head.

"He's too busy wallowing in his own misery. You should call the Dare County Sheriff's office and tell them to meet us at the Outer Banks Hospital in Nags Head."

Angie refocused on Goldbluff. "They'll want to know what charges we're bringing against him."

"That's easy. Attempted murder."

"It'll be his word against ours."

Goldbluff smiled. "We've got the better odds: three to one."

Angie patted the pouch on her hoodie. "And I've got the message in the bottle that might convict Chandler Crane of murder. Unfortunately, we'll need someone well versed in Maya hieroglyphics to interpret it."

"Don't look at me."

"You're not an expert in Maya antiquity?"

He chuckled. "Nope."

"There's a Guardian at the Crane house who claims to be a Maya shaman. He might be able to tell us what it says."

"Honeypot Chen?"

Angie nodded. "Hopefully, he's one of the good guys."

A few minutes later raindrops splattered on Angie's face and the dashboard. "Here it comes." The waves ramped up, and the front of boat bobbed and bounded. Angie felt like she was riding a spirited steed. Lightning streaked down about a mile away, and thunder boomed a second later.

"I'm wet behind the ears when it comes to sailing in choppy water," Goldbluff fretted.

"They say there are some things you can only learn in a storm."

The wind howled, and the skies unleashed a deluge of cascading rain.

"We're about to go to school."

They smacked into a large wave that lifted them off their seats.

"You alright back there?" Angie called out behind her.

"I'm still here," Mee Mee answered.

"I'm sick." Arnold leaned over the side and threw up.

Another large waved whacked the prow, and Angie had to grasp the dashboard to keep from falling off her seat. She heard a big splash.

"Man overboard!" Mee Mee yelled.

Angie whipped around and didn't see Arnold. "Cut the engine!"

The boat slowed to a stop, but the waves continued to rock it violently.

Mee Mee shouted, "He was barfing over the side when that wave hit!"

"We've got to turn back and find him," Angie said.

Goldbluff started the engine and turned the boat in the other direction. The waves slapped its side, threatening to overturn it.

Angie checked the status of the rowboat as it circled by. It sat much lower in the water. *It's probably half full and ready to go under. Crap. We might have to cut the tow line.*

Now the waves were hitting the back of the boat, but they seemed to be easing up. Angie aimed the flashlight across the dark water. *No sign of him.*

From the other side, Mee Mee panned her light over the surface. "He's not over here."

"Try to keep the boat in this vicinity," Angie said. "I think this is where he went under."

"I'll do my best." Goldbluff powered the craft backwards and forwards several times, turning left and then right. The two women scanned the water with their lights. Ten minutes later the storm passed, and the water calmed.

"Where'd he go?" Angie's voice edged with incredulity.

"Davey Jones's Locker," Mee Mee replied.

Angie faced Goldbluff. "We need to call the Coast Guard and tell them what happened."

"Go ahead. I'll widen the circle. The current may have carried his body farther than we figured."

Angie pulled her phone out of her jeans pocket, searched for the Coast Guard's number and made the call. She kept her explanation simple: A guy fell into the water on the Currituck Sound halfway between the Whalehead boat launch and Monkey Island. She blamed the storm and assured them that she and her companions would keep looking until they arrived. Angie figured she could offer additional details concerning the circumstances at some later point.

Goldbluff kept the boat circling in the general area, but Angie and Mee Mee didn't spot anything resembling a person floundering in the water or a floating corpse. Twenty minutes later the Coast Guard arrived. They directed a large spotlight on Isaac's boat as they pulled up beside them.

A guy with a bushy beard called out, "Are you the ones who contacted us?"

Angie stood and faced him. "Yes. My name is Angie Stallone Thomas. My husband is a Dare County deputy. I'm a private detective on an investigation."

"What happened?"

"It's a long story. The guy that fell in the water tried to murder me."

"Are you serious?"

"It's true," Mee Mee said. "I was there."

"Me, too," Goldbluff echoed.

"What was his name?"

"Arnold Crane. He is staying in Nags Head with his grandmother," Angie replied.

"What happened?"

"A water moccasin bit him before he and his partner could do the deed. In the ensuing chaos, his partner escaped, but we captured him."

"Where did this take place?"

"On Monkey Island."

A heavyset bald guy stepped up next to him. "That island is infested with moccasins."

The guy with the beard scratched his head. "If he was

suffering from a venomous snakebite, he's probably a goner. We'll do a thorough search though."

"We'll keep looking, too," Goldbluff said.

"I'll call the sheriff," the bald guy said. "He'll want to know what's going on."

Angie said, "Let us know if he wants to talk to us."

"Will do."

The Coast Guard boat looked to be about twenty-five feet long with twin outboard motors. A bright orange floatation collar wrapped around the entire vessel. For the next two hours it prowled the waters where Arnold splashed into the sound. Goldbluff widened his search, crisscrossing back and forth within a couple hundred yards. Mee Mee and Angie kept their flashlights on the water, but the body never surfaced. When Isaac's boat ran out of gas, Angie checked her watch — 11:08.

"We've been out here for hours," Angie complained.

Goldbluff poured the gas from the two-gallon spare can into the tank. "It's time to head back." He started the engine and pulled up alongside the Coast Guard boat.

"Hey!" Angie yelled. "We're heading back. It's been a long night."

The guy with the bushy beard turned and shined his light at them. "We're not going to stay out here too much longer, maybe another hour."

The bald guy left the helm and stepped up next to his partner. "Sheriff Lucas wants to talk to you-all."

"We want to talk to him, too," Angie said. "Could you tell him to meet us at the Whalehead Club boat ramp?"

"I'll give him a call."

Angie waved, and Goldbluff pulled away. Ten minutes later they approached the launch ramp at the Whalehead Club. Goldbluff shifted into neutral and eased the boat next to a dock near the ramp.

"I'll back the trailer into the water." He climbed over the gunwale and stepped onto the dock. "Just take it nice and slow and guide the boat onto the trailer."

"No problem." Angie moved to the driver's seat and backed the boat up about thirty yards to get a better angle.

Goldbluff headed toward the parking lot. Driving Isaac's old Ford pickup, he made a wide turn and then backed the trailer down the ramp into the water. Angie eased the boat forward onto the trailer and cut the engine. While he turned the crank to secure the boat, Angie checked on the rowboat. Although it had about a foot of water in it, somehow it had stayed afloat.

"How are we doing back there?" Goldbluff asked.

"We're hanging in there," Mee Mee said.

Angie made a chopping motion with her hand toward Goldbluff. "Pull the trailer forward until the rowboat skids onto the ramp."

"Yes, Ma'am. Just say when to stop." He headed for the truck.

By the time they got the rowboat ashore, emptied it and dragged it into the grass, the Currituck County Sheriff showed up. He parked his Jeep Grand Cherokee next to the pickup and got out of the vehicle. A tall deputy wearing a black ballcap stepped out of the passenger side. The sheriff, a wide-chested man with a mustache that made him look like a walrus, approached them wearing a black Stetson hat adorned with a silver-star badge.

"Who's the gal that 'bout got herself murdered?" the sheriff bellowed.

Angie raised her hand. "That would be me."

"Uh huh." He glanced at the deputy and winked. "This ain't no window soapin' Halloween night prank incident. We've got a real crime on our hands here."

"Sure sounds like it, Sheriff," the deputy said.

"A genuine, sociopathic misdeed."

"Ummm hmmm," the deputy mused.

Angie eyed Mee Mee and said in a low voice, "This should

be an interesting interrogation."

Chapter 31
Interrogation

The lawman cleared his throat. "By the way, I'm Sheriff John Lucas. This is Deputy Horace Austin."

"My name's Angie Stallone Thomas." She thumbed to her left. "That's Mee Mee Roberts and Jeff Goldbluff."

"Nice to meet you-all," the deputy said as he pulled out a notepad from his back pocket.

"That's an interesting name . . . Horace," Goldbluff commented.

The tall deputy had a pockmarked face and not enough hair on his chin to qualify as a goatee. "I go with the last three letters."

"Ace?" Goldbluff mused.

"That's right, Ace Austin."

"I call him Arse," Sheriff Lucas guffawed. "Anyway, enough of this chitchat. Tell me what happened."

"I'm a private detective," Angie said. "I was hired to investigate a cold case. My client believed his grandfather was murdered on Monkey Island back in the sixties."

"A cold case from the sixties? Now that's a doozy," Sheriff Lucas said. "Who hired you?"

"Achak Rowtag. His grandfather's name was Ahote Rowtag."

Sheriff Lucas nodded. "I know a little bit about Monkey Island. The Pamunkey Indians used it as a camp for hundreds of years before some rich northerners showed up and built their hunting club."

"Right," Angie said. "Ahote worked there as a guide. He disappeared and his body was never found."

"So you went out there to look around?"

"Correct."

"That island is a rookery. It's off limits to the public. Who gave you permission?"

"The Mackey Island National Wildlife Refuge. I've got the permission papers in my car if you want to see them."

Sheriff Lucas waved his hand in front of his face. "Not necessary. So did you find anything?"

Angie patted the pouch on her hoodie. "We believe we found the evidence that could break the case. It's a note written by the murderer."

"Ain't that a jaw-dropper." The sheriff twisted the end of his mustache. "So who tried to kill you?"

"The same guy who murdered Ahote Rowtag. His name is Chandler Crane."

"Whoa! He'd be older than Julius Ceasar."

"That's true, but he had help from his grandson Arnold Crane. They followed us out to the island."

"How'd he try to croak you?"

"With a large knife. He intended to offer me as a human sacrifice."

The sheriff elbowed his deputy. "Are you getting any of this?"

"Yes sir." He lifted the pen from the pad. "I'm keeping up."

"Good, because it's a whale of a tale." He looked from face to face. "Now are you-all sure this old timer Crane was the one with the knife?"

"Well . . ." Goldbluff said, "he *was* wearing a costume, but that's who he claimed to be."

"A Halloween costume?"

"More like a ceremonial costume," Mee Mee said. "He wore a hooded black robe and had painted his face to look like a skull."

"That's spooky." The deputy stopped writing. "Sounds like the Grim Reaper."

Sheriff Lucas chuckled. "Sorry for laughing, but this *sounds like* an episode of Scooby Doo."

"I don't find it funny," Angie said. "The creep was ready to plunge that knife into my heart until the moccasin bit his grandson."

"Shooooweee!" The sheriff shook his head. "Do you mean to tell me that at just the right moment a snake comes along and bites the boy?"

"It's the truth, Sheriff," Mee Mee said. "I'm the one who tossed the snake at him."

Sheriff Lucas tilted his Stetson hat back, rubbed his forehead, took a deep breath and blew it out with a whistle. "Do you toss venomous snakes at people often?"

Mee Mee shrugged. "Only on special occasions."

"Guess you don't look a gift snake in the mouth." The sheriff turned and faced the sound. "Who fell off the boat?"

"Arnold Crane," Angie said.

"The snakebite victim?"

Angie nodded.

"So the old guy in the Halloween costume is still at large?"

"He took off when Arnold dropped his gun," Mee Mee said. "I picked up the gun and held it on Arnold."

"You must have an attraction to lethal weapons . . . like moccasins and guns."

Mee Mee raised her eyebrows. "They do have a certain allure."

The sheriff rubbed his chin. "I don't know what to think about all this. Let me take a look at that note you found."

Angie reached into her pouch, pulled out the faded paper, unfolded it and handed it to him. Mee Mee directed her light at the images.

Sheriff Lucas frowned. "This looks like a reject drawing from a kindergarten art class."

"Those are Maya hieroglyphs," Angie said. "Chandler Crane claims to be a reincarnated Maya priest."

The sheriff lowered his eyebrows. "This better not be some hairbrained Halloween prank." He handed Angie back the yellowed note.

"No, sir, Sheriff." Angie folded the paper and put it back in her pouch. "There's a crystal skull cult that meets in one of the old beach houses in Nags Head. All this ties into that cult."

"Crystal skull cult?" He gave Angie a doubletake. "I think I smell a flaming bag of dog crap. Now listen, young lady, you've got the Coast Guard out there trolling the sound. And here we are taking time out on a busy Halloween night to investigate what seems like a bad practical joke."

Angie furrowed her brow. "When Arnold Crane's body washes up on shore, you'll know we're not making this up. Check his wrist. You'll find fang marks. Are you going to do anything about his grandfather?"

"What's his name?"

"His name is Chandler Crane."

"If a dead guy with a snakebite floats ten toes up, we'll put out an APB for the Geriatric Grim Reaper. Until then, you're lucky I'm giving you the benefit of the doubt."

Angie bit her lip and narrowed her eyes.

Mee Mee said, "Sheriff, do you need anything else from us. It's almost midnight, and we're exhausted."

He eyed his deputy. "Check their IDs, get all their contact information, and let's head home before the Mystery Machine shows up. I don't have any Scooby Doo treats on me." He turned and walked to the Jeep Grand Cherokee.

After the deputy took down their information, he nodded apologetically and hurried to the sheriff's car.

As Angie watched the vehicle pull away, she said, "We're not going to get much help from the Currituck County cops. Chandler Crane is free to wander."

"Hopefully," Mee Mee said, "he doesn't wander in our direction."

"He just might." Goldbluff said. "He's a man obsessed.

Besides that, he's old. What's he got to lose?"

Angie nodded. "And he wants to get his hands on that blue skull."

Goldbluff tilted his head toward the road. "We better get back to the Crane house. They'll be wondering what happened to us."

Mee Mee raised a finger. "I wonder how much Olivia and Charlotte know about all this."

"Obviously," Angie said, "Arnold got to Charlotte and found out about the AI guy's revelation to me. Once he left, I'm sure they put two and two together."

"It should be an interesting night," Mee Mee said.

Angie placed her hand on her belly. "I'm not going back there tonight."

Mee Mee glanced at her hand. "I don't blame you."

"I want to talk to my husband. Maybe we can get some help from the Dare County cops."

"What about tomorrow?" Goldbluff asked.

"Tell old lady Crane that I'll be there for the final meeting."

"Good." Goldbluff patted her back. "I was hoping you'd say that. You'll have an opportunity to present your evidence. I have a feeling someone dabbled with my capsules when I went on a beach walk with Charlotte. Hopefully, my trail cam caught them in the act. I'll bring the USB stick."

"We'll see if that shakes them up." Angie eyed Mee Mee. "Are you coming home with me?"

"No. I want to stay at the Crane house and keep my eye on things. Don't worry about me. When the sheriff showed up, I hid Arnold's gun." She walked to the pine tree next to the car and picked up the Glock. "I'll prop a chair against my bedroom door tonight. If Chandler Crane comes to call, I'll be locked and loaded."

"You're a brave lady." Angie shifted her gaze to Goldbluff. "Keep an eye on her for me."

He shook his head. "I'm hoping she'll keep an eye on me."

"Call me if anything happens."

"You'll be the first to know." Mee Mee walked over and grasped his elbow with her free hand. "Come on, Mr. Goldbluff, I'm riding back with you."

Angie watched them walk to the old pickup, get in and drive away. *I'm lucky to be alive.* She turned and headed to her car. *I need a night cuddling with my husband. A thousand nights.* She stepped into her Civic, started the engine and drove through the park to Route 12. *What time is it?* She glanced at the digital clock on her dashboard — 12:02. *Two minutes after midnight. The witching hour has begun.* She turned right and headed south.

During the long stretch between Corolla and Duck, she recalled the faded paper with the Maya drawings. She hadn't noticed any markings on the map at the bottom that would indicate the location of a body. However, the words written under the map were chilling: *The sacrifice has been offered.* Now she faced a major consideration: Could Honeypot Chen be trusted? Her instincts told her yes. *Maybe the interpretation will refer to a particular symbol on the map. Then again, maybe Sheriff Lucas was right. The drawings might be nothing more than an obsessed man's childish scrawling.* She shook her head. *He claimed to be the Maya high priest Akna. He sure dressed the part. Hopefully, the drawings were derived from Maya symbols that can be deciphered.*

Passing Duck Donuts, she spotted a tall figure wearing a black hooded robe crossing the street about fifty yards ahead. *It's him.* She slowed the Civic as she passed and noticed his silhouette under a spotlight in the Scarborough Faire Shops' parking lot. *What's he doing here? Maybe he moored his boat at one of the docks along the boardwalk across the street.* She hit the brakes and backed up. The figure disappeared into the shadows under the large building that housed the shops.

Large posts suspended the structure, providing plenty of parking underneath. Angie had shopped there several times at the many stores. *He's cutting through under the buildings to avoid being seen. I bet he rented one of the houses in the neighborhood behind the shops. Should I follow him? I need to find out where he's staying. If the Coast Guard finds Arnold's body, Sheriff Lucas said he'd follow through with an arrest.* She drove another fifty yards and made a left on Scarborough Lane which led to the neighborhood behind the shops.

She pulled off on the side of the road near the exit to the shops' rear parking lot and cut the engine. *If I'm right, he'll come this way and head to his rental house.* She focused on the edge of the bushes and trees that blocked the view of the parking lot. *There he is.* The dark figure hurried across the parking lot exit and up Scarborough Lane. The road ascended a hill for about forty yards. When he crested the top, she stepped out of the car and slipped the Colt .38 out of her pocket.

She jogged up the hill along the edge of the trees. To the left she spotted a medium-sized three-story house. A light from the front porch illuminated a silver Ford F-150 with a boat trailer parked along the side of a wide driveway. He hurried across the driveway and up the steps to the porch. He didn't enter the front door but skirted around the corner. *He's entering through a side door.* Like a ninja, Angie did her best to hustle across the driveway and up the steps with soundless footfalls.

She pressed her back against the wall to the right of the door and edged to the corner. Tilting her head, she listened and heard soft scraping sounds. *What's he doing? Can't he find his key?* More scrabbling sounds followed. *Now's my chance.* She stepped around the corner and raised her pistol. "Don't move, or I'll shoot." When he raised his arms, she noticed an object in his right hand.

"P-Please don't shoot me. I didn't mean any harm."

His voice sounded familiar.

"Drop whatever you're holding and kick it in my direction."

He dropped the object, and it thudded on the deck. He kicked it, and it tumbled across the wooden flooring and into the light at her feet. It was a . . . bar of soap.

"Y-You're the lady in the c-car." His voice cracked like a short-circuited speaker. "I didn't know you lived here. I'm sorry. I'll clean your windows."

Angie lowered her gun, feeling the flush of embarrassment on her cheeks. "Come this way and step into the light."

The teenager walked in her direction as she backed around the corner.

She stopped by the door. "Stay right there."

He halted.

"Where's your scythe?"

"I-I took it home after trick or treating."

"Take off your hood and your mask."

He pulled back his hood, pinched the bottom of his rubber skeleton mask and peeled it over his acne-plagued face.

"How old are you?"

"Sixteen."

"Where do you live?"

He pointed to his left. "M-my parents are renting a b-beach house right down the street."

"Bring your parents back up here with a bucket of soap and water to clean these windows or else you're in big trouble." She thumbed toward the steps. "Get going."

"Yes, Ma'am,"

He sidestepped by her, trotted down the stairs and ran up Scarborough Lane.

He won't be back. She inserted the .38 special into her jeans pocket. *I don't believe I almost shot a kid who was soaping windows. It's the witching hour alright.* She descended the steps and crossed the driveway. Suddenly, she felt an odd craving for chocolate ice cream. *Man, am I hungry.* As she walked down the road to her car, she patted her belly. *I guess you're the one who's hungry. One day you'll be sixteen. I heard raising a teenager is harder than nailing jello to a tree.* She took in a deep breath. *I know one thing: I want to live to find out.* She swung open the door, climbed in the car and drove home.

Chapter 32
Interpretation Anyone?

When Angie turned into her driveway, she felt relieved to see Joel's Ram truck. *He's home for the night.* She checked the digital time on the dashboard — 2:11. *Thank God I didn't fall asleep on the long stretch between the Marc Basnight Bridge and Buxton.* She parked beside the pickup, got out of the car and tromped up the steps to the front door. *He'll be shocked to see me.* She inserted her key and entered.

The yellow lab barked and scrambled into the kitchen.

"It's just me, Rocky. Joel! I'm home!"

About ten seconds later he stepped out of the bedroom into the lighted hallway wearing only his plaid flannel boxer shorts. "Hey, Angie. I never expected to see you here tonight. Is everything alright?"

"I don't know." She raked her fingers through her hair. "Everything is half crazy."

He walked to her and spread his arms. "You look like you need a hug."

"I could use a good hug." She wrapped her arms around his waist as he drew her close. She felt like crying but held back her tears. The warmth of his bare skin and musky smell calmed her.

The yellow lab peered up at them with anxious eyes.

He kissed her forehead. "What happened?"

"You won't believe half of it."

"Sure, I will."

"The Currituck County Sheriff didn't."

"Why not?"

"Like I said, it's half crazy. I couldn't go back to that house tonight. I needed to be with you."

He gripped her shoulders and took a step back. "Let me get you a big glass of milk. We'll sit down at the kitchen table, and you can tell me all about it."

"I'm craving chocolate ice cream."

"Your wish is my command." He led her to the Formica table and pulled out one of the retro chairs. "Plant your bottom right there, and I'll scoop out the ice cream."

She sat and stretched against the back of the chair. "The big bowls are in the top of the cupboard."

"A big bowl it is."

In less than two minutes Joel delivered the ice cream and sat at the table across from her. Rocky laid next to his chair. Between mouthfuls, she recounted the events of the evening: the discovery of the location of the whiskey bottle; borrowing the boat to get out to Monkey Island; confronting Arnold and taking the note; Chandler Crane's attempt at human sacrifice; Goldbluff's arrival and the chaos that followed after Mee Mee tossed the moccasin.

Joel sat back and blinked several times. "Holy stromboli! That's one heck of a bumpy night."

"Especially for Arnold Crane. Too bad for him Isaac's boat didn't have seat belts."

"I wonder if the Coast Guard found his body?"

Angie shrugged. "I don't know. Sometimes it takes several days for bacteria in the gut to produce enough gas to make a corpse float."

"What about the creep with the knife?"

"Sheriff Lucas didn't believe my story. He won't do anything about Chandler Crane until Arnold's body is found."

"That weirdo could be lurking anywhere."

"Do you think Sheriff Walton would alert the Dare County force to keep their eyes open? Maybe assign a couple deputies to stake out the Crane house?"

Joel wobbled his head. "I'll ask him, but I doubt if Crane will be parading around in a Maya high priest outfit. I'll need a better description of him."

Angie clasped her hands to the top of her head. "I could tell you what he looked like when he was younger, but he's old now. A person's looks change. He had a skull painted on his face. He's about six feet tall and in good shape for an old fart. I don't know the color of his hair or even if he's bald." She lowered her arms.

"That's not much to go on." He reached across the table and grasped her hand. "Listen, I'm sure Sheriff Walton will give me some slack if I tell him what's going on. I'll patrol the neighborhood as long as you're at the Crane house."

She smiled. "That makes me feel better."

"Better yet, you don't have to go back to that house."

"Yes, I do. Olivia Crane challenged us to come up with evidence to back up our suspicion of murder." She patted her hoodie pouch. "I've got Chandler Crane's note right here. There's a Guardian at the gathering who may know how to interpret Maya hieroglyphs. I'm hoping he can help us read the note."

"So you don't think the other Guardians are involved in the death of Goldbluff's uncle?"

"No. They may be charlatans, a few might even be true believers, but I don't think any of them are murderers. The Crane family has cornered the market on that misdeed."

"What time are you leaving tomorrow?"

"About ten."

Joel tightened his lips and bobbed his head. "I'll leave about nine and check in with Sheriff Walton. I doubt if he'll complain if I start my shift early and work a few extra hours. I'll be cruising the neighborhood before you get there."

"Thanks, Joel. I knew I could count on you."

"Are you ready to hit the sack, Honey Cake?"

"Overdue. Hope you don't mind, but I'm too exhausted to take a shower."

"Not at all."

"Maybe we can save water and take one together in the morning."

"I'll be up for that."

"Hope you don't mind sleeping next to a grimy girl."

Joel grinned. "I've never been afraid to get my hands dirty."

As they headed for the bedroom, Joel ordered Rocky to go lay down on his doggy cushion in the family room. The lab let out a whimper but obeyed. Angie closed the bedroom door, stripped off her clothes, left them in a pile on the floor, and crawled into bed. In less than ten minutes she fell asleep in her husband's arms.

The next morning after they showered and dressed, Joel cooked a big pancake, scrambled eggs and bacon breakfast. Angie ate enough for two. Drinking her second cup of coffee, she told him about the teenage Grim Reaper.

Joel shook his head. "That boy's luckier than a sunscreen salesman at a nude beach."

"You got that right. I had a nervous trigger finger last night."

"Make sure you take your gun with you this morning."

"It's in my jacket pocket along with the note." Angie checked her watch. "It's a few minutes after nine."

Joel scooted out his chair and stood. "I better get going."

She got to her feet, circled the table, put her hands on his shoulders and gave him a long kiss.

He caressed her cheek. "I love you, Honey Cake."

"Do you know how much I love you?"

"More than bacon?"

She smiled. "I love you so much, I'd walk barefoot across a carpet full of Legos to scratch your back."

He glanced at the ceiling. "I can see that happening in a couple years."

She planted the side of her head against his chest. "This house will be filled with Legos, Barbies and stuffed animals."

He laughed. "Or Legos, toy trucks and plastic army men."

"Maybe both."

"Wouldn't that be a dynamite double-helping." He kissed her again and headed for the door. "Come on, Rocky!"

The yellow lab trotted out of the family room and followed him out the door to his truck.

She returned to the kitchen table, sat on the vinyl padded chair and took a sip of coffee. *Coming home was the right choice. I'm back on solid ground.* She savored the last few drops. *What would I do without him?* Words echoed in her mind from the pastor's message during their marriage ceremony: *Love always protects, always trusts, always hopes, always perseveres. Love never fails.* She smiled, arose and walked to the bedroom. *I guess love isn't finding someone to live with. It's finding someone you can't live without.*

Before she left the house, she slipped into her Columbia fleece jacket with the deep pockets. She checked the right pocket for the Colt .38 and the left one for the note. *Good.* She took a deep breath. *Just making sure everything is in place. I'm good to go.* She headed out the back door to her car. On the drive north along Route 12, a memory from the night before kept invading her thoughts: the large knife hovering above her chest in the hand of the hooded maniac. She patted her right pocket again and felt the form of the gun. *Lord, I pray he wouldn't be crazy enough to show up at the Crane house today.* She thought about her husband cruising the neighborhood. *If he does, Joel will be there to stop him. Love always protects.*

Crossing the Marc Basnight Bridge over the Oregon inlet, she sensed a daunting isolation. The Atlantic Ocean stretched out to the blue-gray horizon on the right, and the wide Croatan Sound extended to the misty North Carolina mainland on the left. Her little Honda Civic ascended the long strip of cement and steel above the clash of sound and sea waters. As the car descended toward the Nags Head side of the bridge, she caught sight of the abandoned Oregon Inlet Lifesaving Station with its lookout tower. The lonely structure loomed a few hundred feet from the edge of the ocean. It stood as a bygone testament to the struggle between life and death. She stared at the top of the tower. The white frames around the dark windows and the white wooden railing gave the parapet the appearance of a skull. A chill rushed through her, and she refocused on the descent to Nags Head.

When she arrived at the Crane house, she caught sight of Isaac shoveling mulch onto a bed of daffodils at the bottom of the steps. She parked behind a silver Audi sedan, got out of the car and hurried toward him. The sun had broken through a spattering of clouds, warming the late morning air.

He wiped his forehead with a handkerchief, leaned on his shovel and eyed her. "Good to see you made it back in one piece."

"It wasn't easy," she said. "I wanted to thank you for lending Goldbluff your boat. He's one of the reasons I made it back . . . in one piece."

"He told me about it. Old Man Crane came calling for your heart."

"Literally."

"Did you find what you were looking for?"

She extracted the faded paper from her jacket pocket and unfolded it. "Did you ever see symbols like these before?"

He nodded. "They're Maya pictograms. There're several books on the shelves in the great room filled with them. Chandler Crane used to study those books for hours."

"I need an interpreter. How well do you know Honeypot Chen?"

He wavered his hand. "A little."

"Can he be trusted?"

"He seems okay. I don't think he's made a pact with the devil like Arnold and the old man. He definitely knows the ancient Mayan language."

Angie heard a horn beep and glanced up to see a sheriff's cruiser pass slowly on Virginia Dare Trail. *That's got to be Joel. He's probably circled the block five times by now.* She shifted her attention back to Isaac. "Could you do me a favor?"

"Another one? What do you want now?"

"If Chandler Crane comes to call, whack him in the back of the head with that shovel."

He winked. "I'll give it my best shot."

Angie mounted the steps, crossed the porch and entered the house. In the entrance hall she spotted a short man with white hair that lapped over his ears. He stared at a photograph in the corner. His white Nehru-collar shirt and white straight-legged pants gave him the appearance of a Hare Krishna holy man. *That's Chen. He's looking at the Ahote photo.*

She stepped next to him and touched his elbow. "Mr. Chen?"

He snapped out of his reverie and faced her. "Yes."

"That's an interesting old picture, isn't it?"

He nodded. "It is one that hides secret."

"What kind of secret?"

"I'm not sure." He patted his chest. "But my heart tells me something not right."

"Your heart speaks the truth to you."

He lifted his silver all-seeing-eye pendant attached to the cord of his necklace. "Ever since you claimed Gavin Goldbluff was murdered, my heart has felt no peace."

"There's been more than one murder."

He glanced over his shoulder at the photograph. "I sense truth of your words, but feelings don't prove anything."

She reached into her pocket, withdrew the faded paper, unfolded it and handed it to him. "Do these hieroglyphs mean anything to you?"

He studied the images for a couple minutes. Then he raised his head and met her gaze, his eyes intense. "These symbols speak of human sacrifice and body buried in secret place. They speak of murder." He folded the paper and gave it back to her.

"Do they indicate where the body is buried?"

He frowned but nodded. "Yes."

"We'll talk later." Angie tucked the note back into her jacket pocket.

"Excuse me!" a woman's voice called from behind them.

Angie about-faced and saw Charlotte standing at the end of the hallway.

"My grandmother wants to talk to you in private. She says it's urgent."

Chapter 33
Below in the Darkness

Charlotte led Angie down the hallway and made a right into the dining area. She walked into the kitchen and passed between a preparation table and a vintage gas stove. Just beyond a stainless steel refrigerator, she halted and motioned toward a wooden door. "She's waiting for you in there."

"What's this about?"

Charlotte shrugged. "I don't know." She reached and opened the door.

Olivia Crane sat in her wheelchair in the back of a large pantry. A bare lightbulb hanging from a wire in the middle of the ceiling lit the room. Shelves on both sides were stocked with can goods, foodstuffs, dishes and cookware. To the right a narrow door broke up the shelving. Angie entered, and Charlotte closed the door behind her.

Angie raised her chin slightly. "You wanted to speak to me?"

She nodded.

"What about?"

"Where's my grandson?"

"How should I know?"

"He left soon after you disappeared yesterday."

"So."

"Charlotte told me about her virtual playmate and the whiskey bottle."

"I see." *She's trying to find out how much I know.*

"He didn't want you to get to that bottle first."

Angie narrowed her eyes. "I'm guessing you didn't either."

"Why do you say that?"

"I met your husband last night."

"And . . . ?"

"He said you are the one who turned him into a monster."

The lines on the old woman's face tightened. "Of course, he blames me."

"You must have pressured him to torture Ahote Rowtag, but that didn't work."

Her body stiffened. "You don't know what you're talking about."

"Ahote didn't divulge where he buried the blue skull. Then your husband went full-on Maya high priest and sacrificed him. You are an accomplice to murder."

"I didn't kill Ahote Rowtag."

"No, but you twisted the killer's arm and then found that note. Maya priests documented their sacrifices with pictographs. You decided to put the documentation into that whiskey bottle and hide it."

"Why would I do that?"

"It was your powerplay to gain control over your abusive husband. You wanted to be the Skull of Doom's Guardian."

"You can't prove any of this."

Angie patted her left jacket pocket. "Oh yes, I can. I've got the documentation."

"That's all I needed to know." The old woman took a deep breath and smiled eerily. "My grandson will stop you."

"Sorry to tell you this, but your grandson is dead. He fell into the Currituck Sound during the storm last night and drowned."

Her eyes widened. "An imposter like you cannot fathom the power we true Guardians possess." Her irises rolled up in her head, revealing only the whites. "The power of resurrection."

The side door opened, and a hulking figure stepped into the room between Angie and the old woman.

He aimed a large handgun with a silencer attached to the barrel at her. "Put your hands up," Arnold Crane said, "and don't make a sound."

Her heart jackhammered in her chest as she lifted her arms. She noticed a bandage on his right wrist, the hand holding the gun. *He swam under water and made it to shore. His grandfather must have met up with him and administered the antivenom.*

"Keep your hands up and hold still." He reached into her jacket pocket and pulled out the note. Then he checked her other pocket, removed the Colt .38 and handed it to his grandmother. "Hang onto this."

She placed the gun in a side compartment of her wheelchair. "Do what you must do."

He motioned toward the dark doorway. "Keep your hands up and go down the stairs."

As she edged by the musclebound man, she caught a glimpse of the old woman's vengeful visage. She looked like a horrid witch from a Vincent Price movie. Turning, Angie focused on the steps that descended into a faintly lit ground floor room. Muffled moaning and groaning lamented from the shadows below.

Arnold poked the silencer into the middle of her back. "Get going."

She started down the steps. *Should I scream? No. He'll shoot me, and no one will hear the shot.* As she neared the bottom, she spied a wooden table with three lit candles. The candles' flames cast wavering shadows against the walls revealing a variety of tools and hardware items: rakes, hoes, clippers, tree saws, cans of paint, brooms. A black figure stood next to a door beyond the table. Cracks of light edged the doorframe. The silhouette stepped forward, and the candlelight licked the skull-painted face of the hooded figure.

He raised his knife and stabbed it into the middle of the table among the three candles. "One by one a light will go out for each of you."

Angie glanced over her shoulder and saw Mee Mee and Goldbluff hanging by their wrists from ropes near the back wall. Both were gagged, and their toes barely touched the cement floor.

"We saved a space for you," Arnold said.

"You can't get away with this. My husband is a Dare County deputy. He's surveilling this house."

Chandler Crane laughed. "I don't fear your husband. He's a paperboy sent by a smalltown publisher to request an overdue payment."

She faced Arnold. "Your grandfather is a nutcase. He'll die waiting to be executed, but you'll face the electric chair."

"Shut your ugly trap," Arnold scowled.

"The world is about to end," Crane said, "and you threaten the next Guardian of the Skull of Doom with judgment? You have no idea what the future holds for my grandson."

"You're crazier than a Scientologist on crack."

The old man yanked the knife from the table. "Enough of your blasphemy."

Arnold held up the faded paper. Here's the note from the whiskey bottle."

"Give it to me."

He reached across the table and handed the paper to his grandfather. Crane unfolded it, pinched it by a corner and lowered it into the flame of the nearest candle. As the fire leapt up, consuming the note, he dropped it onto the middle of the table.

Angie watched it burn, turn black and crumble into ashes. She tightened her lips and tensed her eyebrows. *Honeypot Chen still knows where the body is buried.*

Crane studied her face. "Your evidence has gone up in smoke."

Angie remained silent.

His eyes narrowed to slits. "She knows something."

Arnold glared at her. "Do you know where the body is buried?"

"No."

"She's lying," Crane said.

"It doesn't matter. She'll be dead soon."

"Bring her here, and I'll gag her," Crane ordered.

Arnold gripped her shoulder and directed her toward the table.

The knob on the exterior door jiggled. "Who's in there?" a harsh voice demanded. A loud thud sent the door flying open.

Angie hammered her fist against Arnold's bandaged wrist, and the gun tumbled across the table and onto the floor. Arnold howled and grabbed his wrist. She dove toward the shelving and scoured the floor for the gun but didn't see it. Looking up, she caught sight of a shovel blade as it whacked the hooded head of Chandler Crane. His body slammed onto the tabletop, scattering the candles. He flipped over the table and landed next to Angie faceup. From the light streaming in from the doorway, she could see he was unconscious.

Isaac swung the shovel at Arnold, but he blocked it with his good arm. He managed to grab the handle, yank Isaac toward him and land a hard left uppercut to the chin. Isaac crumpled to the floor. Angie scrambled to her feet and shot out the open door into the sunlight.

Chapter 34
The Chase

A tall dune blocked the view of the ocean. She angled to the left and circled the back of the house. *Joel's out there somewhere.* Glancing over her shoulder, she spotted the brawny form of Arnold Crane about thirty yards back. She churned her legs as fast as they would go, but it felt like a slow-motion dream. She rounded the front corner of the house, cut in between the parked cars and dashed down the driveway. As she passed her Honda Civic, she hesitated. Arnold's thudding footfalls ended any consideration of seeking refuge there. She turned right on Virginia Dare Trail, knowing Joel would still be circling the block. *There he is!* About fifty yards away, the black and white Ford Interceptor headed in her direction.

She glanced over her shoulder. Arnold had closed to within twenty yards. She sprinted down the middle of the street toward the Interceptor. When she neared to within fifteen yards, she cut sharply right onto the sidewalk. She heard a squeal of tires, a loud thud and a crash. She slowed her pace and looked back. Arnold rolled over the windshield, bounced across the roof and tumbled off the trunk onto the street. Joel had swerved, hit him and slammed into a telephone pole. The impact had splintered the pole in the middle, but the wires kept it suspended.

She skidded to a stop. "Joel!" The horn blared and steam shot out of the damaged front end like a geyser. He hung over the steering wheel. *The airbag knocked him unconscious.* Arnold lay on his back. He lifted his head, blinked, craned his neck and focused on her. *He has to be seriously injured.* He rolled onto his stomach and pushed himself onto his hands and knees. *He's . .*

. he's getting up. He stood, staggered a few steps toward her and transitioned into a limping run.

She dashed across a yard patched with seagrass and sand in the direction of the nearest house. *He's not human. I can't outrun him.* The unpainted cedar-sided structure stood on thick posts in front of a wall of dunes. A Chevy Traverse was parked in the driveway near the bottom of the steps. *Please, God, let the front door be unlocked.* Heaving in air, she double-timed it up the steps and across the porch. Several pumpkins and a cornstalk stood next to the door, and a life-size skeleton sat on a stool to the left of the window. Arnold thundered up the steps. She turned the knob and pushed the door open. As she stepped inside, he crested the top and lunged toward the door. She slammed it shut and engaged the deadlock as he banged against it.

Panting like a run-down hare, she heard footsteps pattering behind her.

"Who are you?" a young girl's voice said.

Turning, she saw a ghostly figure and let out a gasp. The specter had long black hair, a pale face and dark circles under her eyes. A line of blood trickled down her forehead. She seemed to hover just above the hem of her spreading white dress.

"Don't be afraid. I'm not a ghost."

Angie shook her head. *It's a Halloween costume.* "I-I-I'm in t-t-trouble," Angie stammered.

A loud thud shook the door, and the girl's body tensed.

"My name is Angie. There's a man on the porch who wants to hurt me. Is there some place in your house I can hide?"

The girl nodded. "Sometimes I hide in the attic when we play hide and seek."

A loud thud blasted the door again, but it held steady.

"Follow me." She spun around and ran into the next room.

As Angie took off after her, she heard a crash and jangling of broken glass. Glancing to her right, she saw a stool tumbling across the entry room—the skeleton's stool. *He's coming through the window.*

The ghastly girl turned left and bounded up a staircase.

"Hurry," Angie said. "He's coming."

She turned at the top of the steps and dashed down a long hallway. Keeping pace, Angie noticed several doors on both sides. The girl slid to a stop at the end of the hall and cut to the right. She stopped on a landing at the bottom of a steep stairway that led to the third floor. "Come on," she huffed. "The attic is up there." Her white dress swished as she scurried up the steps.

An open doorway at the top led into a spacious room. At the apex of a gable, a small window let in a shaft of light that lit the dusty floor just beyond the doorway. Angie made out the dark shapes of old furniture and racks of clothes situated randomly around the murky space. *It's a storage room. Please, God, I pray he doesn't come up here.*

The girl pointed to the right. "Over there is a good hiding place." She hurried around a rack of clothes and dropped to her hands and knees behind a stack of boxes.

Angie knelt beside her. *What have I gotten this little girl into?* She placed her hand on her belly and took a few calming breaths. *Protect us, God, please protect us.*

"There're lots of rooms in this house," the girl whispered. "He might not find us up here. Are the police coming?"

"Yes. They'll be here soon," Angie said in a low voice. "What is your name?"

"Sammy."

"Thanks for helping me, Sammy. Where're your parents."

"My dad moved away, but Mom is in the downstairs bathroom getting ready for the party."

"A Halloween party?"

"Yes. All my cousins are coming over from Elizabeth City."

Angie closed her eyes and lowered her head. *I need to call 911 and let them know where we are.* She tugged her phone out of her jeans pocket. "What's your address?" she whispered.

Footsteps sounded in the stairwell.

Angie raised her finger to her lips.

The girl's eyes grew big.

The footsteps grew louder. Angie rose slightly to see above the boxes and stared at the doorway. *He's almost at the top.* Arnold ascended the last few steps, paused at the top and panned the room. The girl stood. Before Angie could snag her arm, she skirted around the clothes rack. She walked silently through the shadows with her head down toward the shaft of light. Arnold turned in her direction and stiffened. The girl stepped into the light, raised her head and let out a bloodcurdling scream.

Arnold gasped and stepped backwards. His foot slipped off the top step and he tumbled down the stairs. His fall ended with a loud thump and an agonizing wail. Angie rushed by the girl to the top of the steps. Arnold lay on the landing, one leg twisted in an odd direction. When he tried to get up, the twisted leg went sideways, and he let out a hideous howl. He collapsed onto his back, his body trembling.

The girl stepped next to Angie. "Is he okay?"

"No."

"My leg!" Arnold screamed.

"I wouldn't move if I were you," Angie said. "It looks like a compound fracture. If you move, your broken femur might pop right through your skin."

"Help me!" Arnold pleaded. "Call an ambulance."

"Sure thing." Angie raised her phone. "I want you in good health when the judge sends you to the chair."

Chapter 35
A Force of Five

Angie called 911 and reported the wreck, the details of the abduction and the house's address to the dispatcher. The image of her husband draped across the steering wheel flashed in her mind. *I need to get back to Joel.* Remembering her encounters with Arnold, she dared not descend the stairs and try to step over him. *Even with a broken leg, he might try something. Please, Lord, watch over my husband.*

A minute passed, and a woman's voice hollered, "Sammy! Where are you? I heard a scream."

Footsteps echoed in the lower hallway. "Don't go near that man!" Angie yelled. "He's dangerous! Sammy's up here in the attic with me! The cops are coming!"

"Sammy!"

"I'm okay, Mom."

Arnold moaned, "That little devil about gave me a heart attack."

"Don't expect us to feel sorry for you," Angie jeered.

In less than five minutes, Sheriff Dugan Walton arrived along with a deputy. The redheaded lawman stood at the bottom of the steps and eyed Arnold. "Looks like you took a long walk off a short plank."

Arnold groaned, "I need help, Sheriff. My leg's broke in half."

"Did you check on Joel?" Angie interrupted.

The sheriff tilted his trooper hat back and gazed up at her. "He looked okay to me. The paramedics are checking him out right now."

"How about Mee Mee and the two guys?"

"I sent Deputy Cloud to find them."

God, let them be safe. Angie let out a big sigh. "Thanks for getting here lickety-split."

Walton winked. "That's the way we do things in Dare County."

"Sheriff," Arnold whined. "I can't take this pain much longer."

"Quit blabbering and keep still! The paramedics will be here in a minute."

With the lawmen there, she descended the stairs holding Sammy's hand. They sidestepped around Arnold, and the girl ran a few yards down the hall to her mother's waiting arms. They appeared to be quite the combination, the ghost girl and her raven-haired mom dressed like Morticia Addams.

Angie turned toward Sheriff Walton. "I need to make sure Joel's okay."

He waved her away. "You head on down. We'll interview you after we're done here."

She took a few steps and faced the mother. "Ma'am, you've got a brave daughter." Angie knelt and cupped the girl's ghostly face in her hands. "I doubt if you realize it, but you just saved my life."

Sammy gave her a wide smile. "I tried to act like the scary girl in that movie."

Angie nodded. "It was an Oscar worthy performance."

"She's my little Drew Barrymore," her mom gushed.

Angie stood. "I've got to get going." She hurried along the hallway and down the steps to the family room. As she passed through the entry hall, she caught sight of the window Arnold had destroyed. *What an idiot. Did he really believe killing me would solve all his problems? It takes a special kind of crazy to go into murder mode over this occult baloney.* A shudder convulsed her shoulders. *But you read about nutcase murders in the papers every day.*

As soon as she stepped out the front door, she spotted two E-squads, one in front of the house and one thirty yards down the street where Joel hit the telephone pole. Two EMTs carried an ambulance stretcher up the porch steps. She opened the door for them. "Go into the next room and make a left up the stairs. The injured perp is at the end of the hall."

Wearing a blue Polo shirt and shades, the young guy in front nodded. "I hope he's a skinny dude."

"No such luck. He's a gorilla."

"Great," said the heavyset guy toting the backend. "Just what my aching back needs."

"It's alright with me if you drop him."

She closed the door and eyed the blue and white striped ambulance parked by the wrecked Interceptor. Joel sat on the back bumper, and one of the EMTs tested his vision by making him follow his index finger from side to side. She scurried down the steps and jogged over to them.

When Joel spotted her, he stood and spread his arms. "Are you okay?"

"I'm still alive and kicking." She gave him a good hug. "How about you?"

He let out a sharp breath. "My ribs are a little sore."

"Sorry." She broke the embrace and stepped back. "And you've got a nasty knot on your forehead."

A middle-aged EMT wearing black-framed glasses cleared his throat. "We want to take him to the ER and get that bump checked out, but he's a stubborn mule."

Angie stomped her foot. "Joel! Go to the hospital. Head injuries can be dangerous. I'll be along as soon as I'm done here."

"Whatever you say, Honey Cake. But I want to know what happened to that big goon who was chasing you. I swerved to hit him and thought I might have killed him."

Angie shook her head. "You barely scratched his knees. The little girl that lives in that house over there . . . " She thumbed over her shoulder. ". . . she broke his leg in half."

"What?"

249

"It's a long story. I'll tell you when I get to the hospital. Where's Rocky?"

"Deputy Liberatore came by and picked him up. He seems fine."

"C'mon Deputy Thomas," the other EMT said. His shaved head and Fu Manchu mustache made him look like a bouncer. "Step up in the back here, and we'll get some ice on that bump."

The bald EMT secured Joel in the back of the ambulance and closed the door. Blaring its siren, the ambulance sped away. Angie turned toward the house and saw Mee Mee, Goldbluff and Isaac heading in her direction. As they walked toward her, Mee Mee rubbed her wrists, and Isaac shifted his jaw back and forth. They stopped in front of her.

Goldbluff pointed at the wrecked cruiser. "What happened over there?"

"That's where I introduced Arnold Crane to my husband."

"Is Joel alright?" Mee Mee asked.

"I think so. How about you three?"

Goldbluff grinned. "Our arms are about two inches longer, but we survived thanks to Isaac."

"I'm guessing you two were lured into the pantry like me."

Mee Mee nodded. "Then Old Lady Crane unleashed her back-from-the-dead grandson on us."

"What happened to Chandler Crane?"

Isaac said, "He and I regained consciousness about the same time. He picked up his knife, but I still had my shovel. He took off. Guess he didn't want to go two rounds with me."

"Then Isaac untied us," Goldbluff said. "We ran into a deputy out front and told him that Crane was on the loose. He said he'd check around the neighborhood."

"What happened to Arnold?" Mee Mee asked.

Angie recapped the sequence of events that led to Arnold's literal downfall.

Goldbluff chuckled. "Now that's what I call poetic justice: a roided up gym monster done in by a little ghost."

Angie pointed at the Crane house. "I wonder what's happening over there?"

Mee Mee checked her watch. "It's almost noon. Isn't that the deadline Olivia Crane set to present evidence?"

"That's right." Goldbluff extracted a USB stick from his pocket. "I've got Arnold on tape tampering with my capsules."

Mee Mee said, "Too bad Chandler Crane's Maya hieroglyphs went up in flames."

Angie smiled. "I've got a pinch hitter on deck to cover that loss — Honeypot Chen."

Isaac raised his eyebrows. "You showed him the drawing?"

Angie nodded. "He deciphered it and discovered the location of Ahote Rowtag's remains."

Goldbluff pointed his finger at each of them and counted. "If my math is correct, that makes a force of five for the cause of justice."

"Well then," Angie said, "let's go present our evidence."

Chapter 36
The Truth Be Told

Angie tried the handle on the Crane house front door. "It's locked."

Isaac funneled his hand into his pants pocket. "I've got the key." He unlocked the door, and they entered the foyer.

Angie walked to the corner and took the framed photograph of Ahote Rowtag and Chandler Crane off the wall. "A good visual aid always helps when presenting evidence." She led the way down the hall and into the great room.

Olivia Crane sat in her wheelchair near the skull table talking to Charlotte. A siren sounded in the distance. The other seven Guardians had gathered into a couple groups, talking and glancing around the room uneasily. One by one they noticed Angie and her three companions at the back of the room.

"May I have your attention please!" Angie commanded.

The room quieted as the siren faded away.

"Thank you," Angie said. "Yesterday, Olivia Crane challenged us to come up with evidence to prove our allegation that Gavin Goldbluff was murdered. Not only have we acquired proof of that murder, but we also discovered evidence of another cold case murder from fifty years ago." Angie held up the photograph. "The man on the left in this old photograph is Ahote Rowtag. He was murdered and offered as a human sacrifice by the man on the right, Chandler Crane, with coercion from his wife Olivia Crane."

The guardians gasped.

The old woman waved her hands in front of her. "Don't jump to conclusions, my fellow Guardians. You will soon discover that this so-called evidence is nothing but a conspiracy theory." She narrowed her eyes and glared at Angie. "Go ahead. Present your flimsy evidence. True Guardians cannot be swayed by an imposter's ill-conceived speculations. Your house of cards won't stand up to sensible scrutiny."

Angie took a couple steps closer to the skull keepers. "You've heard the sirens and are wondering what's going on in the neighborhood. The ambulance that just departed is taking Olivia Crane's grandson to the hospital. He and his grandfather tried to murder me and my two friends. Fortunately for us, Isaac stopped them."

"Rubbish!" the crone shrieked. "Lies, I tell you. It's all lies."

Angie pointed in the direction of the old woman and Charlotte. "Olivia Crane and her granddaughter lured us into a back room where we were abducted. Why? Because we had the evidence to convict them in a court of law."

Charlotte's eyes widened as she raised her hand to her mouth.

The old woman's lips trembled. "That's easy to say. Show us your evidence."

"It's true," Isaac said. "I'm a witness."

Jeff Goldbluff stepped forward and held up his USB stick. "I have video evidence of Arnold Crane tampering with capsules I placed on the bathroom sink in my room upstairs. He didn't realize his presence triggered a trail camera I had set up behind some toiletries. I am confident that test results will confirm traces of methamphetamine, the same drug used to kill my uncle."

Murmurs rippled among the guardians.

"I didn't know what was going on," Charlotte blurted. "I just did what my grandmother told me to do."

"Shut up, Charlotte," the old woman squawked. "Nothing has been proven yet. Nothing will be proven."

Mee Mee shook her head. "You've got a mounting list of witnesses that say otherwise."

She leaned forward in her wheelchair. "I don't know what my ex-husband and grandson have been up to, but I haven't done anything wrong. You have no proof to implicate me."

Honeypot Chen weaved his way between the Guardians, walked to the back of the room and stood next to Angie. When the room quieted, he said, "I have seen document that tells of murder. It was drawn using Maya symbols many years ago. The pictographs told how god Tohil was conjured and ordered High Priest Akna to offer human sacrifice. It also revealed where body is buried."

"Enough of this foolishness," Olivia Crane said. "Show us the document."

Angie tensed her forehead. "You saw your grandson take it from me. Not long after that your ex-husband destroyed it."

The old woman cackled, "That's a convenient claim. Of course, you don't have it. It never existed."

"Why would Honeypot Chen lie? You called him the spiritual leader of the Guardians."

"You deceived him. You showed him a fake a document."

A door directly behind the skull table opened, and a man with a skull-painted face wearing a hooded black robe entered. Two of the women Guardians screamed as he walked to the table. He spread his hands over the skulls. "Do not be afraid, fellow Guardians. I am the Maya High Priest Akna."

Angie handed Mee Mee the photograph, slipped her phone out of her jeans pocket and dialed 911. When the dispatcher answered, she said in a low voice, "This is Angie Stallone. Tell Sheriff Walton to get to the Crane house immediately. Chandler Crane just showed up, and he's got a knife strapped to his belt."

"I'll call him right now," the dispatcher said.

"Thanks."

Crane pointed at her. "We have imposters among us. Do not fear them or the authorities they call upon to protect them. They have no power over us."

Angie shook her head. *He's gone completely bonkers.*

He reached and picked up the blue skull. "The Skull of Truth is now in the hands of its rightful Guardian. My grandson will soon be the Guardian of the Skull of Doom. The Apocalypse is drawing near, but our unity will bring forth the knowledge of the Atlantean Masters. We will show the world the path to salvation and peace."

Angie shouted, "You are a murderer and a fraud!"

He closed his eyes and held the blue skull above his head. "I am the high priest of the god Tohil. You do not know the secrets that have been revealed to me."

"Tell them the truth," Angie insisted. "You tortured and murdered a man to get your hands on that skull. The Skull of Truth requires that you tell the truth."

He lowered the skull and opened his eyes. "Tohil demanded a life in exchange for the next Atlantean skull."

"And your wife pressured you to commit the act. She wanted power over you and turned you into the monster you are. She was the queen, and you became her pawn."

Crane turned and gazed at his wife.

"Don't listen to her, Chandler," Olivia Crane warned. "She has no idea what happened on that island fifty years ago."

"Then tell us what happened," Angie said.

"It's none of your business," the old woman snarled.

Angie took a couple steps toward Crane. "Are you still under her power?"

He shook his head. "No. The document has been destroyed. She has no power over me."

"Then the blue skull demands the truth from its Guardian."

He bobbed his head slowly. "She was upset that I wagered our house to win the Skull of Doom. But I knew the gods were with me, and I won again." He clasped the blue skull to his chest. "When Ahote betrayed me, she became enraged."

"Chandler!" The old woman pounded her fists on the arms of her wheelchair. "Don't say another word!"

"You see," Angie said. "She still has control over you. Did

she order you to fulfill your duties as the high priest?"

"I'm warning you, Chandler, keep your mouth shut," she seethed.

He lowered the skull, placed his hand on top of it and closed his eyes. Nodding, he opened his eyes and met his wife's gaze. "The Skull of Truth says I must tell the truth."

Olivia Crane sprang to her feet, raised a small handgun and fired at her husband. He dropped the skull onto the tabletop and reached for his knife. She fired again. The bullet struck his shoulder. He staggered backwards but regained his balance. Raising his knife, he took a step toward her. She fired repeatedly until the chambers were empty. He clasped his chest and collapsed at her feet. She dropped the gun, and it landed near his head. Blood spread below his side-turned face and puddled around the gun.

Chapter 37
But You Didn't Shoot Him?

"This is a crime scene," Angie warned. "Nobody leaves this room and don't touch anything."

"Crime scene?" Olivia Crane protested. "I shot him in self-defense! He came at me with a knife."

Angie faced her. "You pulled the trigger before he pulled the knife."

"That was a warning shot."

"He was about to betray you. That's why you shot him."

"Nonsense. I had nothing to do with Ahote Rowtag's death."

"We'll let Sheriff Walton decide when he gets here."

Goldbluff approached the body. "Maybe he's not dead. Shouldn't we turn him over and make sure."

Angie eyed the spreading blood. "She pumped four bullets into his heart at close range. Do you want to turn him over and perform CPR?"

Goldbluff shuddered. "I'll pass."

Angie panned the room. The skull keepers appeared pale and shaken. "Anyone else want to volunteer?"

No one came forward.

"Then we'll let the EMT people handle it when they get here."

Charlotte stepped up beside Goldbluff. "Jeff, I swear I didn't know why Grandmother wanted to talk to all of you in private."

He gave her a sideways glance. "Didn't you wonder what happened to us?"

"Yes, but I had no idea where you went."

"I just realized something." He wavered his finger at her. "You sound a lot like your grandmother."

"Please, believe me."

"We'll let Sheriff Walton decide when he gets here. Geesh. Now I'm starting to sound like Detective Stallone."

"God forbid," Angie smirked.

Footsteps echoed down the hall, and Sheriff Walton and his deputy entered the room with their guns drawn.

Angie held up her hands. "Everything is under control, Sheriff."

He walked toward the body, stopped and looked it over.

Angie moved next to him. "That's Chandler Crane."

"I assume he's dead."

"I'd say he's immortally challenged," Mee Mee said. "But that's from a layperson's perspective."

"I'd agree." The lawman tilted his trooper hat back. "For a Grim Reaper, he sure did bleed a lot. Is that the shooter's gun?"

Angie leaned and inspected the weapon. "No."

"His?"

"No."

"Who's then?"

Angie raised her hand. "That would be me."

"But you didn't shoot him?"

"I did not." She pointed at Olivia Crane. "She did."

"In self-defense," the old woman crowed.

Sheriff Walton narrowed his eyes. "Then how did you get your hands on her gun?"

"I'd love to hear the answer to that question," Angie said.

The old woman took a couple slow steps backwards and lowered herself onto her wheelchair. Shifting her focus around the room, she avoided eye contact with anyone. "I . . . I . . . I'm not going to answer any more questions. Charlotte, call my lawyer."

"Mrs. Crane," Mee Mee said, "you're going to need a good lawyer."

Chapter 38
Back to Monkey Island

A few hours later, around three o'clock in the afternoon, Goldbluff drove Angie, Mee Mee, and Honeypot Chen up to the Whalehead Club in Corolla to meet Sheriff Lucas. Angie recognized the pockmarked face of Deputy Ace Austin but couldn't recall the other odd-looking deputy standing next to him. Deputy Austin removed shovels from the back of the sheriff's car, a Jeep Grand Cherokee. Iron gray clouds had invaded the once bright sky, and a brisk wind kicked up choppy waves on the Currituck Sound waters.

As they approached, Sheriff Lucas said, "I hope this ain't another wild goose chase. That body never did show up."

"He showed up," Angie said.

"At the wrong place and wrong time," Mee Mee added.

Sheriff Lucas laughed. "I heard all about it from Sheriff Walton. I'm just jokin' with you."

Angie forced a smile. "We appreciate your assistance with this expedition back to Monkey Island."

"Who knows." He shrugged. "We might solve a cold case today." He stared at the sky. "More than likely, though, we'll just catch a cold."

"Don't be a doubter, Sheriff." Goldbluff placed his hand on Honeypot Chen's shoulder. "My friend here is a Maya shaman. I'll bet a dozen Duck Donuts that he leads us to where the body is buried."

"I'll take that bet."

"I'll do my best for sake of justice," Chen said.

"I'm sure you'll give it the old college try," Sheriff Lucas gibed. "Deputy Bird's boat is docked over at the pond. Let's head on out."

The original boathouse was erected in front of a large pond across the road from the Whalehead Club. Deputy Bird's boat, a white Scout fishing boat with plenty of seating, was moored to a post along the dock near the boathouse. Like the hunting club, the boathouse had been restored to its full 1920s glory in the Art Nouveau style. Its pink exterior, curved rooflines and louvers gave it a whimsical appearance. They followed the sheriff down a boardwalk that edged the pond. Then he turned left and crossed the dock that led to the boat.

After climbing aboard, Sheriff Lucas and the tall deputy took the two seats in the front. Everyone else found a seat in the back except for Deputy Bird. A short guy with a bulldog face, he sat down at the helm in the middle, started the engine and steered the boat toward the outlet.

Angie gazed at the wooden bridge that spanned the outlet. *Wes and I stood on that bridge two years ago during a missing person investigation.* She remembered the crowd that had gathered on the bridge to see the authorities retrieve a body that had washed in from the Currituck Sound. The sight of the half-eaten, bloated corpse had made her sick. *I felt like quitting that day, but I didn't. I've hung in there. I guess I've come a long way since then. Maybe today the Stallone Detective Agency will reach another milestone: solving a murder and bringing peace of mind to a longsuffering family.* She smiled. *I'd like that.*

Honeypot Chen gave her a friendly nod. "You smile like woman who harbors hope."

"Thanks to you, Mr. Chen. I hope we find Ahote's remains so that his relatives can finally have some closure."

They passed under the wooden bridge and headed for the open waters of the sound.

He gave her an assuring smile. "I believe we will."

"It's funny you mention the word 'believe,'" Goldbluff said. "You seem like a reasonable man. Do you really believe in the myth of the Atlantean Thirteen?"

"I believe, Mr. Goldbluff. But whether reality or myth, I seek deeper truths."

"What are the deeper truths?"

"The importance of showing compassion, valuing dignity, offering peace, and expressing kindness."

"So it doesn't matter to you if the legend of the Atlantean Masters is myth or reality?"

"I don't believe faith is history test."

"What do you mean by that?"

"What happened in history is what happened. No one's beliefs line up exactly with historical fact."

Goldbluff shook his head. "I'm confused."

"Were you there when Almighty One created universe?"

"No."

"Neither was I. It happened how it happened."

"I can't argue with that logic."

"Were you there when Maya people built their great cities or when Moses parted Red Sea?"

"I get it," Goldbluff said. "None of us know exactly how it all went down. Faith isn't about getting an A+ on a history test."

The shaman nodded. "Faith is about seeking deeper truths."

"But what about the Cranes? The skulls didn't lead them to deeper truths."

"No. They saw skulls as path to power. Whether politics or religion, power corrupts."

Goldbluff furrowed his brow. "I guess I've never had a passion for politics or religion."

Mee Mee cleared her throat. "Then how'd you get so corrupt?"

"It just comes naturally."

The ride was bumpy but fast. In less than ten minutes they approached the clearing on the east side of the island. When the bow edged onto the bank, Deputy Austin hopped off the front end and tied the Scout up to the same tree to which Goldbluff had moored Isaac's boat. Honeypot Chen was the last person to disembark. Angie and Mee Mee reached up and gave the older man a helping hand down onto the bank.

Sheriff Lucas straightened his Stetson. "Okay, Mr. Shaman, the show is yours."

Chen peered through the thick foliage. "Can someone lead me to main building?"

"Sure thing," Angie said. "Follow me."

"And watch for water moccasins," Mee Mee warned.

Sheriff Lucas chuckled. "I'm sure you'll attract a few."

Pushing the limbs and bushes aside, Angie made her way to the clearing in front of the hunting club. Herons and egrets squawked and flittered above them. Once he caught up to her, Honeypot Chen turned to his right and eyed the outbuilding, a smaller structure that resembled a cabin. Oversized shrubs grew all around it, and branches lay scattered on its roof. Limbs propped a dead fallen tree against the apex of the gable.

Chen pointed to the outbuilding. "Body is buried near big tree on other side of small building."

Angie remembered going in that direction on the day they found the blue skull. "I'll lead the way. I'm familiar with this path.

"Yeah," Sheriff Lucas said. "You can clear out all the spider webs."

Angie worked her way through wax myrtle limbs and bay bushes to the other side of the outbuilding. There she could see the overgrown path that led to the three large trees where they found the crystal skull. A huge live oak grew about twenty feet from the building. *That must be the tree he's talking about.*

Chen walked to the side of the tree and faced north. He took three steps forward into knee-high weeds. Turning to face them, he closed his eyes and nodded. "Body is buried here."

"Okay, boys," the sheriff said, "If the killer disposed his victim like the murderers on *Dateline*, it'll be a shallow grave. Let's hope so for your sakes. Get digging."

"I'd help," Goldbluff said, "but I just had my nails done."

The two deputies gave him an annoyed glance and began to

dig.

Angie pulled Mee Mee aside. "There's the path we followed to the three trees on Ahote's map."

"Let's hope Crane's map is as accurate, and Chen read the symbols correctly. If we find Ahote's remains, I want to stop by the hospital and let Achak know."

Angie nodded. "I'll go with you. Joel is under observation there. Hopefully, they'll release him later this evening."

"Better to be safe than sorry with head injuries."

"Exactly."

After about twenty minutes of watching his deputies dig, Sheriff Lucas became restless. "That ain't no shallow grave. I'd say they've dug down four feet or more."

"Keep digging," Chen said.

The sheriff screwed up his face. I'll give them about five more minutes, and then we're heading home.

Two minutes later the bulldog-faced deputy said, "Sheriff, we hit something. It looks like the top of a skull."

"Don't break it!" The sheriff leaned and looked in the hole. "Great Caesar's ghost. I think that is a skull. Dig around it. Be more careful than a surgeon removing a kidney."

Angie drew near the hole, leaned and watched the two deputies burrow around the skull with their hands. After a few minutes, they freed it from the sandy dirt.

Deputy Austin brushed it off and held it up. "Looky here, Sheriff. The guy had a gold front tooth. I've never seen anyone with a gold *front* tooth."

"Don't get any ideas, Ace," the sheriff said, "You're a deputy, not a dentist."

Deputy Austin grinned, handed the skull to the lawman and said, "Dentists aren't my favorite people."

"Your smile says it all." Sheriff Lucas cradled the skull in his hands and held it up for Angie and the others to see. "I was wrong, Mr. Goldbluff. We are going to solve a cold case today. Good job, Mr. Chen."

"Thank you," the shaman said. "Ahote's spirit called out for justice from very spot."

The sheriff winked. "You nailed it. I'll give the CSI guys a call and let them take over from here."

"Don't forget, Sheriff," Goldbluff said. "You owe me a dozen donuts."

"No problem. I've got a coupon for a free dozen in my wallet. Duck Donuts is good to us. We're one of their best customers."

"We don't call them donuts, though," Ace said.

Goldbluff raised an eyebrow. "What do you call them?"

"Crime fighting power biscuits."

Chapter 39
Closure

Goldbluff turned into the Crane's driveway and parked his Sorento beside Angie's Honda Civic. Angie didn't see any cop cars. *Sheriff Walton must have completed all the interviews and had the body transported to the morgue.* She checked her watch — 4:45. *The skull keepers cleared out like bootleggers at a liquor raid.* A red Chevy Cruise was parked in front of her car. *That one must belong to Mr. Chen.* An old Ford pickup occupied the space beside the garage apartment. Several large boxes sat in the bed. As she stepped out of the SUV, she spotted Isaac descending the apartment steps with two suitcases.

Goldbluff closed the driver's door and walked toward him. "Where're you headed?"

Isaac stopped at the bottom of the steps and lowered the suitcases. "My brother and his wife have a spare room at their house in New Bern. I'll stay with them until this mess gets sorted out."

Mee Mee joined them. "I guess you won't be coming back here."

"Nope. I spent the last forty-five years taking care of this place. I'm officially retired. Think I'll do some traveling."

"Sorry to interrupt, Mr. Isaac," Honeypot Chen said, "but can I go into house and get my things? I need to catch plane back to Mexico."

"Yes, Mr. Chen. The front door is unlocked. I'll be closing up the place as soon as everybody leaves."

"Thank you, sir." Chen turned and headed for the house.

"Did they arrest Mrs. Crane and Charlotte?" Angie asked.

"Yep. Hauled them out of here in handcuffs about two hours ago."

Goldbluff frowned. "Charlotte, too?"

Isaac nodded.

Angie looked askance at him. "You do realize that she was an accomplice to kidnapping."

"True," Goldbluff said, "but she was also very good-looking."

Mee Mee wagged her head. "Deception always comes beautifully wrapped, Mr. Goldbluff."

"But I still enjoy the unwrapping."

Angie cringed. "We've got to get going and make a stop at the Outer Banks Hospital." She turned toward Isaac. "Isaac, I want to thank you for saving our lives. Without you, we'd be taking a dirt nap right now."

"I just followed your instructions."

"My instructions?"

"You said if Chandler Crane shows up, just hit him in the back of the head with a shovel. So I did"

Mee Mee chuckled. "And you did it with such pizzazz."

"Anyway," Angie said, "we certainly appreciate your shovel-handling skills. I wish you the best in wherever you go from here." She tapped Mee Mee on the shoulder. "Let's get our things and get out of here."

"For sure, and there's one thing I definitely don't want to leave behind."

"What's that?"

"Mr. CBP."

Angie rolled her eyes, pivoted and marched toward the house.

After collecting their belongings from the bedroom, they hurried down the stairs and made their way to the great room. Three skulls remained on the round wooden table: the Skull of Doom sat in the middle, and the blue skull lay on his side, teeth to teeth with Rosey near the right edge.

Mee Mee snickered. "Look how Mr. CBP landed when Crane dropped him."

"If they had lips, I'd say they were kissing."

"You do realize that Rosey and Mr. CBP spent the night together."

"Don't go there."

"Just saying." Mee Mee picked up the blue skull, wrapped it in a towel and carefully lowered it into her bowling bag. "Do you want to keep the skull at your house, or would you rather I hang onto it?"

"I don't want that bonehead at my house. You keep it until we find a buyer."

"That's okay with me. I've got a perfect place for it."

"Where's that?"

"I'll take it to the bookstore every day and place it on top of the pyramid stand for my new mystery book display."

Angie laughed. "Maybe Mr. CBP will use his Atlantean powers to draw mystery lovers to your store."

"I'm counting on it."

They hurried through the house and out the front door. Goldbluff ascended the steps as they crossed the porch. At the top, the three paused and faced each other.

"Well, ladies, we've had a couple thrilling days together."

Mee Mee said, "More like spine-tingling days."

"Thanks again," Angie said, "for showing up in the nick of time on Monkey Island and helping us put the Crane family where they belong."

Goldbluff blew on his knuckles. "Just an average day in the life of the Goldbluffer."

Angie raised a finger. "You know, you'd be a lot more tolerable if you weren't so in love with yourself."

"But then I wouldn't be me. Speaking of love, is Rosey still in the great room on the skull table?"

"She's still there," Mee Mee assured him.

"Good. I was hoping the Cranes didn't kidnap her. I'm sure

she'll miss Mr. CBP. Maybe we should get them back together sometime."

"I don't think so." Angie started down the steps. "Rosey was lucky to get a one-night stand."

Goldbluff spread his hands. "There's always the next crystal skull gathering. Maybe we can all get together then."

Mee Mee stopped halfway down the steps and gazed up at him. "If the world doesn't end first."

Goldbluff winked. "Let's hope not."

They crossed the driveway and climbed into the Civic. Angie backed out onto Virginia Dare Trail and headed south. From the Crane house, driving to the Outer Banks Hospital only took a few minutes. After parking in the visitor's lot, they hurried along the sidewalk and under the large portico near the entrance. The sliding doors separated, and they walked into the lobby and headed to the elevator.

Angie pressed the up button. "He wasn't in very good shape when we visited two weeks ago."

"I know, but he's a tough old mule. Sometimes people refuse to die until they are ready."

The elevator doors separated, they stepped inside, and Angie pressed the third-floor button. "So you think he's hanging in there to hear back from us?"

Mee Mee nodded. "He wants his grandfather's spirit to rest in peace before he joins him."

"Well then, let's deliver the news he's waiting to hear."

The doors opened, and they stepped out, turned left and hustled down the hallway. The strange mingling of hospital smells bugged Angie. *Funny how certain odors get to me now that I'm pregnant.* Feeling a little nauseous, she tried not to breathe deeply.

The door to room 310 stood open. They entered to see Achak sitting up in his bed with a tray of food on the overbed table in front of him. The fluorescent light above him cast an odd glow on his rugged face and long silvery hair. His appearance reflected a deep sense of dignity like the old black and white photos of Native American chiefs.

"You've gained a few pounds," Mee Mee marveled.

Achak smiled. "I'm feeling much better."

"Good," Mee Mee said, "because we have come to talk."

"Have you brought good news?"

Angie nodded. "We found the whiskey bottle."

He leaned forward, eyes widening. "The one from my dream?"

"Yes." Mee Mee placed her hand on top of his as it gripped the bed railing. "You were right. Your grandfather's spirit called out from that bottle."

He gazed up at her. "His spirit demanded justice. What was in the bottle?"

"Some Maya hieroglyphs and a map," Mee Mee said.

"And the map led us to where a body was buried," Angie added.

"His body?"

"Did your grandfather have a gold tooth?" Mee Mee asked.

He curled his upper lip and pointed to his left lateral incisor. "Right here."

Mee Mee smiled. "That's the one."

Achak leaned back against the raised bed, closed his eyes and smiled. After about a minute he sat up, opened his eyes and took a deep breath. He faced them, his skin tone and deep lines on his face like carved cedar. "Who drew the map?"

"Chandler Crane," Angie said, "but he's not the one who hid the bottle."

His eyes narrowed. "Who then?"

"His wife, Olivia Crane," Angie said. "When Ahote refused to divulge the location of the blue skull, she pressured her husband into fulfilling his duty as a Maya high priest. After Chandler offered Ahote as a human sacrifice, he documented it with the pictographs and map in a similar manner to the ancient priests. His wife found the documentation, funneled it into that whiskey bottle and hid it under the floorboards of their bedroom at the hunting club."

The lines in Achak's brow grew deeper. "Why did she hide the bottle?"

"To blackmail her husband," Mee Mee said. "It was a power move to gain sole control of Guardianship of the Skull of Doom. She allowed him to remain in the background as long as he behaved himself."

Achak protruded his lower lip. "He was a weak man."

"Yes," Angie agreed. "Abusive men are weak. Losing the blue skull gnawed at him all these years. When it reappeared, he felt he was its rightful Guardian. Upon his wife's death, his grandson would assume guardianship of the Skull of Doom. Chandler and Arnold formed a partnership to become the leaders of the skull cult. They believed they would be empowered to prevent the coming Apocalypse. The world would recognize their authority."

Achak folded his hands on the overbed table. "Cults can be dangerous. Many murders have been committed in the name of salvation."

Mee Mee nodded. "People are easily blinded by strange beliefs."

He reached and clasped both of their hands. "Thank you so much for all you have done. You are justice warriors. You have fought and won for the living and the dead. My heart is happy and at peace."

Angie felt a warmth surge through her. "W-we wanted to do our best for you."

He squeezed her hand. "And you have."

Mee Mee said, "My friend, I hope you get well enough to go home soon."

"Me, too, although I am not afraid of death. There is good in goodbye."

A ding sounded from Angie's pocket. "That's probably Joel texting me." She pulled out her phone and checked her messages: *I'm in room 302. I think I'll be released soon. Where are you?* "It's Joel. He's in a room right down the hall—302."

"Go see your husband," Mee Mee insisted. "I'm going to visit with Achak a little while longer. I'll stop down in about ten minutes."

Angie waved. "Take care, Achak."

He waved back. "Goodbye, Detective Stallone."

As she walked down the hallway, his words echoed in her mind: *There is good in goodbye. He called me Detective Stallone.* Since she opened her agency, she couldn't shake the sense of inferiority knowing that her business lacked the track record and esteem of a respected agency. Solving the case altered something inside of her. Bringing closure to Achak and his family lifted her to a new perspective. *I am Detective Stallone. I believe I can make this agency fly.*

She entered room 302 and saw her husband relaxing on the raised bed and reading a magazine. "Hey, Stud Muffin, do you mind if I crawl up in that bed next to you?"

"Angie!" he dropped the magazine onto his lap. "I just sent you a text."

"And here I am." She walked to the bed. "Scoot over."

He edged to the other side, and she climbed onto the bed, caressed his cheek and gave him a long kiss.

When their lips separated, he said, "Wow! You just made my jingle jangle."

"Good." She settled onto her back next to him. "That means you're on your way to recovery. I noticed the bump on your head is almost gone."

"Oh, I'm recovered and ready to go home."

"Me, too. It's been a long two days."

"I'm so proud of you."

She grasped his hand. "And I'm thankful for you."

"Wait till the papers hit the newsstands: YOUNG FEMALE DETECTIVE SOLVES 50-YEAR-OLD COLD CASE."

"I had a lot of help."

"You'll be famous."

Angie laughed. "No way." She eyed the magazine on his lap. "What were you reading?"

"*Family Magazine.*" He picked up the periodical and showed her the page.

"*How to Be a Great Father.* Hmmmmm. Learning anything?"

"Sure. I want to be ready when Sammy gets here."

Angie closed her eyes and pictured Joel cradling their baby in his arms. "Being a dad comes with a lot of responsibility."

"Don't worry. I've got it covered. A great dad is a teacher, reads to his children and disciplines with love."

"That sounds about right. Anything else?"

"One of the most important things for a dad to do is show love and respect for mom. Kids notice that sort of thing."

She squeezed his hand. "You know what?"

"What?"

"I think you're going to be a great dad."

A chubby brunette entered the room with a clipboard. Her cheery smile and bright eyes added to her easygoing manner. "Guess what? I've got your release papers here. A few signatures, and you're on your way."

Angie hopped off the bed. "Thanks. We can't wait to get home."

The nurse handed Angie the clipboard, and she passed it to Joel. He went through the paperwork and signed all the forms. Then he shifted his legs off the side of the bed, stood and handed the nurse the clipboard.

"Okey-Dokey. I'll be back in about five minutes with a wheelchair."

"I can walk," Joel said.

She raised a finger. "Sorry. Hospital policy. Got to follow the rules."

"Right," Joel said.

Angie clasped her arm around Joel's waist. "He goes by the book most of the time."

The nurse grinned and jiggled her eyebrows. "But sometimes I bet he's naughty."

Angie smiled and shrugged, feeling her face flush.

A few seconds after the nurse left, Mee Mee entered the room. She put her hands on her hips. "You two remind me of June and Ward Cleaver."

"Who?" they said at the same time.

"Never mind. Let's go home."

If you enjoyed this book and would like to discover how Angie Stallone began her career in the private investigation business, please check out my previous Outer Banks detective series (Weston Wolf Outer Banks Detective Series). In this three-book series, Angie teams up with Detective Weston Wolf to solve a variety of cases full of twists and turns.

Weston Wolf Outer Banks Detective Series

The Roanoke Island Murders: A Weston Wolf OBX Detective Novel

The Singer in the Sound: A Weston Wolf OBX Detective Novel

Kitty Hawk Confidential: A Weston Wolf OBX Detective Novel

Outer Banks Murder Series

The Healing Place (Prequel to Murder at Whalehead)

Book 1 – Murder at Whalehead

Book 2 – Murder at Hatteras

Book 3 – Murder on the Outer Banks

Book 4 – Murder at Ocracoke

Book 5 – The Treasure of Portstmouth Island

About the Author

Joe C. Ellis, a big fan of the North Carolina's Outer Banks, grew up in the Ohio Valley. A native of Martins Ferry, Ohio, he attended West Liberty State College in West Virginia and went on to earn his Master's Degree in education from Muskingum College in New Concord, Ohio. After a thirty-six year career as an art teacher, he retired from the Martins Ferry City School District.

Currently, he is the pastor for the Scotch Ridge Presbyterian Church and the Colerain Presbyterian Church. His writing career began in 2001 with the publication of his first novel, *The Healing Place*. In 2007 he began the *Outer Banks Murder Series* with the publication of *Murder at Whalehead* (2010), *Murder at Hatteras* (2011), *Murder on the Outer Banks* (2012), *Murder at Ocracoke* (2017), and The *Treasure of Portsmouth Island* (2019).

Most recently Joe has completed the Outer Banks Detective Series which includes three books: Roanoke Island Murders (2020), The Singer in the Sound (2021), and Kitty Hawk Confidential (2021).

Joe credits family vacations on the Outer Banks with the

inspiration for his stories. Joe and his wife Judy have three children and nine grandchildren. Although the kids have flown the nest, they get together often and always make it a priority to vacation on the Outer Banks whenever possible. He comments, "It's a place on the edge of the world, a place of great beauty and sometimes danger—the ideal setting for murder mysteries."